DEALING
IN
DREAMS

Also by Lilliam Rivera

The Education of Margot Sanchez

DEALING IN DREAMS

LILLIAM RIVERA

SIMON & SCHUSTER BFYR

NEW YORK LONDON TORONTO SYDNEY NEW DELHI

SIMON & SCHUSTER BFYR

An imprint of Simon & Schuster Children's Publishing Division
1230 Avenue of the Americas, New York, New York 10020
This book is a work of fiction. Any references to historical events, real people, or
real places are used fictitiously. Other names, characters, places, and events are
products of the author's imagination, and any resemblance to actual events or
places or persons, living or dead, is entirely coincidental.
Text copyright © 2019 by Lilliam Rivera
Jacket illustration copyright © 2019 by Aster Hung
All rights reserved, including the right of reproduction in whole or in part in any form.
SIMON & SCHUSTER BFYR is a trademark of Simon & Schuster, Inc.
For information about special discounts for bulk purchases, please contact
Simon & Schuster Special Sales at 1-866-506-1949 or
business@simonandschuster.com.
The Simon & Schuster Speakers Bureau can bring authors to your live event.
For more information or to book an event, contact the Simon & Schuster Speakers
Bureau at 1-866-248-3049 or visit our website at www.simonspeakers.com.
Jacket design by Lizzy Bromley
Interior design by Hilary Zarycky
The text for this book was set in Bell.
Manufactured in the United States of America
First Edition
2 4 6 8 10 9 7 5 3 1
Library of Congress Cataloging-in-Publication Data
Names: Rivera, Lilliam, author.
Title: Dealing in dreams / Lilliam Rivera.
Description: First edition. | New York : Simon & Schuster Books for Young
Readers, [2019] | Summary: "Sixteen year old Nalah leads the fiercest all-girl crew
in Mega City, but when she sets her sights on giving this life up for a prestigious
home in Mega Towers, she must decide if she's willing to do the unspeakable to get
what she wants"—Provided by publisher.
Identifiers: LCCN 2017061248 (print) | LCCN 2018007880 (eBook)
| ISBN 9781481472142 (hardback)| ISBN 9781481472166 (eBook)
Subjects: | CYAC: Science fiction. Classification: LCC PZ7.1.R5765 (eBook)
| LCC PZ7.1.R5765 De 2018 (print) | DDC [Fic]—dc23
LC record available at https://lccn.loc.gov/2017061248

For Annabel

DEALING
IN
DREAMS

CHAPTER 1

PATROLLING MEGA

Tonight feels different. The weight of her absence hits me. On most nights when my crew and I patrol the streets of Mega City, I feel a sense of invincibility mixed with glee. Violence can do that to a person, especially when you're the one unleashing it. At night my crew, Las Mal Criadas, own these streets. Not tonight. We're missing one of our girls, and the warm breeze that blankets my face is a trick meant to seduce me into thinking everything is fine. My soldier Manos Dura. She didn't have to go out like that. No one deserved that ending.

"Go check the building." Truck, my right hand, barks out an order. One of my soldiers sprints ahead. It's been almost a month since the end of Manos Dura, and we're still feeling it. It was Truck who recruited and trained her to be the fifth in our all-girl gang. Manos Dura's specialty was her fists. No one ever wanted to catch them hands. She was good, and now she's gone. The last thing I want to do is be out here patrolling. Such is my lot in life. It's what Las Mal Criadas do. Not for long, though.

"Does she see any stragglers?" I ask Shi. She checks the Codigo5G goggles. The machine is run-down, an old model. We're lucky to have them. Only top crews are authorized to be connected to the server. These Codigos were a gift from Déesse, our beloved leader of Mega City. We have access to the libraries and the ability to transmit.

"She says it looks pretty quiet, Chief Rocka." Shi calls me by the title I earned as the leader of the baddest girl gang in Mega City. I hold the title close to my chest. I intend to keep it.

Abandoned buildings line the streets, empty and menacing. There's no noise except for our boots crunching down on crumbling sidewalks. The nightly curfew is absolute. The people of Mega City are meant to be sleeping in their underground homes. No one is allowed to be out except for crews. From the northeastern tip of Mega City to close to the water, Las Mal Criadas are in charge of maintaining curfew. Other crews take up different sections of the city. We've been at this for five years now. It never fails. We always find a toiler or two aimlessly lost on the streets, such as this woman who is curled in a fetal position against a slab of concrete. Her housedress is dirty. Her hair is a tangled mess of knots.

"What the hell are you doing?" Truck yells. The woman wakes with a startled look. Truck grabs her by the arms and drags the woman to the nearest station. The woman pleads. She's so confused. Truck doesn't bother. She shoves the woman in. Her whimpering echoes up toward the street.

I look away and stare at the Mega Towers, which stand tall, a trio of giant rectangular boxes. The Towers are one of the few buildings that aren't falling apart. There are 536 apartments in the Towers. There's even a school and a health center. Déesse, the leader of Mega City, lives on the top floor. No one is allowed in without an invite. Soon I'll be living there, sleeping in a real bed, not on the dirt floor with Truck snoring on one side of me and another soldier talking in her sleep on the other. To be part of Déesse's chosen guard . . . That's the prize and I intend to grab it. We'll be chilling with the elite, the chosen few, and we will be no different from them. No more fighting other crews and no more dealing with lost toilers. The Mega Towers is where it's at.

It's why we call it breaking night. There are times when you break a person back into sleeping. When the sun comes up, the grueling work begins again for this woman and the other countless toilers, whether it's making the sueño tabs in the factories or running mercados for people to trade for essentials. If you are in a crew, you're not considered a toiler. We are above them.

When this woman wakes up in the morning, she'll be able to fulfill her duties because she'll feel the euphoric remnants from the manufactured dreams made by taking a sueño. Life is monotonous aboveground. Everyone needs to dream in order to survive.

"Does Déesse really live up there?" Nena asks. Nena is our newest recruit, meant to replace Manos Dura. Truck is not convinced Nena has what it takes to be an LMC. She's eleven, almost twelve. She's got a hunger, a strong desire to please, and that's valuable. Still, Nena is too green to understand she shouldn't even be asking me questions. She should be soldiering.

"Recite the Mega City history right now," I say. "You should know this already."

Nena rubs her forehead before speaking. We make every potential soldier study up on the history. No one is exempt. If you don't know your history, then you have no power. That's the problem with the other gangs. They think their strength lies only in their fists. Not my crew. I plan to take them straight to the top, and it will be because we outdid the rest with smarts.

"Before the Big Shake of 2060, men destroyed the city with their greed," Nena says. She looks up with her big eyes and waits for me to give her a nod to continue. "The Big Shake happened and everything was gone.

"We are the daughters of Mega City. We patrol because Déesse's great-grandmother gathered everyone together. She trained women to defend themselves. We showed the men we didn't need them. Mega City was going to be for women. If they didn't like it, they could step."

"Good. Now, why are gangs made up of only five girls?" I circle around her. She stands straight, hands to her sides, stiff.

"There were four who started Mega City with Déesse's great-grandmother. Five leaders total, all women." She smiles to herself, pleased she's getting it right. My other two soldiers, Smiley and Shi, look on. They are waiting for her to slip up. "Also, five means grace."

"And how many gangs are there in Mega City?"

She stops and looks down. Nena doesn't remember the answer. Smiley starts to laugh loudly. They shake their heads. Manos Dura never had a problem when she recited the history. Nena is no Manos Dura. She might have been twelve but Manos never let age get in the way. She listened when she needed to, took notes, and studied them later. When things were quiet, she would ask me questions about everything. Her round face was filled with curiosity.

"Why do we keep her around?" Truck pushes Nena to the ground. "She can't even memorize facts." Nena stands with a rage face. The rage lasts only for a few seconds. She's so young.

"Go light up our way," I say.

A disappointed Nena climbs up the lamppost and uses her mini-blowtorch to light the lamp. She climbs down and jogs to the next one.

"Total waste," Truck says. "We never had a problem with Mano. Mano had the history memorized in a day. She didn't play around." With the mention of her name, my heart starts to hurt again. It's true. Mano was a straight LMC from the first day. She anticipated what needed to be done. How was it possible the one time she needed to be extra alert Mano had her defenses down?

It was the Deadly Venoms. They caught Manos Dura on her way back from partying at the Luna Club. That night we were so trashed. We were victorious in our last throwdown and things were looking up. One more battle with the Deadly Venoms and we would surely secure a spot in Déesse's army. We were feeling good, unstoppable. When Manos Dura left the club early, we didn't think twice. We'd thought she left to sleep off the drinks over at our station. Instead, the Deadly Venoms intercepted her on her way and beat her down. By the time Mano's body was found, there wasn't much left. The only proof we had it was her was the LMC tattoo I personally branded on the side of her head. The Deadly Venoms didn't own up to doing the deed. We had no proof. Death. Our girl. My soldier.

"Want one, Chief Rocka?" Smiley offers me a food pellet. I decline. Smiley deals with the loss by eating. The gold grill covering her bottom row of teeth looks tarnished, not brilliant like when she first made the trade after accumulating so many hundreds of sueño tabs.

Smiley pulls out her cap and tags over a sign made by the Deadly Venoms. Of course they would use an audacious and tacky tag that's barely legible. Huge round bubble letters in their colors of black and pink appear as if written by a toddler. Smiley covers their ink and blazes the LMC in a solid graf style, clean and straight, with our colors of red and gold.

The violence has been steady growing ever since we've been inching closer to Déesse. It's one thing to fight in the public space during monthly scheduled throwdowns; it's quite another to cancel another gang member off hours. The Deadly Venoms are rotten to the core. There's no loyalty. No sense of rules, just anarchy. They've cheated and bashed their way to be placed in front of Déesse. They won't last. They'll pay for what they did to Manos Dura. When that's done, we will be the top dogs of this city. I won't have to bloody my hands on trash anymore. I'll be next to my leader, in her army, keeping Mega City safe from the degenerates who live past the border in Cemi Territory.

"Few more hours and I'm heading to the Luna Club," Truck says. "Screw this patrol." Truck stands tall, with large arms and broad shoulders. It took everyone on my team to keep her from walking into Deadly Venoms' neighborhood and ending them. There are times when Truck reacts so impulsively. She's been handling the death of Mano with more violence. Toilers are getting the brunt of it. Otherwise Truck spends her time partying at the Luna Club. We each have our ways.

Smiley presses her face up against a window of a building. It's a training camp for young girls to learn how to fight. The building is small. There are only a few official training camps in Mega City. The one Truck and I went through is farther east and it is by far the biggest. Families from every corner traveled to the camp in the hopes their daughter would be taken. If you can put up with the brutal training, you are guaranteed a place to sleep and eat. Most young girls come from nothing. The training camps at least teach you how to fight. It's not pretty, yet I made it through.

"Let's wake them up," Smiley says with her mischievous grin. Smiley is short and round. A trickster, she loves to charm people into liking her and then stealing from them with her gold grin. She's also known to bite the crap out of opponents.

"Naw, let's send Nena," Truck says. "Trade her for a better model."

Truck says this loud enough for Nena to hear. Nena doesn't react. Good girl. She's got to learn these insults are only a small part of being one of us. Truck won't relent until Nena gets mad or gives up.

"Remember the time when Manos threw a malasuerte into their dorms. It was raining, and them young girls ran out screaming when the malasuerte blew up," Smiley says. "Manos was ruthless."

Smiley and Shi walk side by side. Their shoulders bump into each other. Manos would have been in the middle. The three of them, always up to no good.

"The girl was notorious. Manos convinced me to give up my Codigo5G because she swore on everything mine was broken,"

Shi says. She tucks her long dark bangs behind her ears. Her frame is slender, which makes her quick and hard to restrain in a throwdown. "Made me think she was doing me a favor."

"Or the time she tricked me into thinking 'Made in China' meant a girl named China made the item," Smiley says. "Got so busted when I tried to trade a pair of jeans I found in an abandoned building and got nothing for them."

I suppress a laugh. "Pay attention," I say instead of joining in. Shi and Smiley straighten up and concentrate on patrolling. I hold back from them and take a breather. The pressure feels worse when they tell stories about Manos. Why didn't I stop her from going? I was too busy having a good time. We have to be on alert 24-7. Always.

"Can't stop thinking about her?" Truck stands by me. Her eyes are red from lack of sleep during the day.

"And you?"

"I won't stop until the Deadly Venoms pay for the pain. For our pain."

"We can't afford to get sloppy," I say. "The Deadly Venoms are in it to win it. Except they don't care how they do it."

"That's why you're Chief Rocka. You strategize while I flex." She pulls off her helmet and goggles. Her dark brown twisted locks now reach the center of her back. I sense a hint of anger in her tone. She thinks I'm being a coward for holding back on the Deadly Venoms. I'm only thinking of our future. Déesse surely heard what went down with Manos. If we retaliate outside of the throwdown, then we appear weak. We lack discipline. There's no doubt the upcoming fight will land in our favor and Déesse will have no question as to who the better crew is.

I continue to walk.

In the distance I can hear music pumping. There's a party going on in the Towers. It's the same deal every night. Not only do Mega City's chosen guards live there, but so do many other elite. Engineers who develop ways to use wind and solar for electricity, urban farmers who create our food pellets, scientists who maintain the sueños to ease people's daily pain. If you're smart and can actually better the city, then Déesse wants you close to her. It makes sense. Most toilers down here can barely read or write.

"Shi and Smiley, go patrol the north side," I say. "Let's finish this up."

My two soldiers walk off. It's just me and Truck. When I decided to create the LMCs, the first person I turned to was Truck. We'd survived the training camp together. She knew me, and I knew her. When I stepped to her about the idea, she didn't even hesitate. I told her about my dream of living in the Towers. This way of life was meant to be only temporary. Although she didn't quite see the future as I did, Truck trusted me enough to follow.

"Nalah, let's hit up Luna Club," Truck says. "We deserve it. Manos would have wanted us to."

Truck is the only person allowed to call me by my real name, Nalah. On the occasions when she does, she speaks as a friend and not as my second-in-command. Hearing my name keeps me grounded, reminds me of our connection. I take a deep breath and slowly exhale. A cold drink and a hot dish. Maybe even a warm bath. The Luna Club sounds like the right type of action I need.

"Where's Nena?" I say, suddenly realizing we hadn't seen or heard her in a bit. The streetlamps she lit still glow. A few blocks away there's only darkness. We listen. Do I hear a muffled cry? Truck gives me a look, and we bolt forward. We slow down when we hear Nena's voice. I give Truck the nod, and she pulls back, finds a concrete slab to crouch down behind and waits. Ready.

"Help me, Chief Rocka," Nena says. Her tiny voice is a scratchy note on this hateful night.

A few yards ahead of me is a guy. He has one arm wrapped around Nena's neck. With his other arm he yanks her hand back so hard tears stream down her face. Dumb girl. How did she get caught up in this stupidity?

I knew in my gut Nena needed more training. She wasn't ready. Nena wanted to prove she was down. Now look at her. I'll need to knock this guy out because Nena can't soldier. Damn her for being such a rookie.

"Please!" she yells.

I tilt my head and start strategizing.

CHAPTER 2

HIT 'EM UP

Nena is in a serious bind. With every cry, the man smirks. This guy thinks he's got one up on us. He doesn't see my girl Truck holding a tricked-out tronic aimed right at his junk. He thinks he got lucky tagging Nena. The foolish act is going to be his downfall. I just need to give Truck the sign and it's lights out.

"Let her go," I say.

"I'm not scared of you," he says. "I don't care. I'll break her little neck."

Nena's arms flail about, trying to land a hit. She's unable to make contact. I need to cut her loose soon before she truly freaks and trips him into committing a fatal act. It was only two days ago when we showed her how to break free from a bear hug by stomping the enemy's feet. Those hours of training are completely wasted if she doesn't calm down and formulate her next move. I'll think for both of us.

"That soldier you're holding is mine. You hear me?" I keep my hand steady on my weapon, my beautiful silver tronic, and point the laser beam at him, creating a neon pink dot on his forehead. The tronic produces nanosecond electrical pulses meant to knock a person out. We don't have enough juice to kill anyone, but it's more than enough to cause a blackout.

His eyes dart wildly, as if he's waiting for backup. He smells of a loner. Only fearless crews come out at this hour. Girls only. There is none more fearless than our crew. This guy is a fluke.

I shoot above his head. He barely flinches. Nena screams. I should shoot her instead for causing such a ruckus.

"The next shot is going to be your face," I say. My black curls sneak in front of my goggles. I keep steady. I don't want to make any sudden moves.

"I'm not here for her," he sputters. "Who are you? What's your name?"

He wears green, a common color for most toilers. However, his overalls are ripped and covered in muck. He looks to be in his midthirties, way older than me. The tattoos on his knuckles are slightly faded. I can barely make out the *T* for *toiler*. There's no way he's a worker. The men in Mega City are relegated to manual labor; they work in the factories, hauling trash to the dumps. If they're smart—scientists or engineers—Déesse will invite them to be a part of her inner circle. This guy is exhibiting none of those traits. He's a garbage dweller

13

scrounging for whatever he can steal. He's found a live one in Nena.

"I'll let her go as soon as I find . . . um, I'm looking for . . ."

He has a hard time completing his sentence. He must have snuck up on Nena when she tried to light our path. We taught her to use the large slabs of crumbled concrete as cover or to walk alongside the multitude of empty buildings. You can never be too sure if another crew is hiding, holding their buffalo stance on a desolate lot, waiting to jump you. We're here to make sure no one makes false claims on our section of the city. With Déesse living in our neighborhood, life for us is way easier and more comfortable than in other parts of the city. We've got the best boydega clubs and a better selection at the mercado. Unfortunately, we divide the neighborhood with the Deadly Venoms. A temporary thing until we beat them in the next throwdown. The other sections of the city can't compare. Crews have tried to muscle in. They fail every time.

"You're breaking curfew," I say. "Everyone in the city is asleep. You need to join them."

I inch closer to him. His eyes and lips are awash in blue. Soon his skin will turn an ashy gray. I should have known. He's an Anonymous Nervous Toiler, an ANT, a toiler addicted to sueños. Sueños are meant only to ease people into sleep and to alleviate pain. Weak people abuse the tabs and end up wanting to live in a euphoric state of fantasy forever. I've seen the strongest succumb to the temptation. From the looks of his disheveled state, this ANT's desperate for another trip into dreamland.

A message from Truck appears on the screen of my goggles, asking permission to attack. I let her wait. I don't want the mess. He'll harm Nena. The ANT's smirk disappears and becomes a grimace. Just what I thought. He's in pain. Nothing but an ANT caught up in the sueño cycle, where there are never enough tabs to keep him going. I have no pity.

"Okay, relax. We can work this out. I'll help you find the person you are looking for." I slowly lower my tronic. He loosens his grip on Nena. He's doing exactly what I want him to do. That's right. Keep thinking you're winning this fight, ANT, keep dreaming.

"See, I'm listening to you," I say. "No problem."

His stormy eyes are so focused on the tronic, he doesn't notice how my other hand reaches behind for my baton.

"Legs up," I say calmly to Nena.

Kneeling, I throw my baton toward his leg just as Nena pulls up hers. The baton hits his ankle with a loud *thump*. He buckles down in pain while Nena manages to break free. As I step to him, the ANT rushes toward me. I don't wait to see if he has a weapon. I grab hold of his arm and kick him where my baton landed. The pain is enough to cause him to cringe. While holding his hand, I turn away from him, pull him toward my back, and bend my knees. He's lighter than I thought, light enough to flip. His head makes a horrible smacking sound as the ground knocks the wind out of him. Without missing a beat, Truck catches up to us, straddles him, and gives him a punch to the side of his head. As quickly as it began, the ANT is out for the count. Too easy.

I'm only a few feet away from him, and his stench makes my eyes tear. I adjust my goggles to cover my nose. This ANT is our third victim of the night. He better be my last.

"I didn't know he was behind me. I swear, Chief Rocka," Nena says. "I'm so sorry. Please, don't get mad at me. I didn't see him. It's not my fault."

"Shut up, soldier! You should know better than to let an ANT take hold of you," Truck yells at her. "You're never going to be a true Mal Criada. We should send you right back where we found you."

Nena tries to muffle her cries, nearly hyperventilating with the effort.

"Do your thing, Nena," I say firmly. She's the youngest in our outfit. She has to wise up. Get hard or get dumped.

Nena wipes her tears with the back of her hand while Truck looms over her. She removes her bomber jacket and ties it around her waist, exposing her thin arms covered in thick metal cuffs similar to the gold cuffs I wear. She puts on her gloves and walks over to the ANT. She empties his pockets.

"He got used tabs," Nena says in a shaky voice. "Garbage. Garbage. Garbage. Wait. There is an object around his neck."

She pulls out her knife to release the item.

"Can I keep this?" she asks.

Nena dangles a necklace in front of me—a miniature black fist charm hangs from a crude leather cord. Wait. I've seen this charm before. Where? I scan my head, going over the other gangs. Is it an emblem from another crew? No. I've never seen anyone rock this fist. So strange.

"Give me that." Truck grabs the piece from Nena.

Truck is never one to play it cool. If she's not unleashing blood on an enemy, she's turning on those who are close to her. It's hard to keep her anger in check. We've been together since we were recruited by one of Déesse's scouts when we were seven, almost ten years ago. I vaguely remember my recruiter. She had a nice smile. There was nothing hard about her, not what you would expect from a person whose job was to find the roughest. I never saw her again. She must be in the Towers. Recruiters continue to go station to station, assessing families with daughters. Not every girl is selected. You can't be sickly or harbor any weird flaws. Only a lucky few can catch a break. The girls who aren't selected must figure out how to make themselves useful—work in the sueño factories, feed the soldiers.

"What are you looking at?" Truck yells.

Nena quickly moves away from Truck after getting caught staring at the guy. There's not a day that goes by without Nena getting scolded for not paying attention. She quickly gets distracted. Nena searches for members of her family—an aunt perhaps, a distant cousin? As Nena tells it, she woke up one day and her parents and younger brother were gone. A note was left with the word "Cemi." Nothing else. How can a family just pack up and head toward violence and uncertainty in Cemi Territory when Déesse provides us with everything? Nena's family is probably dead by now.

I went through a similar period when I was Nena's age. My sister did the same thing to me. She left without so much as a word when I was six. I didn't even get the courtesy of a note. Ten years ago. I don't feel the loss. Once a person crosses the border, they are as good as dead. The crew is Nena's only family and mine.

Nena snaps a picture of the ANT. I watch as she taps with frustration at her Codigo5G, cursing how the equipment isn't working right. The Codigo will scan faces of Mega City residents and see if there's a match. I listen for noise. Any person hiding might be connected to him. It's deadly quiet. We are alone on this street. Truck twirls the necklace. A slight feeling of anxiety grows inside of me. I can't place the fist.

"His name is drawing up blank," Nena says. She cocks her head to the side. Nena has the tendency to end her sentences as if she's asking a question and not answering one. "Searching the other libraries? I'm not having much luck. He has no people. I'll do a search on the necklace."

Nena takes another picture. I adjust my choker and stroke the embossed LMC lettering, a gift given to me by one of

Déesse's assistants after our last throwdown. I study the ANT. His appearance holds no clue, just dirt and blue lips cracked from dryness. His body jerks from sueño withdrawal. Most men will show their preferred gang with ink on their right arm. His arms are bare.

"Whoa," Nena says. "You're not going to believe this. Seriously? This is crazy."

"Spit it out," I say.

"The necklace belongs to the Ashé Ryders."

My heart sinks.

"The Ashé Ryders," Truck says. "There's no way this skinny mocoso is associated with the Ashé. No way."

"Have you ever met an Ashé?" Nena asks. "In the flesh?"

Nena instantly regrets asking the question after the scowl Truck throws her way for trying to start a conversation. No one in my crew or anyone we know has run into an Ashé Ryder. The stories on the Ashé are legendary, from conjuring natural elements to destroy their enemies to burning their dissenters alive. The tales are bogeyman stories, though, told to keep people in check. Apparently, the Ashé Ryders were a regular crew until they started to get too big. This happened way before I was born. I learned about the Ryders history while training in the camp to become a soldier. Greed is what Déesse said was the root of their collapse. They were run out of Mega City many, many years ago for going against the people and starting a riot. Now they're in Cemi Territory, or what's left of them. No one ventures outside of Mega City for fear of running into an Ashé. Déesse's army has kept the borders tight and everyone in Mega City safe within. The degenerates who live outside in Cemi Territory serve only as reminders of how lost they are in their brutality. There is no sense of community, only violence. The same violence almost destroyed Mega City. Ashé Ryders are no different from the hundreds who chose anarchy over order.

"We should try to wake him up," I say. "Ask him where he got it."

"Why?" Truck says, annoyed. "He probably stole it."

"Are you questioning me?"

Truck steps down while Nena stares nervously at her boots. After a few seconds of awkward silence, Truck walks over to me, speaking quietly so that Nena will not hear.

"Nalah, we are both beat. We need to chill," she says. "This ANT probably found the necklace and wanted to trade it for more sueños. I'm telling you, he's not worth it. Right now all I see is an addict. We follow Déesse's orders and slip him a tab so he won't crash too hard from withdrawal. Okay?"

I take a deep breath and slowly exhale. I'm letting my emotions cloud the correct action to take. Truck is right. But I can't seem to shake that I'm missing a sign. Why is this silly necklace stirring doubt in me? As if this addict holds information I should know. It's dumb. I must be tired. It's been a long night. The sun will soon rise. Breaking night will be over. I need to check in on Shi and Smiley.

I study the ANT again. His grimace stays plastered on his face. I'm being paranoid. It's a simple charm representing a crew that no longer holds any power in Mega City. The old-school ways of doing things were destroyed in the Big Shake. The past is truly dead. There's only Las Mal Criadas, our leader, Déesse, and my goal to make it to the Towers.

"Okay," I say. "Mark him."

Nena takes out her cap and tags our letters on his left arm, our normal procedure whenever we run into a guy with no allegiance. When he comes to, he'll forever bear the mark of the LMC on him, an indicator to everyone we crushed him first.

"I'll take that."

Truck sulks as she reluctantly hands me the necklace. Although the black fist charm is small, it weighs heavily in the palm of my hand.

This is my city, and I intend to defend it to the end. There are throwdowns to bet on and boydegas to party in. No one goes without, not even the addicts. There is a citywide distribution of food pellets. An abundance of underground stations for families to live in. You cobble together a crew of strong girls and create a life worth living. It's simple. This is due to Déesse's vision. We owe her. Maybe this necklace will prove valuable.

Nena creeps over with a shy smile, the remnants of her

assault already forgotten. Her eyes are large and green, almost alienlike. She's tiny for an eleven-year-old. I want to protect her. Her skills for soldiering are sorely lacking. I'm giving her a chance because I believe, in time, she can be a strong LMC. It's probably a weakness on my part.

"It's pretty," she says. "You think Déesse will want it?"

I rub her shaved head, feeling the tattoo still raw from when we branded her last week. Her green eyes pop against her sunburnt skin.

"He didn't hurt me," she says when I inspect the emerging black-and-blue marks around her neck left by the ANT. The bruises will only get worse by tomorrow. At least she'll have a good story to tell the others.

"Sure he didn't," I tease. "It seemed as if you were handling the situation, especially when he had his arms wrapped around you."

I'm reluctant to walk away.

"Do you think it's enough to get us to the Towers?" Nena asks. "We've beaten those other crews. That's got to be enough."

"Stop asking Chief Rocka stupid questions," says Truck. "You're never going to live in the Towers. You can't even follow orders. Keep quiet and move."

Nena scurries to gather what's left on the ANT to sell. I remember when I was as young as Nena, a skinny thing trying to roll with the big girls. I got beat down so much when

I spoke out of turn. I soon learned to punch first and punch hard.

It was the fight in me that made me Chief Rocka.

In our weekly newsletter from Déesse, there are always images of former Mega City residents who took their chances in Cemi. True violence. Body parts. Real hunger. The Ashé Ryders have stayed in Cemi Territory with the other degenerates for years. Now is not the time for them or anyone to appear.

"Let's roll."

"If the Ashé Ryders are itching to creep into Mega City," Truck yells, "they're going to have to contend with Las Mal Criadas!"

"Mal," I yell.

"Criiii-adas!" Nena and Truck respond with our signature call.

I shove the necklace into my pack and head toward the direction where Smiley and Shi should be waiting.

CHAPTER 3

BOYDEGA DREAMS

We stand in front of the entrance to the Luna Club. Doña Chela squints at us. She wears her usual uniform of a grungy bathrobe and slippers. She's an old-timer. We've lost many bets trying to guess how old she is. Doña refuses to reveal her age. It doesn't help that she's missing various teeth and that her hair is a disheveled nest dyed a putrid green.

"Bendición, Doña." I ask for her blessing. My tiny show of respect is mandatory. She owns the most popular boydega club in Mega City. I must shower her with love even when my crew is one of her regulars.

"My girls been playing rough tonight, huh?" Doña inspects us with her lime-green eyes made to match her hair. I wonder how much she was willing to trade to get those colored contacts. Those who live in the Towers love changing the color of their eyes. Doña probably has a Tower connection for petty beauty accessories like this one. She points a chubby finger at me. "Where are the rest of your girls? Chief Rocka, you should let them have fun, too."

Provocative images of guys in various forms of undress cover the walls of the boydega from their latest calendar, the Papi Chulos of Luna Club. One papi flexes his muscles, another admires himself in a full-length mirror, and another sucks on a lollipop. When I was young and lived in the training camp, papi chulo trading cards were given to those on good behavior. I collected the cards and traded with others, professing my undying love for my favorite. My preference always leaned toward the papi dressed as a scholar by way of thick, black-rimmed glasses and an open book on his lap. He looked smarter and hence more approachable. The chulos here are kept forever young with a fresh crop of candidates willing to strike a pose.

I peel off my jacket, remove my cuff, and thrust my arm under the detector. I can't shake the uneasiness I've felt since the run-in with the ANT. I sent Nena, Smiley, and Shi back home. Nena's carelessness caused the rest of them to get screwed out of papi action.

Doña Chela offers a toothless grin when the mandatory bell rings the rank of our crew. Only the top-five gangs gain VIP entrance to this particular club. Everyone else who wants to party in the Luna Club must contend with begging for access. If you're not VIP, expect to wait hours to get in, if you get in at all. The embedded numerical rank placed under my skin is proof of our worth. With every throwdown, Déesse and her inner circle determine your crew's rank. There are currently about fifteen registered crews in Mega City, each ranked in order. Unregistered crews are not worth a mention.

I've been to underground boydegas when Las Mal Criadas were just starting five years ago. The chulos were so ugly and dirty. There are Mega City residents who don't approve of boydegas, which is hard to believe. Instead they cut loose with the Rumberos over by the water. A religious group, the Rumberos spend way too much time dwelling in the spiritual mumbo jumbo instead of reality. They are a small, forgettable bunch.

The Luna Club is legit. There's good food, music, and potent drinks. There are sueño tabs too, if you are into that. My crew stays far away from sueños. We keep our minds clear of manufactured dreams. It's a decree I made when I started the gang. I've seen firsthand how sueños can destroy a person.

I won't stay long tonight, though, just long enough to return to my normal self, not shook because of a dumb charm.

"What other mocosos are here trying to uglify your home, Doña?" Truck asks as she checks in her weapon. Truck loves the club. Here, the chulos think Truck is the bomb. She plays drinking games with them or wrestles. She's generous with the papis to the point one summer I cut her off for trading too much of her sueño supply. Sueños are our top currency. With every throwdown won, we get paid in tabs. Since Déesse provides us with food and we carve our own shelter, there is no need for old-school money. Still, we can't spend tabs carelessly. That summer the battles were pretty dull, so Truck went kind of nuts with boredom. She handed out tabs as candy. It got so bad I had to block her from entering the club for a whole month. Nowadays I allow her a little bit of leeway. Not much.

"Nobody's here, just a couple of my girls. Quiet. I think everyone is getting ready for this weekend." Doña accepts my sueño tabs and chucks them into her purse. She calls gang members, no matter what affiliate, her girls. Doña doesn't have any children of her own, although she gives a motherly vibe. I don't have that type of relationship with her and I don't let my soldiers be seen that way. We don't need mothers. We only need each other.

"We've got a special tonight," she says. "If you buy two, you get the third chulo at half price."

There won't be any sales on the day of the throwdown. In fact, she'll make renting a papi twice as expensive. That's when everyone will want papi action. I'm glad the club is empty. For the most part, boydegas are neutral territory. No one is supposed to fight. Of course, things get stirred up from time to time. How could they not when you have rival crews hanging in one spot? Not tonight. Everyone will save their aggression for the throwdown this weekend.

The booming bass from a popular song rattles the gilded

mirrors lining the stairs leading down to the club. I catch my reflection and see the long, jagged scratch left by the last lost toiler. Kicking her felt justified. My black curls lay limp. I look tired and run-down, much older than sixteen.

"Ugly," Truck says. She ruffles my curls.

I follow her down the stairs.

Giant paper animals hang from the ceiling: massive tigers and lions, pandas, and kangaroos, each with a maniacal grin. When the place is jumping with people crushed side to side on the dance floor, Doña Chela usually invites the victors to bash the giant animals and shower the partygoers with candy laced with "happiness." Unlike the synthetic sueños, the candy has a natural high consisting mostly of THC. On this subdued night the giant animals stay put. The massive piñatas turn their heads as if they are watching us.

Truck elbows me. A couple dances in the center of the club. I recognize the Deadly Venom colors, black and pink, on the drunken girl. The chulo she leans on tries his best to keep her steady.

"She's by herself," Truck says. I shake my head, signaling to Truck she's not worth it. The couple continues to dance. I sit at our table a little away from the dance floor.

"What's going on with you?" Truck says after taking a large gulp from her drink. "You've been with a sour expression. We need to get pumped for this weekend. It's on!" She pats my back hard.

The throwdown this weekend is by far our most important one. We've sparred our way to this very moment, beating other crews and proving we're the best. The Deadly Venoms are hopefully the last obstacle for us to overcome before we step to the Towers. The stakes are too high for us to mess up.

I want to live in the Towers. It's what I've been dreaming most of my soldiering life. We've never been this close to having this dream realized. I sense—no, I can see—it becoming my reality. No one else sees it as clearly as I do. Truck is too busy thinking of what's going on right now, beating so and so, drinking and fooling around with chulos. I'm thinking about our future, of my whole crew's destiny. Battling gangs for a measly crumb is dead. Once we're set up in the Towers, we can watch other crews bash each other's heads. Truck is wrong in thinking this weekend's throwdown with the Deadly Venoms is just another fight. We are not only avenging Manos Dura's death, but we are proving once and for all we're worthy enough to live in the Towers.

"We can't just beat the Deadly Venoms. We've got to put them on display," I remind her.

"Don't stress, Rocka. We got this. It's a wrap!" Truck stands. "We got this. I'm going to—"

"No, we don't got a thing." I pound my fist on the table. "It's important we show we're smart. You feel me?"

Truck settles back down into her seat. She places her hand on my shoulder, a rare gesture that would embarrass others.

Truck is fearless that way, not afraid to show a bit of vulnerability.

"Don't worry. I'm here. We'll get to the Towers," she says. "No one else comes close. They're even proclaiming our name."

It's true. Most walls across the city are tagged with our initials, LMC. More and more residents are sporting our colors of red and gold as a show of solidarity. The LMC has a reputation of playing things straight and fair. Even if the attack to Manos was never proven to be by the Deadly Venoms, it was cause enough for most of the residents of Mega City to despise them. I should feel good about this. Then why do I feel as if my plans are held by the thinnest of ropes? Anxiety rises, gnawing at me, telling me the bloody favors I've made along the way will never be enough.

I look at Truck. There is never any doubt, only confidence. I wish I were like her.

"I won't sleep until I hear it straight from Déesse," I say.

"It's a done deal—"

"No." I cut her off. "We need to be laser-focused. If we are not careful, we'll end up old-timers, homeless, unable to contribute to Mega City after one too many throwdowns. We've got to protect ourselves and shape what we want our tomorrows to be."

"I am," Truck mumbles after a pause. She pulls her hand away and gestures over to a chulo to bring us more drinks. If Truck is nervous she'll never tell.

"What are you tired cows doing here?" The drunken Deadly Venom pulled away from her chulo and now points at our table. The drink is giving her courage.

"Let's go dance," the chulo urges. The Deadly Venom refuses.

"No. I want to talk to them," she slurs. "Las Mal Criadas are a bunch of played-out girls who can't fight. Just wait until you see what we are going to do to you."

This Deadly Venom is barely twelve. There are no scars or marks on her. She must be a new soldier, as green as Nena. I want to warn her, to tell her no matter how many soldiers she knocks out, there will be another one waiting to strike her down. I want to tell her she's young enough to bail. This life is definitely not for everyone. The sueño factories aren't that bad. There's time to carve a decent if boring life as a toiler. Instead, I keep quiet.

The Deadly Venom lunges toward us. She bumps into our table and tips over our drinks. Truck looks at me. To let this soldier go would mean to show weakness. It doesn't matter how green she is or if she acts alone. I must play the part. I get up and shove the Deadly Venom hard. Before the young girl has a chance to figure out her next move, I straddle her and throw a flurry of punches to her side, then toward her chest and ears. The girl tries to protect her face. I stop when her blood covers my knuckles.

"Go home or I'll end the night with you," I say. "Tell your leader we are ready for this weekend."

The papi chulo helps the Deadly Venom up. He muffles her cries with his hand. The giant piñatas grin their paper smiles at me.

"That's what I'm talking about." Truck laughs. I do not join her. Stupid girl probably hasn't been fully initiated into the Deadly Venoms, so she's here trying to make a name for herself. What a fool.

We eat our meal in silence. When I'm done, I retreat to the rented room and leave Truck with her chulos.

I submerge my bruised body into the scalding-hot water. Hot baths are so rare, the cost of having one in the Luna Club depends solely on the whims of the owner. Since it's a slow night, Doña charges only a few of my tabs. It's so worth it. My body aches from the patrol.

"Do you want me to read to you?" he asks. The papi chulos in Luna Club don't go by names, just by type. I've nicknamed him Books because of the glasses he wears, although I'm sure he wears them only for show. I don't know anything about him except he has a calming effect.

"No. Can you work on my neck, please?"

"Of course. Whatever you want," he says.

I've never seen Books outside of the club environment. I don't even know how he looks in regular clothes. I go to him because he knows right away what to do. A hot bath. A massage. It's enough to slow down the adrenaline racing through my veins. Books is tall and slender with dark brown eyes that stand out behind the glasses. He knows well enough to wear a tight green T-shirt to make them pop even more.

"Have you heard?" Books whispers in my ear.

"What are they saying?" I ask.

"They say there's a new crew coming into play."

If Books expects me to react, then he's at a loss. Not even in front of this harmless chulo will I reveal how I feel. Surely the next person who rents this room will be given a lowdown on my reaction. No. I act as if I don't have a care in the world and wait for him to continue to spin his tale. I won't have to do much to coax Books to talk.

"Really?" I say with a hint of boredom.

Books pours more hot water into the bath. The steam creates a fog around the room, shadowing the lit candles. Besides the tub and a couple of mismatched tables, the room is pretty bare. Doña rents more elaborate suites for role-playing. I detest those types of entertainment.

"Yeah. Apparently, they're coming to topple Déesse," he says. "Nobody wants to see her hurt. Déesse's been so good to us."

There's a hint of sarcasm in his tone. Life as a papi chulo can't be easy. Dealing with rowdy crews. Always being charming and at their service. Still, there's no reason to hate on Déesse. Being a papi beats working in the factories or mercados. Books also can't deny that a threat to Déesse is a threat to what we've built.

"Be careful. You seem to forget we owe Déesse everything," I say. "Besides, new crews are constantly being formed. It took my crew two years to be registered. Another four to get to where we are at. This is just talk. Probably a crew trying to create buzz without doing any real work. Nothing more."

"You're probably right," Books says, wiping the steam from his glasses with a red handkerchief. "Then again, people seem to think this crew might have a bit of leg to them."

"And who are these 'people' you keep mentioning? They seem so knowledgeable," I ask.

There are only a handful of crews that truly count. Most two-bit players don't stand a chance. These lowly nobodies believe if they can hold a weapon in one hand they can use it.

He places his glasses back on and reveals a smile. This grin is familiar. He doesn't fool me. Books is trained to be a lover. This tempting smile won't work on me because this is business, and I don't pay extra for alluring games. I'm trained as well, just on other things.

I face him and hold his stare until he looks away.

"People say a lot of things, don't they? This talk is just toilers trying to shake things up in Mega City," he continues. "It's been a while since we had a good throwdown. We wait for you to rescue us from boredom."

Books resumes the massage.

"Right. I'm more than happy to provide the proper entertainment for the masses." I try my best to read him. He's not giving me much information. "What else are they saying?"

A smart papi, he ignores the question and continues to knead my neck. He hums to himself while he works

"What are you humming?"

"An old song. Ever heard of Graciela?"

"The singer?" I say. "Vaguely."

Graciela Divina. I remember how I loved her name. It sounded so regal. She was popular back in the day. Old-timers adored her. Her makeup was always the same—three elaborate buns and blood-red lipstick. Her most popular song was called "El Fuego me Llama."

"She was beautiful. A voice unlike any others. Truly special. Can't get the song out of my head. Anyway, it's not important. You're tense," Books whispers. "I'll get you a pot of relaxing tea. I'll be right back."

I'm relieved when he walks out of the room. No more talk about crews and throwdowns. I close my eyes.

It doesn't take long for my thoughts to turn to Manos Dura. No one can argue that Manos was a fierce fighter but there was a side of her that few saw. Manos carried with her a picture of the Towers. At night, she would pull the picture out when no one was looking and kiss the image. "I just want a place where I can look out the window," she once told me. "When I have that, I can stop running the streets, You know?" I can see the face she would make when she stared at the picture.

She was full of hope. Her dream was mine and I failed her.

How I wish the day had played out differently. We knew the consequences of being in a gang, Manos included. The violence is real. Tronics are meant only to shock a person. This doesn't stop crews from using other weapons. When one of your own is brutalized the way Manos was, it's hard not to follow suit.

Soon I'm spiraling into more heartache, where my thoughts shift to my own family. Mother and her pain, when she was so deep in her sickness, right before passing away. Her lips blue. The signs were there. I can see them now. I was too young to regulate the sueños, to make sure she took the right amount. An overdose could have easily been avoided if only I'd had help. Where was my father? It's impossible to even remember him. There isn't a feeling of a father. He's a ghost, if he existed at all.

Then there's my sister. The moments when I can see her are so rare that when she appears I hold my breath for fear I'll lose the memory forever. In this memory, I'm crying, reaching out to be comforted. I must be six years old. Close to seven perhaps. When my emotions seem to overtake my everything, my sister appears out of nowhere, her head popping up as if by magic. She has a full head of crazy curls, similar to mine. The only difference is her hair is light brown, not inky black. Her skin is dark, and she has a warm smile. Her full lips mouth words to a song I no longer recall.

The vision lasts for only a moment and I feel a comfort I never get in the real world. There's a sense everything and everyone will be safe if I just stare at this funny girl with deep brown eyes and a slightly crooked smile. Soon the smile is gone and she is serious. I stare at her lips. I can't make out the words or why she is so upset. There are tears in her eyes. She tries to tell me something urgent. I don't know what.

This is my slim recollection of her. There are certain scents that conjure her to me from time to time. The smell of the sidewalks right after a light rain can do it. A vague sense that perhaps we played together outside. A feeling of joy. I don't know why I'm thinking of her. It's been so long.

There are times when I'm not even certain if this memory is mine. Perhaps I stole it from another person—as with the other items I've taken throughout my soldiering life. I don't want to believe that. It's my sister, my only sister, before she abandoned me for Cemi Territory. Her name is Yamaris. I hated her for so long. Now I don't even think she exists.

I reach over to the charm tucked in my jacket. I turn the necklace over and notice the small initials engraved along the arm of the fist. The letters *AR* for *Ashé Ryders.*

The plan is to show Déesse the charm. She'll know what to do with it. Truck is right. We're so close to our goal. I have to focus on this weekend's throwdown. If there was a real threat, we would have been told. Mega City is tempting for the wild ones in Cemi Territory to want to try to bum-rush. With Déesse's military hold, degenerates who try to break through our borders fail. Those in Cemi Territory are just not organized enough. As for the LMC, we'll beat the Deadly Venoms. Déesse will welcome us into her military fold and into the Towers.

I roll my shoulders a bit to shake off the tension. The water is already losing its heat. I continue to rest.

"Missed me?"

That is not Books's voice. I reach for my baton. It's back where I left it when I checked in.

I'm naked in a tub and about to get jumped. This is not how I'm meant to go out.

CHAPTER 4

SAINTS AND SOLDIERS

B efore I can turn, the person jams a weapon to the base of my neck. This fool is on a serious mission. My heart races. Is this connected to the Deadly Venom I just bashed? Retribution? Where is Books with the damn tea?

"What the hell do you want?" I say.

There is only silence. I search the room. The candles are too far away. The necklace is the only thing I have. What good will a leather strap do if I can't reach the person's neck to strangle them with it?

"I asked you a question." There is only a slight chuckle. It's not enough for me to determine who he is or to tell if he's tall or short, alone or with an army. I can't smell him either, since the room has the powerful scent of jasmine meant to create a soothing effect. How does a sweet fragrance smell so deadly now?

"There is no way you passed a tronic through Doña Chela, so this object you're feeling my neck with is harmless." This gives him the cue to use the weapon to caress my hair. He is playing. If this person had wanted to stun me, he would have done so long ago.

Maybe Doña Chela got confused and thought I wanted a little extra with my massage. The club caters to every type of "game." This idiot probably thinks I paid for this show. He strokes my hair again.

Coming to the Luna Club was just another bad call. Add it to the endless questionable decisions I've made tonight. Letting Nena roll ahead of us instead of staying close during our patrol. Allowing the ANT to mess with me in ways I can't pinpoint. Because I was too wrapped up in flashbacks of my family, this guy caught me with my guard down. I can't fall victim the way Manos did. I need to think quick, because it's me or this guy.

When he pokes me again, I make my move. I inhale deeply and duck my head into the water. As I go down, I grab hold of him and pull as hard as I can. I drag his upper body into the bath. Gushes of water splash everywhere. I waste no time in whipping my body around and using my strength to keep his head in the water. He thrashes violently. Everything around me disappears as I concentrate on using my anger to keep him down. He kicks and makes gurgling noises. The room no longer exists. The candles. The papi chulos. Time is at a standstill. I won't let him breathe.

The rage of having a punk disrespect me rises. No one touches me. No one invades my space. I hold him down. Harder. Harder.

And then it hits me. My eyes focus away from my hands and examine the person. The familiar build. The clothes. Holy Mega. I know him.

"Santo!"

I lift his face from the water. He coughs uncontrollably and spits. The cough soon changes into laughter. Santo drops to the floor and cradles his stomach in between gulps of air.

"Have you lost your damn mind!" I yell. "What is wrong with you?" I could have killed him. What he did was dangerous.

He laughs and flashes his almost perfectly straight teeth, which shine against his olive complexion. The more he cracks up, the more I want to slap him. I get up and wrap a towel around my waist. When he won't stop laughing, I kick him. Hard.

"Hey," Santo says. "Is that any way to treat a brother?"

I kick him again.

In his hand he holds a harmless decorative figurine, a statue he probably grabbed from the hallway. Idiot. Although Santo calls himself a brother, he's more than that. He's been on Las Mal Criadas' side for a long time, ever since the day he approached me after a battle and commended me on my skills.

He kept coming around, offering me tips, better weapons. The friendship became something more. We are not partners or in love—don't believe in love—we just have a strong connection.

"What are you doing here?" The initial shock has worn off. I throw him a towel.

"I should be asking you the same thing. What are *you* doing here with a chulo?" he says. "You don't need him when what you need is right here."

I slap his cheek playfully. He takes off his wet shirt and places it against a seat. His arms are covered in ink. You can spend hours reading the elaborate tattoos on his body. There are quotes and symbols, animals and beautiful women. There's a story behind each design. He even has LMC letters inked on his right arm. I did the tattoo myself. Everyone in Mega sees the letters and knows he stands with us.

Santo pulls me toward him. We smile at each other. I'm happy to see him even after the stunt he pulled. Soon we will be together in the Towers. Me and him. There will be no need to pretend he doesn't play favorites even when everyone can see it as plain as day. Santo leans in for a kiss. His callus-free hands and soft full lips remind me of my future.

"You didn't venture out of the Towers to reprimand me for hanging with a papi." I pull away and put my clothes on. "What did you do to Books anyway?"

Santo shakes his head, giving a look of disapproval. "I sent the boy to Truck. She needs that trash, not you. This place makes you weak," he says. "You're wasting your energy when you have bigger things to be thinking about."

Wow. He's here for less than five minutes and he's managed to cut me with a dose of harshness. This anger must be jealousy. What is there to be jealous of? I don't worry my head over what goes on in the Towers. He's free to do what he wants with who he wants. Our connection is built on openness. It has to be. There's a whole lot of baggage that comes from being Déesse's only son. Struggles I am privy to when he shares. Those moments are rare.

"I'm sorry if my being here makes you uncomfortable. Next time you want to see me, send a message on the Codigo instead of springing up unannounced," I say. "Now, drag your sorry ass out of here and leave me alone."

"I didn't come here to talk about papi chulos." He hands over my pants. "We're cool even if these places are pathetic excuses for fun."

I snort. Fun? He should talk. I've heard of the craziness that goes on in the Towers. The lavish parties, scenes, anything you want to happen can happen with the snap of a finger. Of course, Déesse would never admit to the debauchery. We hear about it down on the streets. That's why so many people want to have access. Live the high life and do what you want without any repercussions, without having to deal with hard labor. Everyone has their own way of coping. Most people work under the burning sun or in the factories. Others pay with fists. I would rather fight than work in one-hundred-degree weather, the sun beating down on me day in and day out. Until I make it to the Towers, the boydega clubs are my sanctuary. Who is he to judge?

Santo caresses my arm. This is his way of sort of apologizing without having to say a word. I lean in to his hand. I don't want to argue. Too much has happened tonight. I don't want to end with Santo mad at me. I need him.

"Where are your guards?" I change the subject.

"I'm here alone."

When Santo leaves the Towers, he usually travels with at least two bodyguards. This is unlike him. To come and look for me when he could have easily sent me a message only adds to the seriousness. I search for clues and find none. He holds my stare, the only person who can.

"Who did this to you?" He lightly touches the scratch under my eye. He kisses my forehead and then gently kisses the cut.

"What's going on?" I ask.

He pulls away and picks an uncomfortable stool to sit on. I can tell he's nervous by the way he toys with the lit candle, dipping his hand in the melted wax without flinching from the pain.

"As promised, you are to meet with Déesse this weekend," he says. "I'll take you to her after the fight. Before that happens, I need you to do one thing."

I let out a sigh of relief. This is what I've been waiting for, to be able to speak to her in person. Only she can grant access to the Towers.

Residents in the Towers are sent packing when they fall out of favor with her. Santo's been letting me know when there's been a vacancy. There is a weekly newsletter that lists people who are kicked out of the Towers and the reasons why. Infractions can be anything from not pulling your weight to starting beef with others. Santo has been giving me copies of the newsletter although he's not supposed to. There are a few apartments available, enough room for my whole crew to create a new home. Those apartments won't stay vacant for long. Finally, we can make a move.

"I need you to fake the fight."

Wait. What the hell did Santo say to me? I must have heard him wrong. He didn't ask me to throw a battle. Did he?

"Your crew will let the Deadly Venoms win this weekend. There will be no victory for you," Santo says. "You've got to let them win."

Is he high? I will never let my crew throw a fight. Never. We've bashed our way to get to this point. How would we look if we played chicken? No one would ever take us seriously. He's got me wrong.

"It won't happen. We aim to win." I vigorously dry my hair. "You made a mistake. Las Mal Criadas are no punks and, by asking, you're insulting me."

He stands and grabs my shoulders, forcing me to face him. "This is no joke. You can't win."

This can't be. I pull away. "Why? Who benefits from this?"

We've never been approached before to throw a game. If we had, the person would have been trounced for asking. By doing so, we lose credibility. How would we look in front of Déesse if we decide to cave in unless . . . ?

"She's asking us to pull it, isn't she?"

Santo returns to playing with the candle wax. I have my answer. This is wrong on so many levels. Why is she asking me to do this? I need a reason, because right now the signs point to hell no.

"This doesn't make sense. My crew is meant to prove we can beat the Deadly Venoms. I've been leading them toward this, and now you're telling me to fake the fight. I don't get it. Why would Déesse ask me to do that?"

He can't even look me straight in the eye because he knows this is trash. What a joke. I can't go to my crew with this. Déesse has been straight with the people of Mega. Straight and fair. Why is she playing me?

"What's the deal?" I search for answers. Santo has his city look on, a hard and cold expression. Not even a tiny glimpse of why, just a furrowed brow. "Tell me, Santo. If you're my brother, then you'll tell me what's going on."

He traces the lettering on my choker and pulls me in real close, so close I can feel his breath on my neck. He gestures to the door. The rooms here are being recorded. Of course. How foolish I've been. Doña Chela sits listening to our whole conversation.

"This is coming from her," he whispers. "Déesse has her reasons, and she's not sharing them with me. I'm sorry."

Santo holds me tight, and I try to decipher the meaning behind this setback. As top crews, the Deadly Venoms and Las Mal Criadas must occupy the same neighborhood. The neighborhood is clearly divided. The Deadly Venoms patrol along the 2 Line, while we are on the D. The 2 Line is a sweet section of Mega City. No lost ANTs, just decent toiler families trying to get by. The D Line covers a bit of the border, which means breaking night is riskier.

Even with their better section to patrol, the Deadly Venoms have gotten sloppy lately. They force certain families to pay tribute to them in the form of trade. Protection "offerings." Crews are meant to guard the citizens of Mega, not steal from them. The families they've been gouging are promised access to the Towers or a better living situation. The Venoms are even dangling medical supplies to these families, drugs only Tower residents are privy to. When the Venoms fail to provide what they promised and the families are brave enough to complain, they use violence to shut them up. People are too afraid of the Venoms to say anything to Déesse. These families are begging for us to retaliate.

If the Deadly Venoms are messing around with the rules,

then it's only fair the better crew rises up. I don't understand.

"What if we don't?" I whisper.

"I think you know the answer."

I do. There will be no Towers for us. The chance to join her special guard will be squashed, and Las Mal Criadas will be stuck doing the same old crap, patrolling borders for lost toilers.

This isn't right. What did Las Mal Criadas do to get on her bad side? Did my crew overstep their boundaries? I rack my brain, going over recent events in my head, seeing if we tripped. I will tear the whole crew apart if I find one of them messed up our chances over a dumb mistake.

Santo pulls away.

"What's this?"

He takes hold of the black fist necklace. I try to snatch it back. He quickly moves farther into the room. Santo dangles the charm by a candle to get a closer look. He concentrates as if he's waiting for the necklace to speak.

"It's none of your business," I say.

Adrenaline pumps through my body again. Keep it together. The plan was to find a way to get the charm to Déesse. This still holds true, although it looks as if my goal is slipping farther away from me.

"Where did you get this?" Santo twirls the charm. I reach for it again. He's too fast.

"Stop trying to change the subject." I try my best to be

vague, sensing Doña Chela sits in a remote room watching us as if this is her own private novela being performed live.

"This doesn't look familiar. AR. AR." He mouths the letters. "They must be a new crew. What did your intel get on it?"

Any other day and I would freely share my findings with Santo. His connections have gotten me things other crews can't ever afford. Not today. I'm taking this straight to Déesse. Now more than ever, I need the charm to be valuable. Besides, if he's not willing to tell me why his mother wants us to pull the fight, then I'm not willing to tell him what I know about the charm.

I punch him in the gut, not too hard, just enough to send a message.

"Okay, okay."

He hands the charm back. I tuck the necklace deep in my pocket.

"So, how are you going to play this?" he asks.

This isn't the first time he's been a messenger for his mother. At least he came to me and didn't send some random assistant instead. This proves Santo is an ally. Since the directive comes from his mother, I can see why he can't divulge her reasoning. I respect this. He has to side with his blood family. As for me, I must decide whether I'll be a true follower of Déesse or whether I choose another path.

There's no option. Las Mal Criadas will fight the Deadly

Venoms. If Déesse is asking me to lose, then she must see an objective that goes beyond the throwdown. I don't know what that is. I have to believe she will take care of us in the long run. She hasn't proven otherwise.

When my mother died, Déesse came to see me. Only a few hours had passed since I found my mother's body unresponsive. I was alone in the underground home she claimed for us, unable to formulate my grief. I was so lost. I didn't know what to do next. Déesse entered the room with no entourage. No guards. I had never spoken to her before. I was just a young punk with no reason to be close to such a goddess. Yet, here she was before me. Déesse took hold of both my hands and made me a promise.

"This pain will pass, and what will remain will be the loving moments between you and your mother. Don't blame her for how she handled this life. A broken family is hard to heal. Now it's your responsibility to honor her and forge a new family. I promise to take care of you as I take care of my own daughter. Because when you hurt, I hurt."

I will never forget what she said. Those weren't just words. I felt them. Although I never spoke to Déesse after that day, she kept true to her promise. A beautiful ceremony was held for my mother in the courtyard for everyone to see. My mother died of a broken heart. When my sister and father left, where else could Mom turn for her pain? Déesse understood that Mom wasn't an addict. She was just confused. It was an accident.

"I believe in Déesse. She will take care of my crew," I say. "I will do what she asks me to do."

Santo nods with an air of indifference. As much as he wants to pretend he's one of us, down with the cause, he's living a privileged life. He's royalty, whereas I'm just one notch above a toiler. Las Mal Criadas will toe the line. We have to. Déesse holds the key to our fate.

"I'll see you on Saturday, then," Santo says. "Suerte."

"I don't need any luck."

He heads toward the door and turns with a serious expression. "Always with the last word. Sorry, not tonight." With that, Santo leaves.

I thought Déesse wanted a crew that stood for righteousness. So be it. Las Mal Criadas will go down this weekend whether we want to or not. I'll fake the fight and let the Deadly Venoms win. I'll lie because lying will save us.

CHAPTER 5

CHANCE WITH DESTINY

The three tall buildings that make up Mega City Towers have the shape of a giant letter U. It's the only complex to survive the Big Shake with minimal damage. Those who live in the Towers get a gorgeous view of the courtyard that lies below at the center of the U shape. Only Tower residents have access to the blooming flowers and shady trees inside the courtyard. There's even a playground for kids. On most days, the rest of Mega City can peep enviously through the gates and admire the luxury of having such a green space. Not today. Today is the last Saturday of the month. The gates are wide open for the throwdown. The courtyard is overrun by Mega City people.

As we enter, red paper flowers rain down from above, covering the floor in scarlet, the color of my crew. I look toward the hundreds of windows that make up the Towers and to those tossing the flowers. The chosen ones. They smile and laugh, secure in being far away from the toilers down below. Can't say I blame them. No one wants to be near regular ol' toilers, sweaty and reeking from hard labor. The sun will soon set and a cool breeze will serenade us. If only the breeze could gather me and place me next to the luminous people above. I hope the potent drinks flow tonight. How closely will they look when I give up the fight? I hope not too closely.

Across from us, the Deadly Venoms present their game face. They're dressed in black, with mugs painted in their trademark skulls. When they snarl, they flash their neon pink mouth guards. I take a hard look. Which one of them did Manos in? Who threw the last punch? It's going to take everything to throw this fight now that they stand before me.

"Hey, Deadly Dumb Dumbs!" I yell to them. "You goofs need to sit down. Take all the seats. You're looking janky."

Around me, several toilers laugh and jeer at the Deadly Venoms without fear of repercussion. This is the only time when throwing shade is not only encouraged, but it adds to the whole spectacle.

"We're going to shred you to pieces," counters one of the Deadly Venom soldiers. How original. These idiots deserve to be crushed. The worst fate for any crew is to be dull, and the Deadly Venoms are the dullest.

"You cows are played out, you and your skull faces," yells Truck.

"Suck my tip!" they scream back.

As we trade insults, the toilers behind us yell out who they will bet against. A girl sells wooden dolls made to our likenesses. Other vendors trade drinks and delicacies normally found only in the Towers in exchange for sueño tabs. Seats are free, but toilers will gladly give up their spot if a good trade presents itself. Everyone is in on the action.

Two crews battle it out fist to fist. Five girls against five girls. Technically it should be a pretty clean fight but crews are known to bring extra help with them. Sticks. Bats. Rocks. Fight whoever you want to fight except for the leaders. The leaders of each gang must end the throwdown by battling each other. It is a show, and that is what the masses expect. Schedules are determined in advance. There are lightweight throwdowns for baby crews starting out and main events like ours.

Ask any old-timer. They will reminisce back to when large sporting events were held as a way to bring people together and to invigorate the cash flow. They forget how most of those events were catered to men. Déesse brought back these competitions with a twist—women only take center stage. The throwdowns are reminders that we have strength equal to or more so than men. For crews, these battles are a way to position themselves and gain favor with those above. A battle won can mean a better line to patrol or entrance to the best papi chulo clubs. Losing can mean being stripped of your status and delivered to a weak toiler job.

"This is going to be the end of Las Muchas Muchas," says

Destiny. "Yeah, I'm looking right at you. Santo's squealing sucka."

Destiny is the leader of the Deadly Venoms. Funny how her name sounds so queenly. Doesn't go with the person who beats her crew with a large gold cane while gorging off their findings. Destiny surrounds herself with a young, shredded group. She makes sure they're desperate, a real hungry bunch, willing to accept her beatdowns in exchange for whatever measly piece she tosses their way. I can't believe I have to lose out to her. Faking this fight when Destiny is literally the worst piece of trash in Mega City.

"I'm going to take that gold cane and shove it up your ass," I say. "You're going to be my very own piñata."

More and more people stream in. Children climb poles to get a better view. There's a real surge of energy emanating. A sense that a harsh and bloody show is about to go down. My girls stretch their bodies. Get limber. It's on us to teach Destiny and her crew a lesson in the name of Manos Dura. They have their rage faces on.

Last night, I couldn't find a way to tell my girls about Santo's proposition, not even Truck. Instead, I gave them a pep talk to end all pep talks. I used words like "sisterhood" and "the Towers" and "making our dreams come true." I spoke the truth, for the most part. Because I end the fight with Destiny, I will lose to her. Individually, they can save face. As for me, I will go down. When I do, the LMCs will lose.

Nena gently tugs at my jacket and whispers, "She's here."

A hush spreads across the courtyard. Eyes are glued to the balcony. School is in session. I hope once I see Déesse I will understand the task before me. I tried to figure a way out of this. The roads lead right back to me playing the sucker tonight. I have to trust Déesse.

Déesse steps onto the balcony on the first floor of the Towers. She wears a flowing dress in neon colors so bright that those with the bad luck of being far away can see her. Her braids reach the floor and her arms are encased in large gold cuffs. Even the freckles that cover her face and neck add to her breathtaking beauty. I'm not the only one who carved freckles on their skin to imitate her. Every girl wants to be her.

Standing next to Déesse with a sour expression is her daughter, Sule. She has no freckles.

"My beautiful children! If you hear me, let me know. If you feel me, scream it to the sky," Déesse says. Everyone, including myself, yells so loudly our throats most certainly burn.

"All who hear me, far and wide, know that we are in this world for one thing, to make this life right. When everything around us was being destroyed by those lost in their blind ambition, we didn't cry. We didn't ask, 'why?' No, children, we got up and got to work."

Although Déesse begins each throwdown with these same words, I never tire of hearing them. It reminds me of my own power. I can do anything if I put my mind to it. My destiny is not fixed. It is manifested.

Déesse continues. "Today I want to talk about our hands. These hands. Back then we relied on others to make our things. Food. Clothes. Weapons. Globalization, they called it. A fancy word. A big word. It meant not looking within our own talent and relying more and more outside. How do we feel about that?"

There is a chorus of *boo*s.

"Everything made in Mega City is done by us, for us. We reuse every single scrap. Repurpose every item. With these hands, no one can stop us."

"Say it, Déesse," yells Truck.

Her words wash away my anxiety. My mother once told me how hard life was for her when she was a child. Hunger and disease wiped out many families. Violence was rampant. It wasn't until sueño tabs were created that the city turned around. Food pellets have the essential nutrients a person needs. It was Déesse and her family who worked on a way to produce them on a large scale. She shared the knowledge with everyone.

"They, the money people, the liars, the men, they destroyed the homes we had. With our hands we now have a new place. Don't ever forget we did this together and we are going to continue to build a better future. Together."

How can one woman bring so much hope simply by speaking? Old-timers say Déesse learned the art of oratory from her great-grandmother. Listening to her speak, I am reminded of how my future can be reshaped, even if I'm living off of trades or sleeping on dirt floors. If Déesse wants me to throw this fight, I'm willing to lose if it means I'll eventually be closer to her.

"Today is a special night," Déesse says. "Each month we prove we are triumphant in the streets. We can come together and defend our home. This isn't La Casa de Déesse. No, children. This is our house! And we protect it with this."

She raises her fists, and everyone goes wild. Déesse waits for the roar to subside.

"Go ahead, Sule. Speak to your sisters."

Only a few toilers, mostly out of pity, welcome Sule with claps. She mumbles so quietly. Those behind me scream at her to speak up. Sule repeats herself. No one can make out what she's saying. This only makes her fumble even more. She huffs and reveals a flash of anger that causes a few of us to laugh.

Anyone else in Sule's position would love to be dressed in such beautiful clothes, to be part of such a beloved family. Not Sule. I don't know how Déesse can produce such a plain, boring daughter. There's a joke going around that if you want to insult a person's beauty, just tell them they are "pulling a Sule."

"We are very happy to be here tonight," Sule says. "To, ummm, for these fights."

She practically throws the microphone back to her mother and walks farther into the balcony so no one can see her. Poor

Sule. She doesn't have her brother's smarts or her mother's looks. She can't even fight, although her mother has arranged for the best soldiers to try to work their magic on her. Kind of a waste if you ask me.

Santo stands beside Sule. He's dressed in armor although he will never fight because of his gender. What type of conversation did he have with his mother? Will Santo lose respect for me for throwing the fight?

This angers me. Screw him and screw me for allowing my thoughts to be tied to what he thinks. There's only the goal. There's no room for feelings.

"As you know, these streets have been patrolled by two of my most trustworthy crews. Las Mal Criadas are a true bunch." The crowd goes crazy. They don't let Déesse finish. She begins again.

"Las Mal Criadas are a true bunch. They're the Bad Girls. The E-ratic Commanders, the Wild Ones. With Chief Rocka as their leader, these soldiers have taken many a crew down with their strength and wisdom."

Toilers behind me pat my back. It feels good to be loved.

"The Deadly Venoms have been by my side for a while. The Mighty Demons, the Thunderous Bandits, the Female MCs. Destiny has shaped her crew in her likeness—forward crushers. Now *they* are the ones to beat."

Everyone screams around me. The noise deafens to the point where the sounds blend into one.

"Of the two, only one will stand. The victors will be placed on my right-hand side."

The time has come. A toiler picks up the clave and begins the rhythm. The "ta-ta, ta-ta-ta." My crew begins the chant, our chant. Las Mal Criadas' call to action, in synch with the clave.

"Mal-Mal, Mal-Mal-Mal."

The repeating chant is soon joined with the sound of the congas. The thumping of the same beat over and over again. It follows the rhythm of my pulsating heart, the sound of my crew's heart. I join in on the chant and focus on every word and what they mean. To be bad. To be born into this world for only one thing—to cause pain. Yes, I'll lose this fight, but first I'm going to cause Destiny's crew misery.

We line up in formation. To my left, the muscle of my crew, Truck and Smiley, take up space. Smiley wears a gold grill, one that marks the victims she bites with an "LMC." Her hair stands in multiple directions. Her lips are lined in bright red. Nena stays close to the middle, right beside my girl, Shi. Shi may be short, she's also super fast, a quality most people underestimate. Her long black bangs conceal most of her face.

I take one more view of the Towers. Those nameless strangers shout and throw petals down. Soon I will be among them.

"Don't forget, LMC. This is our moment," I say to my

crew. "Stick to the plan. Remember, we are sisters, family, and we look out for each other."

I face each of them. Tap them on their shoulders. They are ready.

Déesse nods to Santo. He will light a malasuerte signaling the start of the throwdown.

I focus on Destiny's grotesque lips and wait to hear the explosion. Destiny voices foul curses. Those are the lips I will punch for the times she called me Santo's whore. For insulting my crew. For disrespecting my house and the house of Déesse. And for killing Manos Dura. She will pay right before I lose the fight.

Boom.

Her crew gallops toward us. What a bunch of chicken heads. They fan out into a semicircle so Destiny stays protected behind them. My crew's mission is to wipe them off one by one. Everyone is up for grabs except for Destiny. They have no clue about my plan to fake this fight.

I take the first Deadly Venom with a jab to the stomach. I finish her off with several kicks to the groin. Before I can charge toward Destiny, another Deadly Venom jumps on my back. She's a crazed devil, yelling indescribable noise in my ear and ramming her fists onto my head. I try to flip her over. It's a no go. Instead of a bear hug, she's now going for my eyes. A baby recruit who thinks she's got a chance with me. Not tonight, young gun. I push back, forcing us both to fall backward. When we drop, I elbow her in the ribs. While she catches her breath, I turn and straddle her body. I rain a flurry of jabs on her, destroying her face until her lip splits and her eyes roll back.

Quick tally on the LMCs. Nena is being tag-teamed by two Deadly Venoms. Smiley comes to her rescue, takes a big bite out of one of them. Nena gets her bearings back and is able to get in a couple of good blows. A Deadly Venom holds a bag by her side. This is a tip I gave my girls before the fight. The Deadly Venoms are known for storing shit and rubbing handfuls of it into their opponent's mouth. Disgusting and effective as hell. Nena sees the girl and outsmarts her by jumping on her first. The shit bag falls from her hands. I don't wait to see what happens next.

Truck tackles another. Destiny continues to hide behind her people. What a joke. To lose to her is a tragedy. My insides burn at the thought. I'm not sure if I'll be able to pull this off. Pride usually gets the best of me and it's directing me to win. I'm reminded again of the task when I take a quick glance at the Towers.

"You're mine."

The massive giant heading my way is Destiny's second-in-command. She goes by the name La Chiquita. There's nothing small about her. There's only one weak spot on her, her thick ankles.

La Chiquita grabs me by my collar and lifts me off my

feet. I struggle to break free. The girl has been working on her biceps. Truck wields a bat and breaks it on La Chiquita's back. It only causes her to slightly loosen her grip. La Chiquita doesn't even wince. She just laughs.

"Damn, Chiquita, cut back on the sueño mixers for once," I say, then kick her while Truck is crouched behind her so she topples over. Before La Chiquita gets up, I grab my baton and swing it at her ankles. Chiquita coils, screaming bloody murder as I hit her again.

Finally, the path is clear. Destiny is left unguarded. I glance at Déesse. She speaks to Santo. There must be a question of whether I'm going to go through with the plan. With the adrenaline rush, it almost seems too easy not to.

"You punk ass. When's the last time you've been in a fight, you cow?" I yell. There's no one left to protect Destiny. Sweat pours from her, clamping down her ratty hair. "How much have you stolen from innocent people? You're the losing end of this crew."

The crowd can't get enough. I enjoy seeing Destiny cower. Humiliating her is easy. I have to let her win, no matter what. Focus, girl. Focus. Destiny has to win.

I stride up to her and punch her on her side. Wrong move. My hand crumbles. She's wearing protective armor. With my strong hand useless, she flops her body on top of mine, sending me reeling back to the ground. She's going to try to smother me.

"Where's Santo now?" she grunts.

Her body reeks of greasy food and armpits. She's going to kill me with her stench. I head butt her. When she doesn't move, I try biting her ear. She pulls away before I give a good crunch. There isn't much time. She barrels over to me again, wielding a cap. She throws it. I dodge out of the way.

That's when I see him. The ANT we took down the other day. The one with the charm. He's here and he's walking over to the field, ignoring the violent action before him. The ANT's stride is long and determined. His eyes are wild, and he's looking right at me.

"I need to speak to Déesse," His screams are guttural and deep. A desperate person. Toilers try to stop him from entering the field. He shrugs them off. Others laugh and think at least this can be a comical obstacle to the throwdown. I'm not laughing.

With my mind distracted for a second, Destiny takes the opportunity to punch me in the gut, knocking the wind out of me. Even while she hits me with one jackhammer after another, I strain my neck to see where the ANT goes.

"I need more sueños!" He grabs at the toilers around him. Clawing at them, determined to be heard. They push him away. He is a pesky nuisance.

The ANT forgoes entering the field and instead argues with the guards. He tries to get the attention of Santo, and it appears as if he's succeeding. Santo no longer watches me getting my ass kicked. Instead, he has turned to see what the commotion is with the ANT.

I flip away from Destiny for a second and run toward Santo. I can't have the ANT mess my game up when it comes to giving Déesse the charm. Whatever lie he spews might hinder any progress. I barrel toward him to shut him up.

I've forgotten the one thing I've taught the LMCs: Never give your opponent your back. Destiny grabs my ankle, and I fall flat on my face. Gravel etches into my skin. She pounds my back. Holy Mega.

I look up. Santo leans toward the ANT. What is he saying?

Destiny lets go of my legs after a smashing kick. I stand up to knock her out, completely forgetting my initial plan to lose. She stands her ground with a baton in her hand, the exact same one I used to pull down her own people. Destiny is about to take a big swing, right to the side of my skull. There's only a second, a second that transforms into an eternity as I watch Destiny's demonic grin display her pink mouth guard. She takes a swing. Everything goes in slow motion. The baton comes down, down, down.

And then it's lights out.

CHAPTER 6

THE HEALING GAME

M y hand reaches up and finds my head completely wrapped in bandages. The events leading to my current situation come to me in succeeding snapshots. Although I feel drugged, the image of Destiny smashing my head slowly comes into focus. How did I make it out of there without brain damage or death?

A tired toiler hovers over me, probably counting the hours when she can go home.

"Water," I half whisper, half grunt to her. The toiler ignores me.

Destiny clocked me because I was too busy trying to stop the ANT from reaching Santo. So dumb. The ANT doesn't have anything on me. Now I'm stuck in this room with my head wrapped up. Who knows what else is missing from my memory. I let an ANT get the best of me, and the worst part is, I got sucker punched by Destiny. I was supposed to lose this fight. The hope was to make myself not look like too much of a chump. Who knows how bad off Las Mal Criadas are. Did I screw our chances to get to the Towers?

"Hey, you. Water."

The toiler pretends not to hear me. She fiddles around with a tube connected to my arm. Never once addresses me or offers a drink. She exits before I can gather the strength to throw something at her.

Everything hurts. Even my eyebrows. At least I'm not dead. I got to get out of here. I don't feel safe. I try to lift myself off the bed. The pain is too much. There's no way I'll be able to leave. I search the table next to me, hoping to find a syringe I can use as a weapon. This tube connected to whatever poison they're pumping into me has to go.

As I draw my breath in to pull the tube out of my arm, I hear the rattling of the doorknob. I've got to move. One. Two. Three. Pull.

Nena storms into the room, rushing to my bedside with tears and snot rolling down her cheeks. She wails hysterically. I can't understand a word she says. Right behind her is the rest of my crew.

"Chief Rocka! Chief Rocka. Oh my God. I thought you were dead. They wouldn't let us see you, and I kept telling them I would do them in. I told them they couldn't keep us away from you."

She notices the blood pooling around my arm. The tube dangles on the side of the bed.

"She's bleeding!" she yells. I wince at the sound of her voice, as if Destiny once again wields a baton to my head.

"Please shut her up," I say.

"Damn rookie. You never know how to act." Truck pushes her away. "Step aside."

Smiley chuckles while Nena wipes her snot on her shirt.

"Sorry, Chief. I tried to keep them at bay. They wouldn't hear of it," explains Truck. "Besides, they wanted to pinch."

Smiley opens her jacket to reveal a new stash of medical items she conveniently hijacked. If there's an angle to work, Smiley is the one to find it.

"May I?" Shi asks. She examines my arm. Shi is the type of girl who doesn't say much. At the training camp, Shi was quiet to the point others thought she was unable to speak. It's the quiet ones who are usually underestimated. After we left the camp and started striking on our own, Shi stepped to us one day. She let me know a rival gang member was about to jump one of my girls. Shi didn't ask for anything in return. When the information was confirmed, Truck and I knew we wanted Shi to join the LMC. At the time we were heavily looking into completing our group. Smiley was already on board. With Shi by our side, we just needed to find our fifth, which we did when Truck recruited Manos Dura.

Shi brushes away her bangs from her eyes and pulls out a bandage roll from inside her jacket. She starts to wrap my bleeding arm. She's good at tending to our wounds after fights.

She also has the intel on the latest medicine available in the mercado. Shi's our doctor when there are no doctors to be had.

Even with Nena sobbing, I'm glad they're here. My family.

"You're living the life," says Smiley. "At least you got a bed."

Smiley rocks a black eye and a couple of stitches above the other. I bet the person got it worse under her hands.

"I look and feel wrecked," I say. "I'm dying of thirst."

Nena runs out the room before being told to do so.

"So, how long have I been here?"

"Two days," says Smiley. "My chillas on the inside gave me the lowdown. I made sure you were being well taken care of."

They tell me I'm in one of the healing centers located near the Towers. Toilers can never afford these places. Neither can crews. After battles, we patch ourselves up and hope for the best. Buy or steal whatever makes us feel better. Why am I in this healing room? Is this a prelude to the LMC moving to the Towers? A little taste of what's to come? I hope so. The room is not as opulent as I expected. It's still better than any room I've slept in.

Nena returns with water. She's no longer crying. Her eyes jump from Truck to Shi to Smiley and then back to me. She's nervous. So am I. Two days lying on this bed. Who knows what machinations have occurred outside this room with regard to our livelihoods.

The silence continues until Smiley can't stand it. She's

the opposite of Shi. Smiley will talk to the point of dizziness.

"What else you got in here? Any good drugs?" Smiley says. "We can use a few happy pills. Am I right? Especially after dealing with those Deadly Venoms."

It doesn't take long to notice my crew is keeping secrets. Even when Smiley tries to make light of the situation by telling a joke of how she conned an old lady into giving her food, she can't face me. No one wants to break the news. Whatever apprehensions or fears they are feeling, they won't say.

I give Truck the look. This is a conversation I must have with her alone. The rest of the LMC take the hint and leave. It's time for real talk between me and Truck. I need to know what's the deal before anyone else decides to surprise me.

Truck closes the door as they exit. Concern is written all over her face.

"Tell me," I say.

"You messed up. You got beat down by a lazy, no-good trick in front of everyone," Truck says. "Not only that, but you punked out. As if this was your first time throwing down."

She's not holding back.

"The Deadly Venoms. It was ridiculous!" Truck raises her voice. "What the hell was going on out there? You lost focus. We swore to get even in the name of Manos Dura. The rest of your crew held their own. You were too busy paying attention to I don't know what."

Truck wasn't privy to Déesse's plan. She's got every right

to be mad. My dream to live in the Towers is her dream too. I sold it to Truck first. When we both left the training camp, we did stints with other crews to see if we wanted to join them. None of the leaders of those crews had any real plan for the future. They only concentrated on how to hold on to their small section of the city. I could fight. So could Truck. We had mad skills. It's not enough. I knew we needed to join Déesse's elite soldiers to ever be invited to live in the Towers. If I was going to make that my goal, then I had to build a crew who would follow me there. I pushed them harder than ever before. We are almost there. She can't even see it. Why else would I be set up in this healing center?

"You told us we had an in for the Towers. This was *the* fight for us. I plowed down those Deadly Venoms to make room for you. You think it was easy? What do we have to show for it? Nothing. We're back to zero."

I close my eyes and wait. I need to know what happened after I blacked out. Did the ANT reach Santo?

"Are you done?" I whisper. Every move hurts. "Did the ANT say anything to her?"

"ANT? What ANT? To who?" Truck says. "What are you talking about?"

"The one who was trying to speak to Santo. Didn't you see him?"

Truck flashes me the expression she reserves for sueño addicts. She thinks I'm losing it. It doesn't matter. The ANT was probably tossed to the side. Good. We should be in the clear.

"What's the word on Déesse?" I ask.

Truck hesitates.

"I heard she's disappointed. We are on the wack list. The Deadly Venoms are on top," she says. "We need to go, Nalah. My gut tells me we've got to leave."

Without waiting for a response, Trucks gathers my belongings. She opens the drawers and finds my clothes. She does this in rapid formation, understanding there isn't much time for us to leave before facing the inevitable letdown from Déesse. I can't go. There's nowhere to go. Besides, I lost the fight. That was what Déesse wanted. Santo promised I would meet with his mother. I'm so close to the Towers.

"Stop."

Truck doesn't listen. What is it with lying down on this bed? Everyone ignores the patient.

"I'm facing the future as a fighter," I say. "I don't run."

Defeated, Truck lets the clothes drop back to the drawer. She knows I'm right.

"So, tell me one thing. What happened? That wasn't you fighting," Truck says. "You could have broke the heifer in half. Be straight with me. What's going on?"

No one gets to question my leadership, not even my best friend. With what strength I can muster, I sit up.

"Listen, soldier, you and me are tight. No doubt. Get this

straight—I won't explain my strategies to you," I say. "There is a why for what happened in the throwdown. Now is not the time for me to break it down. I will when I will. Till then, I need you to keep your side clean. I'm Chief Rocka. That makes you my right hand. Be my right hand, soldier, and don't ever question my moves again. You got me?"

Truck opens her mouth to curse me out. She stops. "Yes, I got you, Chief Rocka."

It's not in me to keep much from Truck, not when it comes to the crew. I'm asking her to go blind on this one. Plus, I'm pissed off. She's not the one who got thrashed by Destiny.

"Toss me my clothes," I say.

Tucked inside a hidden pocket is the Ashé necklace right where I left it. This will help us. I'm riding on it. I put on my pants and store the necklace safely inside. I hope I'm right.

Truck walks over to my side of the bed. She places a hand over mine and gently squeezes. There is anger and confusion. There is also tenderness.

"I ride or die with you," she says. "For as long and as far as you want." Truck understands and I'm grateful.

There's a knock at the door. Smiley sticks her head in.

"Déesse is heading this way," Smiley says. "And la fea is with her."

This is it. I'm going to find out our fate. Did the ANT create havoc? Did throwing the fight mark an entrance into the Towers? Or am I right where I was at the bottom?

"How do I look?" I ask.

Truck grabs a wet rag and wipes the sleepiness crusted in my eyes. This is how I know I got the right soldier. Truck will stick by my side. We're sisters. Pissed off or not, she will always be there.

"Wait by the door," I say to her. "No beef. Be on the alert, though."

Truck nods and leaves the room.

There's nowhere to turn and I'm too weak to do much of anything. I try to brace myself. Santo told me the LMC must lose in the throwdown. We followed instructions. This rising anxiety will choke me.

Minutes later, Déesse enters with an assistant, her daughter, Sule, and a soldier. With her entrance, the room changes from smelling sterile and bland to musky and fragrant. She wears a long yellow tunic with linen pants underneath. Her braids are tucked under a yellow headwrap. Déesse's arms are weighted down with her signature cuffs. She gives me a warm smile.

The only conversation I've ever had with Déesse was right after Mom passed away. I was so young and clueless. Soon afterward the training camp became my second home. I found purpose because of Déesse.

Here she is again. Those dazzling freckles are in front of me once more. It's hard to believe.

"We should clear the front. Toilers are crowding the hallway." The guard makes an obvious dig to my crew. She knows we are not toilers. I stare her down. It's hard to throw a mean face when you're lying on a bed.

"My crew stays where I stay." I say this to Déesse. Her guard doesn't exist. There's only Déesse. "They're under lockdown, so there will be no ruckus on our part. We left the violence on the courtyard. I give you my word."

"Of course we believe you," Déesse says. She nods to the soldier and waves her away. There won't be any beef. Truck will make sure of it.

"How are you?" Déesse asks. She unexpectedly grabs my hand. Anyone else and I would have found a way to draw closer to claim the knife Déesse keeps by her side. Anyone else and I would have hurt them. The only thing I can think of right now is how Déesse is asking how I'm doing. She's worried about me. The tension releases from within, and I allow myself to sink more into the pillow.

"I've never seen anyone take such a hit. That skull of yours must be made of concrete," she says. I try to join in and laugh. It hurts too much.

She shakes her head.

"No, no. Destiny did quite a number on you. You're lucky Truck was there to pull the baton away from her. Too bad Truck wasn't quick enough. The tip of the baton still managed to smack the side of your head. . . ."

This is why Truck is so pissed. She always had my back.

Sule toys with my bedsheet. Nervous or bored, I can't tell. She doesn't want to be here. I don't want her to be here either. And where's her brother? Is Santo out there waiting, or did the sucker leave me high and dry?

"Thank you for coming," I say. "You didn't have to."

"Nonsense," Déesse interrupts. "You're one of my children. Besides, we have business to attend to, don't we?"

With that, she lets go of my hand. Déesse sits down. I hadn't noticed when her assistant placed two chairs for her and her daughter. These are no ordinary chairs. They are elevated so no matter where or with whom she's talking, Déesse will be seated slightly above them, with the legs of the chair dangling off to the side.

"I'm happy for the Deadly Venoms," I lie. "They're obviously a better crew."

Déesse laughs. She faces her daughter, who is dressed to match her in a bright yellow satin dress. The color makes her look sickly. This is the first time I'm taking a real good look at Sule. Her makeup is so heavy. It's practically caked on.

"Sule, tell Chief Rocka what the Deadly Venoms are doing."

Yellow lipstick covers Sule's thin lips, causing her teeth to appear stained. She rolls her eyes. This must be a topic that's been on rotation.

"They've been stealing from me," she says.

"Not you," Déesse corrects her. "Us. They're stealing from

everyone. They're thieves. They're the worst kind because they think they're pulling it off. Stupid kids."

"Right, us. Yes," Sule says. "They're stealing valuable things and instead of stopping them, we're allowing them to continue."

Déesse displays a frozen smile. Her daughter's tone is so disrespectful I'm embarrassed for her. If she's known about the Deadly Venoms stealing, why did Déesse ask me to fix the fight? It doesn't make sense. If we had won, we would have gotten rid of them for everyone's sake. I choose my words carefully because my thoughts are spinning. I'm not sure where I stand.

"I'm sorry to hear that. The LMCs are a true bunch. Working for you would be an honor we would never take for granted," I say. "We can get rid of the Deadly Venoms. I'll make it our mission to do so."

"It breaks my heart when my children are deceitful," Déesse says. "For Mega City to survive, we must rely on each other. As sisters, we have no choice."

Déesse taught us how Mega City is a circle and everyone must fulfill their role in keeping the sphere strong. When one person ventures away, the circle weakens.

"It doesn't make sense when children choose to hit those protecting them," Déesse says. "One crew blatantly steals while the other, the other acts far more selfishly."

Her statement trips me up.

"So tell me, Chief Rocka," Déesse says. "Who will you leave behind?"

My heart races. What is she talking about? Did the ANT reach her and tell her about the charm?

"Sorry, Déesse?" I say.

Déesse's gaze stays fixed on me. She asks me again, and I don't know how to respond. This is going wrong. What is the correct answer? I should have listened to Truck and left this place when I had the chance. Now it's too late.

CHAPTER 7

ON A MISSION

Déesse's not talking about the drugs my girl Smiley stole only a few minutes ago. This is bigger. I rack my brain trying to decipher what she's getting at.

"The LMCs haven't been forthright. Wouldn't you say?" Déesse says. The assistant doesn't bother looking away from her Codigo. She pounds into the machine, completely oblivious to what is happening. Déesse's daughter caresses the bedsheet. There is a moment when it appears as if Sule is about to nod off. Is she high? What is going on?

"I'm not sure I'm following you," I say. I try to sit up straight, to exude strength. It's not working. I feel vulnerable. My girls are right outside the door. Why do they seem miles away?

Déesse continues to smile. "Santo tells me you no longer want to protect my streets. He says you've grown tired of doing the work."

I breathe a little. She thinks I'm abandoning the toilers of Mega City because I want to live in the Towers. That's far from the truth.

"The streets are my life. It's where my heart is," I say. "I would never leave behind the people of Mega City. It's just not possible."

"Why do you want to live in the Towers?" she asks.

This is a test. If I respond by saying I want to sleep in a real bed, then I'm being selfish. How am I different from Destiny, who steals from innocent people? She wants what she wants. A better life. Material things. How different is that from me wanting to live in a nice place? I take my time and think.

"I want to serve the people of Mega City as a soldier in your army," I say. "The LMCs have fought and beaten the best crews. There is no denying we are warriors. We can also take orders. Your army's mission is to protect our borders. It's my mission to do the same, to make sure everyone is safe. I'm ready to continue this work in your army."

Déesse gives a slight nod. I answered correctly.

"What if I allow only one LMC in the Towers?" she asks. The assistant stops pressing into her Codigo. Sule stares at her shoes.

What kind of trick question is this? I can't leave my crew. If I live alone in the Towers, how long before I can send for the LMCs to join me? Is that even on the table to discuss? I try to calculate. I can't play my girls. I won't. What makes the LMCs valuable to Déesse? We're smart and we see the big picture. I dig in my pocket and show them the charm. They concentrate on my offering.

"I found this on a toiler four nights ago. I knew the medallion would be worth more to you than the guy. I thought you might want to see it."

The assistant reaches for the necklace. I drop the charm on her delicate hands.

Déesse's benevolent smile disappears and is replaced with a serious expression. She calmly takes the medallion from her assistant and gestures for her chair to rise closer to the glowing light above the bed.

The room goes silent. No one says a word.

"Do you know what the fist stands for?" Déesse says after a long, uncomfortable pause. She addresses no one in particular. "It's called an azabache. Many used to think this black fist was a talisman meant to protect the person who wears it from harm. They were wrong. This tiny fist symbolizes hate. Odio."

It's hard to read Déesse when her chair is so elevated. I'm unable to see her. She speaks in an even tone. I can't tell if she's angry or if I did the right thing by giving her the necklace.

"You must know it belongs to the Ashé Ryders. Correct?" she asks. I answer her with a yes. My back is damp with sweat. I don't know why I feel as if I'm being interrogated. Sule perks up. Maybe she enjoys seeing how freaked out I am.

"What do you think?" she asks. From my vantage I can see her twirling the necklace.

"I think it's an old trinket," I say. "He probably came across it accidentally and thought he could trade it for sueño tabs."

"You didn't look close enough. Right beneath the AR is an engraved number. The year when it was presented to the wearer. It is right there," she says. "This is a relatively new charm, and it's found its way into our city."

She slowly brings the chair back to its original floating position. Déesse holds tight to the necklace. Her lips are pressed together. No smile. I feel the tension rise in the room. How can an innocent black fist bring such uncertainty? Déesse lets out a long sigh.

"Do you know the story of the Ashé Ryders? Not the tall tales. The truth?"

I stay silent and wait for her to begin.

"After the Big Shake, Mega City was in shambles. It didn't take long for people to see the source of destruction began with men. The Big Shake happened because of their drillings and their need to take from this earth. In order to rebuild, we came together to form a new existence. It wasn't hard to convince everyone. And for a time, we were united."

She continues. "A small group wanted to do things differently. They began sabotaging our livelihood, letting men make decisions on their behalf. Using violence against their own. They lusted for power," she says. "That's how crews came to existence. People wanted to take sides. Silly, if you think about it, when we have the same goal—to survive."

"So that's how the Ashé Ryders were born," I say. "Why would they want to destroy Mega City?"

"Why do the Deadly Venoms steal?" she says. "They think to be powerful you must stomp on those weaker than you. I asked you to lose to the Deadly Venoms because I wanted to see if you can control the brutality needed in a throwdown for a cause bigger than yourself."

I stare at the azabache. It holds a different meaning now.

"This is the third medallion I've seen in a month. It's clear to me there are sympathizers willing to risk bringing this into Mega," she says. "Passionate enough to stir the hate. The fear is not of the Ashé Ryders trying to step into Mega. My army is animal raw. We hold the borders tight. However, we must cut the disease before it spreads, before toilers start to think the Ashés hold a better way of living. That is a danger."

"Everyone is afraid of the Ashé Ryders even if they've never met one before," I say. "A charm won't entice me to leave everything and everyone I love for Cemi Territory."

I feel the need to defend the toilers. They are not as weak as she's implying. I've walked close to the borders many times. I can hear the wild cries and moans coming from Cemi Territory. Fires burning bright. There is only discord. Even Déesse has spoken on the true horrors that await those who choose Cemi Territory over Mega. Unbridled violence. Who wants that?

"How old were you when we took you in to train?" Déesse asks.

Before I can answer, the assistant pipes in. "She was seven years old. Father and sister are missing," the assistant says. "Mother is dead."

I want to throttle the assistant. No one speaks about my family, and here she is spilling my personal history. My blood family doesn't exist. They are only whispers. I don't even have a solid recollection of my father. Not a vision, not even a feeling. As for my sister, she comes to me only in one flimsy dream.

"Where is your family?" Déesse asks. "Where did they go?"

"They are dead," I say. "The LMC is my only family."

"What happened to your sister?"

"The LMC are my sisters," I say. "I only have the LMC and Mega City."

Memory is a tricky seducer. It dances with you, flirts with you. Ultimately you are alone. These dreams of my sister are a cruel trick meant to sway me away from my goal.

"I don't know what the Ashé Ryders are up to. How many are there? What are their plans for Mega City? These trinkets are an indication that innocent toilers are being used by them," she says. "What do you think we should do?"

Déesse is asking me for my opinion. Strategy, like a soldier in her army. I am this close to fulfilling my true role. I take my time in responding.

"We need to venture into Cemi Territory and find what the Ashé Ryders are up to," I say.

Déesse's smile returns. "I need an aggressive crew to do this. This is no ordinary mission. A crew must infiltrate the Ashé Ryders and report back to me," she says. "We need to know what they are trying to do."

"Mami—I mean, Déesse—can I go? Please, I'm not feeling well." Sule stands from her chair, forgetting she's elevated, and falls to the ground.

Déesse ignores her daughter's request. Sule is an idiot for asking. I detest her. Déesse sits here giving me a real talk and Sule can't even shut up for a second. I can see it now. Sule is an addict. The heavy makeup tries to conceal the gray skin. How long has she been in this state? Perhaps this is the reason why Déesse has such sympathy for addicts when her own daughter is unable to get off the sueño cycle.

"Mami?" Sule asks.

The assistant casually hands Sule a sueño tab. Sule's eyes meet mine. There is a rage in them. She wants to check out right in front of her mother. No wonder she is such a failure as a daughter. What does it mean to be unable to fight or lead? Déesse is all-powerful, flawless and true. Sule, on the other hand, cowers behind drugs.

Sule takes the sueño tab. She even grabs my glass of water. After swallowing it, she goes back to her seat, which is now grounded. Her focus returns to her shoes. It won't be long before she rides off on her sueño trip. To see her in this state makes me feel sorry for Déesse and Santo. What a burden she must be to her family.

"You can count on the LMCs to take care of business," I say. No pause. No half stepping. "We'll travel to Cemi Territory and find the Ashé Ryders. We will take care of it."

Déesse brings her chair down. "This won't be an easy task. The skills you've learned patrolling Mega City won't come into play in Cemi Territory. It's a whole other beast. You understand, don't you?" Déesse gently lays her hand on my shoulder. "Are you sure you are ready?"

"Yes, Déesse," I say. "We'll enter Cemi Territory for our people. We will look for the Ashé Ryders and gather as much intel as possible. The LMCs are the strongest crew in Mega City. We are meant to lead the way."

"Find the Ashé Ryders. Gain their trust. Let them think the LMCs are abandoning Mega City. I know you can fake a fight. I saw it with my own eyes," she says. "I have faith in the LMC and in you, Chief Rocka. You are our hope. Return victorious and you and your whole crew will be welcomed into the Towers."

Déesse's word is bond. Now my word is bond. The LMCs must carry this mission. We must protect the city no matter what.

"We won't fail you," I say.

Those freckles. She practically glows. Soon I will be near her. The Towers are within reach. My heart soars. It's really happening.

"The sooner you leave, the quicker we can welcome you back," she says. "What do you think? Seven days to go there and come back—that should be more than enough time."

Then she hands me back the necklace. "You'll need this."

Déesse programs the chairs to exit first. Déesse follows and then the assistant. Sule lingers behind. It's funny how the assistant and Déesse both pay Sule no mind. How far is she into her dream state? It doesn't seem too far. Sule looks sad.

"Such important decisions shouldn't be made in haste," she says.

What in Mega is she talking about? It must be the sueños. I have the strongest urge to hurt her. She better not ruin my chances with her cryptic statements.

"Ashé Ryders," she says with a chuckle. For a few seconds Sule closes her eyes, relishing the trip she must be embarking on.

The assistant reenters the room. "Come, Sule. She's waiting." The assistant places her hand on Sule's arm to guide her to the door.

"Take care of yourself," Sule says.

A princess with everything at her fingertips squanders away her opportunities in fabricated hallucinations. No wonder Santo never speaks about Sule. I will never be a burden to anyone. The LMCs can face whatever comes our way. We do so because we have no choice. Sule can hide behind her mother.

I won't lie. I'm scared. I've never crossed the border. Here

I am about to head to the worst place ever. Cemi Territory swallowed my sister. Probably took my father, too. I've never understood what would make a person enter Cemi voluntarily. There are no boydegas. No papis. No fun. Just hardship. Who would choose that? Deep down I believe my sister and father are dead. There's no grief for that loss. It happened so long ago. Blood family doesn't necessarily equate a connection. I saw this happen in the training camp. The closer you are to your family, the harder it is to become a fighter. When I entered the camp, I came completely alone. My focus was razor sharp. Other recruits wanted to run back to their parents. Babies. Searching for comfort when there was no room for softness.

I would never have imagined a simple throwdown with a crew would lead me on this insane mission. Am I capable of lying on such a scale? To pretend to be an Ashé Ryder ally? There's no question. I must.

First I need to find the ANT.

After leaving the camp, I joined a couple of crews to gain experience, take notes. Soon enough I ventured out on my own. Throwdowns upon throwdowns. I risked my body until everyone in Mega knew who the LMCs were. I've managed to overcome each obstacle thrown my way.

Now this.

How much longer can my dream of living in the Towers be kept from me? This must be the last test. My final obstacle before I can rest.

The streets are eerily quiet, which causes me to tighten my guard. We left the healing center right at the start of breaking night. We don't have to travel far. I continue to feel on edge.

A wall that once proclaimed our victories has a pink slash across our names. Deadly Venoms are claiming space and scratching us out. With one major loss, our rep is taking a hit. Only shows we need to do right by Déesse or we will never be back up. Without me having to say a word, Smiley covers up the names with new ink. THE LMC FOR LIFE.

Nena bumps into me. She walks so close it's as if she's afraid to lose me. She should stay in Mega City. Oversee our home. Nena is so green when it comes to fighting. She needs more training. There is not enough time. Then again, we might need her. The more fists the better.

Nena smiles at me. Those big, innocent eyes of hers. How will she react when I tell her we're heading into Cemi? What will my soldiers say? Will they tell me I'm a fool? Will they

CHAPTER 8

QUEENS OF THE UNDERGROUND

H ow to begin? Hit the station first, and then tell my crew. When my crew entered the healing room, they knew right away not to ask questions. It wasn't the time nor the place to hatch out what Déesse just proposed. Instead, they helped me gather my things in silence. We quickly left the room. Now we are on the streets, and I'm trying desperately to wrap my head around what the necessary action should be.

Find the ANT. Travel to Cemi. Locate the Ashé Ryders and pretend to join them. My life revolves around evading dangerous scenarios. The future seems so hazy when it should be crystal clear. I've done everything by the book. In the training camp, if they asked for twenty push-ups, I did thirty. When learning how to fight, I would pick the biggest girl even when I knew I would get beat down for being too small. I did what I had to do to stand out.

say no to the plan? I wish I didn't have to make these types of decisions.

We reach a gate that blocks the entrance to the 183rd station. Truck and Shi pry open the gate to create a gap large enough for us to squirm our bodies through. Inside, it is completely dark. We stand still until we adjust to the darkness. Soon we are able to make out the stairs leading down to the tunnel. Nena uses her mini-blowtorch to light the way. We listen to make sure there are no signs of toilers trying to move in. We've found one or two stragglers before and kicked them out. That's how Nena came to us. Soon after Manos Dura was iced, Nena showed up asleep on the second step, curled up like a lost puppy. Truck threw her out. Nena came back the next night and the next. She was determined to be accepted into the LMC. Every night Truck sent her flying. On the sixth day, I let her in. Truck was angry with me when I made the decision. We were grieving over Manos. Nena appeared when I needed to go beyond the hate that wanted to consume me. When I focused on Nena, the feeling of hopelessness dissipated.

More steps lead further down. The perfumed smell that recently emanated from Déesse in the healing room is now replaced with rust and rotting rodents. We eventually reach a cement wall. For most stragglers, the adventure to try to set up house in our station ends at this point. Once they make it here, the station appears to have no further access.

Smiley hoists Nena up. Nena lifts an unsuspected grate hidden behind a pile of broken cement. She pushes her body through the small grate and disappears. The sound of dripping water can be heard in the distance. It was Shi who located this station for us. She managed to dig deep in the Codigos archives and find this unassuming place overlooked when walking aboveground. We didn't create this tunnel. I'm pretty sure it was a random old-schooler who did it. With Shi's help we were able to locate the right openings, create new traps, and make it our home.

"She's taking too long." Truck shakes her head. "Manos used to make it to the other side in less than five minutes. She's too slow."

A couple more minutes pass before Nena dislodges a side entrance visible only to the LMC. To enter we must go down on our knees and crawl. It's a complicated procedure to get to the place we currently call home. It's worth it. When the LMC first started, we lived in crowded stations with hundreds of other families. There was no privacy. You had to hold tight to your belongings because people would easily steal them.

The LMC moved from there to other stations. Crews tried to bum-rush. Mini battles played out. It took a few tries before we located this one. It was empty. Within a couple of days we cleaned house and moved in.

"Fix that." Truck points to the broken glass spikes sticking out of the ground. Smiley kneels and replaces the spikes with new ones. Once we pass through a short hallway, we drop down to an open space. A few more feet left.

For the past six months, the steel car bearing a faded letter "D" on the side of it has been ours. Along with the concrete and steel, there is actual growth down here. A slew of plants manage to grow inside. Shi says it has to do with these panels installed in the ceiling. She said they were once called heliostatic panels and they somehow deliver sunlight from above ground. The plants add a nice bit of green even though we barely tend to them. Smiley thinks they are just glorified weeds. Funny how even in the darkest of places, life manages to break through.

The LMC pile into the rusty car. They light candles and place their offerings on the altar. Mementos from before they became an LMC are gathered in a corner. Smiley puts a sueño tab by the image of her mother. Truck drops a blue stone by a crude sketch of her brothers. Shi leaves a piece of paper with a word on it that only she knows. Nena drops a food pellet in front of a ragged worn doll. I cut a piece of my head wrap and place it on a fabric once part of my mother's dress.

"Line up," I say. My voice sounds hoarse. I'm still in pain from the throwdown, and I have a pulsating headache. Why does it feel as if weeks have passed me by? Manos. The ANT. The throwdown. And Déesse's mission. So much. I must find the right words. I will use anger to give me courage.

"Las Mal!" I shout.

The girls respond, "Criadas!"

I say it again and they yell back, louder each time. Their voices echo against the steel walls. Why can't our voices create a ghost army of LMCs?

I stare hard at each of them.

"Most of you have been rolling with me for the past five years. Have you got trust for your chief?"

They shout back, "Hell yeah, Chief Rocka."

I pace in front of them. Giving each of them the business. They are either with me, or I go on this search without them.

"A threat is coming to Mega City, and it's on us to track it down," I pull out the Ashé necklace. "This holds the key."

Each hard face looks straight ahead except for Nena, who sneaks a look at the azabache she helped discover. Our eyes meet, and she quickly goes back to her stance.

"An unknown ANT came to Mega City wearing this medallion. When we did a Codigo search, he turned up with no history. No family. No name. No ties to a specific crew, except for one we swore no longer existed. The medallion is called an azabache," I say. "This necklace belongs to the Ashé Ryders.

"Déesse believes the Ashé Ryders are coming through. We don't know the plan. We don't even know how many are in Cemi Territory. It's on the LMC to uncover what the Ashé Ryders are up to. If they pose any type of threat to Mega City, our people need to know."

"The ANT is now on our radar. Find him first. Then we head into Cemi Territory to infiltrate the Ashé Ryders. We gather as much intel as we can and return to Mega within seven days. When we're done, we're good to go to the Towers. Déesse gave me her word."

I let my talk sink in. No one blinks.

"Open floor," I say. "Speak your mind."

Smiley is the first to step forward. This doesn't surprise me. She's the talker of the bunch, and she will quickly be forthright.

"Why go to Cemi Territory?" she asks. "Only degenerates live there. The Ashé Ryders, if they even exist, are probably a bunch of wannabes. What does it matter? Our borders are guarded by Déesse's army, and it can't be beat."

Smiley turns to Shi to see if she will back her up or not. Shi won't lie. She doesn't make her decisions by gut. She only goes by intel.

"I've been following the rumblings, and they've recently shifted," Shi says. "There's a definite uneasiness on the streets. The stories have been a steady flow since a little before our throwdown. People are starting to fear that the Ashé Ryders are coming to invade the city."

"The Ashés aren't real," says Nena. "Right, Chief Rocka?"

Her voice quivers a bit. I can't have this weakness, not when I need every ounce of courage.

"If they aren't real, then there's no problem," I say. "We

need to find out for ourselves. That means locating them. It also means if they are real, we have to pretend we're down with their cause. Gather information. Then bounce without getting caught."

Truck keeps quiet. She will listen to everyone first. Her mind is racing. So is mine. I'm a tightwire about to snap. To go through these variables with my crew is making me doubt my decision.

"We are going in there blind," Smiley says. Her grill glows against the candles. "We don't know how many are true Ashés and how many are just renegades talking a big game."

"Why doesn't Déesse send the Deadly Venoms instead?" Shi asks. "Why us?"

I give it to them straight. What has been rolling in my head since I spoke to Déesse.

"We're the baddest. You don't send a weak-ass troop to take care of business," I say. "You send the best, and that's us. The LMC. There's no doubt in my mind this is the reason why."

Shi looks at Smiley. They contemplate what I've said.

"Or, maybe, we are the ones who lost the bet." Smiley says. I knew she would voice the concern rattling everyone.

"How are we going to pretend to be down with the Ashés?" Smiley shakes her head. "That's traitor nonsense."

"It's not as if you don't spend your soldiering days lying to get what you want," I say. "It's your specialty."

"What if we don't go?" Shi asks.

"You can stay in Mega City," I say. "It also means you are no longer an LMC."

"For real?" Nena says, barely above a whisper.

I walk up to her. Her scared face so close to mine. "For real."

"Right," Smiley says. "It's this hell or Cemi hell. What do you say, Truck?"

We look at Truck. Her mind churns the possibilities in her head. She stays erect and tall in her buffalo stance. It's hard for me to read her. She's mulling everyone's words. Weighing the options. What makes sense for our crew? I value Truck's opinion the most. If she doesn't agree to go with me, I'm not sure what I will do.

There is a long pause.

"I don't know what you guys are chirping about," Truck finally says. "If Déesse has the smallest inkling the Ashés are coming to Mega, this means they're coming for us. Let's meet them before they get the wrong idea that Mega is open for any weak crew to stroll in. Them chickenheads won't know what to do when they meet us."

I can't suppress a smirk, because Truck is crazy and that's why she's my down-for-anything girl.

"I don't know," Nena says. "I mean, why can't we wait until they show up here?"

Nena hems and haws. She's the only one making noise.

"Don't go," I tell her.

"Then I won't be an LMC," she says, ending her sentence as a question.

"It's on you. It's on each of you to come to your decision," I say. Open floor is over. They must decide to stand with me or walk. "If you want out, take your stuff and go. If you want to bring order to Cemi Territory, then come correct."

No one breaks their stance. They are with me.

A slight nod from me to Truck and she begins. "You heard what Chief Rocka said! We got us a mission here. Gather what you need. We are on the move."

There's a hint of glee in the air. Electric energy. We are heading toward Cemi Territory. My girls are going to be by my side, the only way I can do this. We gather around and start strategizing. This is definitely crazy. I don't know what we will find in Cemi Territory or what to expect from the Ashé Ryders. One thing is for certain: We are going in with our fists clenched.

CHAPTER 9

SEARCH PARTY

We haven't been back to the club since before the fight. My gut tells me we won't be welcomed. It happens to every crew after a throwdown. Mega City residents give the losers the cold shoulder. This frostiness won't last long, just long enough until the next throwdown is promoted. When we were newly formed and not well versed in fighting, it happened to the LMCs. We'll have to bear with it. The people will turn around. Mega City is a fickle girl.

"Que quieren?" Doña Chela asks. She glares at us from behind her encased storefront, speaking as if we're toilers asking for scraps.

"Open this door," Truck says.

When she refuses, Truck bangs the gate. Doña Chela, in her putrid-pink getup, jumps back. She's scared, although not enough. How quickly we've fallen from grace. I place a hand on Truck and motion for her to step back. Now is not the time to lose allies, however flimsy they may be.

"Bendición, Doña. I'm sorry. Truck has to learn how to respect our elders. It is what Déesse teaches. You hold our city's wisdom."

Doña does not budge. I'll speak to her financial side, since that's where her heart is.

"We need a quick bath. Food. How much?"

Her arms stay crossed in front of her. She eventually scribbles down numbers on a piece of paper, acts as if she doesn't remember exactly how much the items we're requesting are going to cost. I want to rip the green wig from atop her head and make her chew on it.

"I will need this many sueños. Plus, you can't stay for long," she says. "The Deadly Venoms are coming, and I don't want any trouble."

She asks for more than double the tabs we usually pay. As much as I hate to give in to the exorbitant price when we need to conserve tabs for our journey, I hand them over. The Luna Club is the center of Mega City. Only the illest can pass through these doors. This also means information is being freely relayed to the papis inside. When it comes right down to the order of things, Doña Chela doesn't matter. She won't be the top dog forever. Similar to us losing face because we lost the throwdown, Doña Chela and the Luna Club will fall victim to the rotating tastes of our city.

Inside, the papis try hard to contain their excitement in seeing Truck. One stern glance from Doña Chela and their demeanor changes. We're given the service of only one papi each, which is fine by me. Truck lets out a stream of curses that can be heard from above the booming music. We eat our food quickly and separate to our rooms.

Books waits for me with the bath already drawn. "Do you want me to read to you first?" he asks.

"No. Just the bath please."

He helps me undress. That's when I see the mark. I grab his arm and pull up his sleeve. There it is. "DV" in large letters. He's been tagged.

"You're with the Deadly Venoms now, huh?" Papi chulos aren't to be branded. Destiny's crew is tagging everything, including my favorite papi.

"I'm with you," he says. "No one else is here."

Books feels the temperature of the bath and takes off his glasses to wipe the fogginess off his lenses. Without them he looks tired. The last few days must have been intense. The wild parties the Deadly Venoms must have had. And now the tag. It's never crossed my mind before how similar our lives are. Books and I hustle in ways that are not for the weak. Bruises from throwdowns and unwanted tattoos. Marks of two people trying desperately to get by.

"Enjoying your new branding?" I ask, unable to hide my misguided jealousy. Why am I getting so worked up? I pay for his service. He treats me right. For reasons I can't place, I'm confusing this transaction.

"Branding is very important for crews," Books says, rubbing the raw tattoo. "I'm here for everyone to enjoy. This can easily be taken off."

I take note of the anger in his voice. I recognize the edge very well. He hates the Deadly Venoms as much as I do.

"It's over, you know? Destiny and the rest of the Deadly Venoms."

He snickers, and I'm mad at him for laughing. We were the shit before and we'll be the shit once again. There's no time to convince Books he can bet on me. I'm here on far more urgent business.

"What have you heard about the Ashé Ryders?" I ask.

Books gives no recognition to what I've said. Instead, he pours me a cup of tea and one for himself. He adjusts his glasses. How long have I been coming to him? Even if the glasses are fake, he seems smarter than the other guys. I can tell by the way he maintains his personal collection of books. I've even contributed to his stash. Whenever I come across a book I think he might like at the mercado, I have it sent to the club.

"Not much. Mega City pushed them out," he says. "They don't exist."

He's lying. The room is probably being watched by Doña. Books is not stupid enough to place himself in a bad situation.

I hold my hand out to him so he can help me into the hot bath. When he's close I ask him again, this time quietly.

"What do you know?"

"Nothing concrete. Only that the Ashé Ryders are on the come up and they want to shake the way things are done," he says. "Equality for everyone."

People can't be serious.

"We have it so good here," I say. "It doesn't make sense."

"How long do you think the Deadly Venoms, and the rest of the crews, will last?" he says. "Maybe Mega City needs a change."

I'm in a healing center for a couple of days and the masses are jumping to absurd conclusions. So now the Ashés are coming to make things right? The Ashés are identical to the Deadly Venoms, only worse because their absence has made them seem invincible.

"What do you think will happen to the papi chulo clubs, to the Luna Club, if what you say is true?" I say. "You'll be sporting an AR on your arm instead."

"Whether I'm Destiny's or working for Doña Chela, it doesn't matter," he whispers. "No one will be free until everyone is. That includes you."

He's been reading too many of his old-school books. I am free. The LMC may be down in the dumps now. It's temporary. The night is mine to break. There aren't many soldiers who enjoy the freedoms I have.

I turn to face him, letting water splash on the sides of the tub.

He's so close. What is going on behind those glasses? Is he trying to offend me? I want to kiss his lips, be reckless. Confess my fears. Be the type of person who burdens their papis with their dramas. That's never been me. I keep my secrets close. There he is, staring at me with secrets of his own. He wants to dismantle this city. This makes him dangerous, even if it is only words. This also makes him more real to me, more than just a regular papi. What kind of dreams does Books have? Are they similar to mine? Does he envision more to this life than the Luna Club?

"What is it you want?" I ask.

He takes his time. "I want to make you comfortable while you are here."

"Right," I say, disappointed. He must follow the script. It would have been nice to be presented with an alternative answer. Maybe a bit of hope before my journey. Too bad.

"Have you seen this ANT?" I reach to my Codigo and show him the image. He shakes his head.

"The Rumberos are always attracting an interesting group of people."

The Rumberos? A religious group searching for answers in the intangible. I can see how an ANT might find solace with a bunch of spiritual fools. The Rumberos are a small enough group to be ignored by Déesse. Because of their size, they move around quite a bit, with one caveat—they set up their tents by water. The tents are a perfect place to hide out in.

"Are you sure?" I ask.

"Do you want me to read?" His response is an indicator he's through providing me with answers. Fine. I got what I could. I'll go back to the role we were destined to play.

"Sure. Go ahead," I say. Books picks up from where he last left off.

But what interested Dorothy most was the big throne of green marble that stood in the middle of the room. It was shaped like a chair and sparkled with gems, as did everything else. . . .

I let myself follow the journey of a girl lost in a weird, upside-down world. Books's soft-spoken voice describes a complicated journey. Hints of what Cemi Territory may hold for me.

"You need to leave!" Doña Chela's grating voice breaks me from my relaxed state.

I get up, and Books hands me my clothes.

"I hope you find what you're looking for," he says.

Who knows when I will see him again and how things will change.

"It might be a while before I visit. Since I'm leaving, tell me this one thing," I say. "What's your real name?"

He takes off his glasses and rubs the bridge of his nose. "My name? I don't remember." His smile can't hide the sadness behind it. He's lying again. Everyone wants to keep their past to themselves. He'll keep his secret, so no one, enemy or friend, can snatch it from him.

"Do you want to take the book with you?" he asks.

"No," I say. "Save it for me. I'll be back."

He nods, and I walk out.

I find my soldiers gathered around a girl.

"C'mon, Gata, you know I'm good for it," Smiley whispers in Gata's ear. Gata came through the training camp, although she never could dig deep into the buffalo stance. She would rather hang on the sidelines waiting for the winners to appear. Gata has no allegiance to any one crew. She's a type of free-lancer who attaches herself to whoever is on top. Just last week that person was Smiley. There are plenty of freelancers who hang with top crews. Thirst Fans is what they are called.

"Meet me tonight and I promise I'll make it up to you." Smiley flashes her mood teeth guard, which changes color with an emotional shift. Gata seems to be enjoying the attention.

"I want to help you, Smiley. I don't have it in me," Gata says. "I'm already meeting Destiny at the Luna Club. How would it look if I appeared with you? The only currency I got is my word and my ass."

"Destiny? She ain't the one. C'mon, now," Smiley says. "We go way back. I mean, last week it was just you and me and the DJ playing your favorite song over and over. I did that. Not Destiny."

Gata's not taking the bait. She gives off a nervous vibe, afraid of being seen with us. The circle of information is shrinking. There's only a small window before it closes for good.

"I'm sorry, baby," Gata says. "I can't help you. I don't know a thing about an ANT."

Truck grabs Gata by the hair. The *meowing* back and forth is getting old, so I'm not mad at Truck for finally moving things along. We usually don't witness this dance between Smiley and her sources. We're probably ruining this for her. Smiley likes Gata, and Gata feels the same about Smiley.

"Stop wasting my time and give us the word before I rip this long, pretty hair," Truck says.

Smiley shoots Truck a look of anger. They've got their own ways of working the streets, and Smiley can't stand the way Truck works hers.

"Okay! Okay," Gata pleads. Truck lets her go, and Gata immediately fixes her hair. "I might have heard about the guy you are looking for. He's on a celestial trip with the Rumberos, wailing. What else is new? That's what the Rumberos do. They wail. No fun whatsoever. Not you, Truck. You love to party, right?" She pushes up against Truck.

Truck shoves her away. Truck hates when girls use their bodies to try to manipulate situations. Déesse believes women no longer need to rely on their beauty and sexuality to get by. I agree as does Truck. What a person looks like shouldn't weigh in on how they navigate this city. The male gaze is dead. Gata is aware of this yet she still enjoys pissing Truck off. Smiley slides Gata sueños for trading and sends her on her way.

Books was right. We need to visit the Rumberos next. What we're currently wearing won't do. We need to change.

"Truck and I will go," I say. "The rest of you head to the mercado and take care of the provisions. Remember what I said—divide the list and make sure no one is onto what or where we're going."

"I can help with the Rumberos," Nena says. "My father fell in with the group for a bit, so I know what it's about. Wearing blue. The lyrics to most of the important songs. It's a call and response, so you . . ."

"Shut up," Truck says.

"I can help," Nena mumbles.

"What did you say?"

"Nothing, Truck," she says. "I didn't say a thing."

There's a change in Nena's response. A bit of anger mixed with defeat. Nena is growing tired of being yelled at by Truck. That's too bad, because Truck won't stop until Nena pushes back with all she's got. Truck did the same thing to Smiley and to Shi before her. You can prod the young ones too hard. I've seen girls from other crews beg to enter the LMC after being driven to the edge. There's a fine line to follow when molding an LMC. Nena is reaching that point.

Truck and I differ in how to handle new recruits. I think each girl can be shaped into what we want. Violence isn't the only path to take. Truck isn't Chief Rocka for a reason. Her anger gets the most of her. The arguments we've had have almost come to blows. There are times when I wonder if she wants to be the leader of the LMCs. I see the way she scowls at my decisions. She doesn't approve of the way I'm handling Nena. Truck thinks I'm getting soft. That's not the case. Each recruit is different, and if Truck were smart she would see that.

"Nena, give me the intel on the Rumberos."

Her smile glows. She only wants to help. The black eye from the fight is barely visible. "They wear blue for the ocean," Nena says. "You wear blue or you won't be able to go in."

I let her continue even though Truck huffs beside me.

"Once you enter, there's only drumming and wailing," she says. "You're conjuring the spirits. No one is there to fight. It's peaceful. He took me once. I remember dancing."

Rumberos are not considered crews. The tents are more a poor woman's version of a boydega, where residents can meet and let go of their aggressions. It makes sense the ANT would hide there. He can suck on sueño tabs without anyone caring. Now that he no longer has the azabache, what more can he do?

"Also, be aware of the really young girls," Nena repeats. "They consider some of them, umm, vessels. I think that's what they call them. They're messengers, and they might have messages you do not want to hear."

Truck's head is tilted to the side. She doesn't believe a word Nena is saying. Neither do I. It sounds pretty ridiculous.

"Good work. Now go with the others and make yourself useful," I say. Nena's smile remains as she runs to catch Shi and Smiley.

"I keep repeating myself. The girl is a waste," Truck says. "We should trade her before we leave."

"Be patient," I say. "She'll surprise you one day. Watch."

Truck doesn't see it. Each girl at one point didn't seem much. Now look at Shi and Smiley. I can't imagine life without them in the crew. They're so essential with their own strengths. Shi and her quiet way of gathering intel. Smiley and her mischievous way of cheating and winning. Nena too will prove to be irreplaceable, just as Manos Dura did. Manos was a fierce fighter but she also had mad love for toilers. When she thought I wasn't watching, she would give her food pellets to the littlest ones in need. The streets loved Manos. The same will happpen to Nena. She'll find her groove. I'm sure of it.

"Yeah, maybe," Truck says. "Or maybe we're carrying her."

She walks ahead. Truck is anxious. Back at the D, she tried to tell me how she felt about this new directive from Déesse. I shut her down, stating there wasn't time to talk. I don't want any doubts placed in my head, even from my right-hand girl.

CHAPTER 10

SPIRITUAL BACHATA

My tronic sits nestled in an inside pocket of my all-blue jacket. Truck can't find a spot for her weapon. She prefers her tronics big and bold. She decides on a small tronic tucked in her boot. We don't need them. The Rumberos aren't about that life. Still, it never hurts to be ready. I can hear the rumbling sound of congas playing.

As we approach the tents, the smell of burning sage is so overwhelming I start to cough. Two Rumberos sway at the entrance. Their movements are so languid, I wouldn't even consider them real guards. They don't hold any weapons or even have a rage face. Instead they greet us with warm smiles.

"Everyone is welcome here," one of the Rumberos says. "We only ask you enter with love and an open mind."

Truck snorts behind me.

"How many tabs?" I ask. There has to be a payment to enter. I'm sure of it.

"Tabs are worthless here. This place is created to build community. Are you part of this community or are you against us?"

What kind of question is that? I want to tell her shut up with her weak-ass words. I won't because this is the start of our journey, and if I have to pretend to be down with these religious freaks, so be it. I face Truck and smile my widest grin. Truck rolls her eyes. Then she copies me.

"We've come only to build and connect with our people," I say. My syrupy words make me sick. I better get used to them. The success of this mission will depend on the lies I spew to make myself fit in.

The guards are more than happy to let us in.

A never-ending row of congas takes over the back of the tent. Women of all ages play the instruments with enraptured faces. To abandon themselves so fully to a spiritual movement is my worst nightmare come true. How can anyone believe music or chanting can elevate you to a better state? There is no higher plane in sight except for the Towers, and those buildings are undeniable. My hands can touch the structure. Closing your eyes and searching for the divine is a useless task. There is only what is in front of me, what I can feel and see with my own eyes. To think otherwise is to live in a fantasy. You might as well take sueño tabs and call it a night. I find solace knowing my tronic is close at hand.

Truck and I separate. There must be a hundred people

crammed inside the tent, way more than I had anticipated. People young and old move to the music. Not everyone is wailing. Women are muttering prayers to themselves. Others groan. It's a sea of blue.

These toilers want to check out of reality. They don't understand how heavens won't save them. Only their hard hands, their fists, can be their salvation. We built Mega to be what it is through our intelligence, not through supplications. I want to scream this to them. They are lost within their endless spiritual dance.

I walk to each person, hoping to find the ANT. There are too many people. The worst are the kids. Kids who will soon be of age to enter the training camp. For Mega City to be safe, we need to keep the borders secure. Without new recruits, who will keep Cemi Territory outsiders away? It's been years since haters have tried to bum-rush the city. The last time the haters did, they caught the force of Déesse's army. We can't sustain this success if kids aren't taught how to defend themselves.

I asked Santo once why Déesse allows the Rumberos to live aboveground and worship in such a fruitless way. I even offered our services to help close down the tents. He was abrupt in his response. Shutting the Rumberos will only make their religious fervor stronger. So what if a few toilers want to escape and temporarily live in a limbo state? They're not harming anyone, is what he said. I'm not so sure.

A young girl, about six years old, begins to hop up and down. She pounds her tiny chest to the rhythm of the congas. I've seen her before. She sells wooden dolls made to the likeness of various crews. I purchased one from her a long time ago. On the streets of Mega the girl appears timid, selling her dolls. Not here. In here she almost appears ageless.

She hits her chest hard, and with that the conga players start to beat even faster. Others gather around her, creating a protective circle to guarantee enough room for her to dance. As the girl spins around, those closest to her touch the top of her head. What is it about her that makes everyone here want to connect with her? I see Truck. She's way over on the other side of the tent, barely visible in this ocean of blue.

The girl begins to moan, and her wail rocks the room. How is this even possible? She must have a microphone on her.

A group of elderly ladies press against me. Their movements are no longer gentle. I push back with force. I'm going to faint from this oppressive heat. I want to tear off these clothes.

Where's Truck? I need to get out of here before I pull my tronic and start emptying it on everyone. I don't want this uncontrollable feeling. This rapture is menacing. A threat.

The girl continues to go around in a circle. Around and around. I am mesmerized by her movements. Is she the vessel Nena mentioned? I don't believe in religion. Calling for a powerful being? Music and dancing are useless actions. No one should have the time or privilege to engage in such frivolousness.

I need to get out of here. I push past the elderly women to get to Truck on the other side. I don't care if I'm crossing this stupid circle. The ANT we are looking for is here, and these Rumberos are blocking my way. I don't want to call the spirits. I don't want to be sucked into this vortex, a black hole that takes you nowhere.

As I walk across, ready to bash a head in if I have to, the girl grabs my arm. I try to pull free. She has a steady grip that doesn't belong to such a tiny person. She draws me closer to her even when I'm doing everything I can to pull away. When she doesn't let go, I reach for my tronic. I come back empty-handed. My piece was stolen. It could have been anyone. I am powerless.

"He's here. He has your answers." The girl sings these words to me. A song that goes with the drumming. She won't let go of my hand. Her deep dark eyes bear down on me. What does she know? She must be on a celestial trip, a sueño? It can't be. Kids don't suck on tabs.

"Let go. This is just a dream." I try to reason with her. "You're on a trip."

With this, she smiles. "You will not win this fight. Stay

here with us and call for the spirits to heal you. Stay here or you will not return to the city as Las Mal Criadas. The LMCs will perish and so will you."

She lets me go, and the circle engulfs her. She's swept away before I can ask her more questions.

"Wait! Come back here!"

I push the ladies protecting her. They refuse to part. The drumming increases and so do the lamentations. They're singing in unison—a song that sounds eerily familiar.

I will follow you, child. I used to know the way.

I can't place the tune. From where?

It's as if hundreds and hundreds of people are singing the lyrics. I start to feel light-headed. What is going on? The music is hypnotizing. Taking me down. Was I slipped a sueño tab? The rhythm is taking me in. Maybe if I stay here, I will no longer fight. This isn't the Towers. Still, it could be home. The girl said I will perish. If I join the Rumberos, I won't. I can live with them forever in this space where only the strong can connect to the other world. If I learn the song, I can follow the path of the Rumberos.

"C'mon! I got him!" Truck pulls me away before I truly lose myself.

"Wait . . . No . . . the girl . . ." I plead with Truck, not wanting to stop the dancing.

"We got to go." Truck yanks my arm hard and, pushing her way through the people, she thrusts me into the far end of the tent.

"This will snap you out of whatever you're in." She splashes water on my face. Slowly, the spiritual force fades away.

"You didn't feel that?" I ask. My head is groggy.

"What are you talking about? I didn't feel a thing, just mad annoyed by the singing and the heat. Your head injury is messing with you."

Stupid brat. It wasn't drugs. It must have been the temperature and the noise that got me dizzy. What the hell does the kid know? Using vague words so she can play to my weak side. It's a trick. My injury is causing me to make foolish moves.

Truck leads me to a smaller tent. In a corner, the ANT sits clutching a conga to his face. He looks completely lost. His clothes are torn. He sings a song to himself. I can barely make out the words.

El fuego me . . .

The ANT doesn't even notice when Truck and I grab his shoulders and lead him to the entrance. When we reach the opening, it finally dawns on him what we are doing. The ANT tries to get away.

"Let me go! Let me go!" He screams. I give him a shot from Shi's drug arsenal. The guards notice the commotion and block the entrance. Truck pulls out her tronic.

"Back off," Truck says. "He's coming with us."

The guard lunges toward Truck. She stuns her with her tronic. The Rumbero falls. The other stays frozen, confused.

They are by far the worst guards I've ever witnessed. We cut out.

After a few blocks, I dump the ANT to the ground. Truck empties his pockets and checks his vitals to make sure he's not too far into sleepy land.

"Are you okay, Nalah?" Truck asks. "You seem spooked."

I don't want to think about what happened inside. I can't dwell on the girl and her dark proclamations. "How long before he wakes up?"

The ANT starts to jerk his body around. Soon his saucer eyes are open. He's pissed he's not back in the tent.

"Remember me?" I ask.

He shakes his head. I give him a sip of my water. Under the streetlight, I can see him a lot clearer. The blue outfit is dirty and stained. He's malnourished. Underneath the dirt, though, there's a tiny glimmer of who he must have been before he got hooked. He's beautiful. Not in the papi chulo sense. No, his beauty, or what were his looks, are in a different category. It's sad how time and sueños can destroy a body.

"What about this?" I show him the azabache necklace. He's no longer in a daze.

"That doesn't belong to you," he says, and foolishly reaches for the trinket. Truck punches him in the stomach.

"It's ours now, ANT. Truck is going to ask you questions," I say. "Every time you answer with a worthless comment,

Truck here will practice her jab." Truck won't give him much time to catch his breath.

"Where did you get it? I don't care if you stole it. I just want names, a place."

He shakes his head. Truck hits him. He doubles over.

"It doesn't matter. Keep it. I messed up," he says. "I wasn't strong enough."

"How did you mess up?" I ask.

He cries now. Big sobs. So pathetic. Truck is about to punch him again. I tell her no. In between his cries, he speaks. His long greasy hair covers his dirt-encrusted face.

"I thought I was stronger. I thought I wouldn't be lured by the sueños. I was wrong, even after all these years."

"Do you hear him?" Truck says. "Leave it to an ANT to play victim while reaping the joy of sucking on tabs."

"Zen. Zen," he cries. "I shouldn't have come. I wasn't strong enough."

Truck and I can't follow.

"Zentrica," he says.

Truck pipes in and asks him more questions. He refuses to answer anything other than cry over Zentrica.

"Who is Zentrica? Is she in Cemi Territory?" Truck asks. "Is that where you came from?"

He starts to mumble. "My home. Los Bohios," he says. "I never should have left Cemi."

Bohios? Truck taps the words in her Codigo and waits for the information to come in.

"It's a dwelling, old-school, as in way back in ancient times. The structures are made of wood," says Truck. She shows me an illustration. "Maybe it's not literally a dwelling. Maybe it's the name of the place."

Are the Ashé Ryders living in Los Bohios? There are so many questions. I wish this ANT weren't so far gone into his addiction. I kneel down.

"Is Zentrica an Ashé Ryder?"

This is the moment of truth. He's not holding back the tears. I hope he doesn't hold back this vital piece of information.

"Yes. Zentrica is the leader of the Ashé Ryders."

Then it's true. The Ashés are real. This is the confirmation we needed. We are heading in to Cemi Territory, and Los Bohios will be our destination.

"Why did Zentrica send you to Mega City? When we met you the other night, you said you were looking for someone. Who was it you were looking for?" I ask. "What were you meant to do here?"

"Zentrica didn't send me. I came for the sueños. I needed to fix. I thought Déesse might help me get more. Déesse is the reason why I am the way I am."

He blames Déesse for his addiction. Freaking ANT. He failed to use the tabs correctly. It's not Déesse's fault if a person becomes addicted to them. For the majority of Mega City, they can control the intake. What makes this guy think he's special?

"Aren't there sueños where you live?"

"Sueños are the devil," he says.

Truck nudges me. This is the angle. He thinks sueños are bad even when he can't stop taking them.

"You are right. A city freely dishing sueños can't be the city for us. You saw our fight with the Deadly Venoms. You saw how it went down," I say. "We are on the outs with Déesse. There's no point in staying here, not when the odds are stacked against us."

"It's true," Truck says. "We are not down with the way she's running this city. We are ready for a change."

"Let us help you get back home, where you belong," I say. "Show us the way to Los Bohios."

There is an inkling of a smile. I can't tell if it's from the sueños or from what we've said. Maybe it's a combination of both.

"I won't be able to get back without help," he says. I know what he means by help. He'll need sueños to get him by. Not a problem.

"We will take care of you," I say.

"Wait until you meet Zentrica," he says. His eyes are closed. "You'll fall for her too."

We're losing him to the dreams. Zentrica. The person I

must align myself with. I search the Codigo. The screen comes back blank. Who is Zentrica? Will we be able to deceive her?

Truck picks him up and throws him over her back. We're heading to Los Bohios, and this ANT is going to be our guide, whether he knows it or not.

CHAPTER 11

READY OR NOT

The ANT sits on a rock, chewing on a stick meant to ward off his craving. His next hit won't be for two hours. It's hard to figure him out. He seems so resigned to this new circumstance of traveling with the LMC. He gives only the smallest of morsels—a street name here, a landmark—whenever we ask about Los Bohios. Shi says this must be due to the sueños screwing with his memory. She's probably right. It doesn't stop Truck from threatening to cut his fingers off. Violence doesn't seem to work on a man who appears to be holding on to such little hope.

I look up. The sky is an unbroken darkness. No moon to keep watch over us. No clouds. There are too many worries, too many "what-ifs" racing through my head. I try to play them out, close the gap of the unknowns. The azabache is nestled in my pocket. I calculate our odds.

My Codigo blinks red. It's Santo. He wants to see me.

Where was he when I sent him a message a couple of days ago? He never bothered checking in to see how I was doing. My name was dirt. Now he wants to see me. No. It's too late. I ignore the request. It blinks again.

"You should answer that." Truck motions to the Codigo.

Part of me wants to write him off but I'm not stupid. I shouldn't. He is too important in the scheme of things. Santo holds sway with his mother. I need to make sure we stay on their minds while we are away.

"Anything wrong, Chief Rocka?" Smiley asks.

"No," I say.

Truck raises her eyebrow. "Who knows what Santo might have for you? Only way to find out is to talk. We'll wait for you by the border."

She's right. He's only five minutes away. "I won't be long."

The toilers I pass are leaving work and heading home. A couple of them give me a nod hello. To avoid my path, a man crosses the street. He's smart to stay clear. Men have been taught to defer to crews. His reaction is a show of respect.

I pick up the pace. The lights from the Towers glow brightly. Breaking night will soon begin. We agreed to leave then. I walk toward the courtyard where Santo said he would be waiting. The place is desolate. There are no red petals blanketing the ground. No sign of our recent battle there. Instead, there are posters advertising the next throwdown. Baby crews I don't even recognize. Mega City will go on without us.

Santo leans against a cement wall. He's not alone. Three guards wait with him. I chuckle at this. The last time I saw him at Luna Club he was all swagger. Unafraid to travel alone to the boydega. Now he comes with heavy protection. I return to being angry. Where was my brother when my head got kicked in by Destiny? Where was he when Déesse presented this mission? There's enough hurt inside me that I want to hit him. Yet I walk foolishly forward. Why? Because there is a history between us. Even if he hides behind these guards, there is a satisfaction in knowing I am valuable enough to merit this meeting.

Once the guards see me, they grab hold of their tronics and aim.

"What's up, Santo? Scared I might ruffle your hair?" I ask. "You were the one who reached out to me." He nods to the guards, and they put their weapons down.

"Leave us," he says.

Santo is starting to grow a beard. He's trying to make himself look tougher. He doesn't need to, not when he walks around with guards protecting him. It's not the first time he's tried to mask his face. The new fuzz always seems to coincide with drama at home. As if he can conceal his feelings behind this growth. What's going on in the Towers that has him hiding?

"Did you come here to try to convince me not to go, or are you here to give me a pep talk?" I say. "Either way, I can't take you serious with that facial hair."

"Always with a smart mouth. That mouth isn't going to work where you're going."

"What do you want, Santo? I have things to do."

He hesitates. We are in a different space since the last time we saw each other. I try to disguise the awkwardness between us with harshness.

"You don't have to live there." He motions to the Towers. "You can stay and become a toiler. I can hook you up at one of the factories. There's no need to prove a thing to me or to anyone."

"Are you trying to slip me up?"

This must be yet another test from Déesse to see how loyal I am. I'm not going back to square one. My path is straight. Sure, he can help me nab a miserable job. I would toil while he chills with another crew. It would be the end of the LMCs.

He doesn't understand. I belong right by him, in the Towers, because Déesse chose me. He's playing mind games, trying to bring doubt. My place is beside him, not below him.

"This is my only way of surviving. My crew counts on me to lead them through this last obstacle," I say. "You don't get it. Never mind. Just make sure my bed is ready."

I turn to walk away. Santo grabs hold of me. If he tries to kiss me I will definitely punch him. This emotional display won't change my plans.

"I'm sorry this is happening," he says. "It sucks being the best, don't it?"

"Don't worry, Santo." I try to pull away. "I promise to bring you back a gift from my travels."

Even with my smile, it's hard to ignore the lump in my throat. I don't want to leave Mega, to leave the streets I know so well for a complete unknown. There is a routine to breaking night. I'll miss the green flowers growing inside the D without much help from us. I'll miss entering the Luna Club with swagger. I'll even miss this hug from Santo confirming how much he doesn't want me to go.

"Do you know what you are doing?" he says. "I can't help you."

"Like you helped me when I was in the healing center? It's too late to show you care." His heart is pounding. So is mine.

"I'm not abandoning my sister. Here." He hands me a large bag of sueño tabs and a card. "This shows you where you'll be able to cross the border. As for the sueños, you'll need to connect with the Gurl Gunnas. They're going to want to trade."

I've heard of the Gurl Gunnas. They are sellers that create pop-up shops in boydegas to trade in high-end items. Codigos. Beauty items. Objects available only in the Towers. I worked with their leader Vanessa a while back. Before I had Santo, Vanessa got us used Codigos. She did right by us. We gave her the set amount of sueños and she gave us what we wanted. No drama whatsoever. I didn't know the Gurl Gunnas lived in Cemi Territory. I just thought they were similar to freelancers.

"Why are the Gurl Gunnas allowed to move back and forth from Mega City to Cemi Territory?" I ask. "What's the deal?"

Santo strokes his beard. "They have an understanding with Déesse. It's not important. What's important is that you are ready to barter. You can't go far into Cemi unless you go through them first."

I try to decipher the type of understanding the Gurl Gunnas have with our leader. What benefits do they hold, and who are they serving in Cemi? Do they know about the Ashé Ryders? If they are out there, they must. They will be invaluable to us. I accept Santo's bag.

"Get my place in the Towers ready. The LMC are staying right there." I point to the vibrant building. "Get it ready, Santo."

I give him a kiss on the lips. The beard tickles me. I won't linger. There is no room in my life for sentimental good-byes. Santo will be here when I come back.

Most of the fences located around the border of Mega City are juiced, electricity meant to fry anyone who tries to enter the city. Not in this section. The electricity in this section of the fence is spotty, going in and out. No one else is privy to this bit of information. They don't have Santo.

"We should be in the clear," Shi says.

Nena jumps the fence first. We pause to admire the vast amount of garbage awaiting us. A while back, Déesse declared there be an "Only Mega" Month. Residents were encouraged to throw away items with any reference to the old ways. "Made in China" or "Made in India." If these places exist, we don't know or care. Déesse told the residents that we should be proud of the accomplishments we made with our own hands. Everyone got rid of objects—furniture, appliances. Items proved to be too essential were to be refurbished. The original source of where the item was from had to be erased. When the dumps in Mega City overflowed, people started to toss the items over the border. Hence, the garbage.

"Let's go," I say. We climb over the fence. The ANT is sandwiched in the middle.

We wear our Codigo goggles. The stench from the rotting garbage is too overbearing. Not wanting to weigh ourselves down, we carry only the essentials on our backs.

"Eyes open," I say.

We're heading into a space where we've never ventured before. In Mega we've memorized the streets. We know each corner. Here I feel vulnerable. We're open targets for any loose crew eager to make a name for themselves. I've heard of a couple of them. They are so basic. I don't want us to start this journey by appearing to be lame ducks waiting to be clipped.

"How far we've got to go?" Smiley asks the ANT. He shrugs.

Without so much as a warning, Truck lightly pushes him.

"Back up off him," I say. I have to remind Truck to keep

the blows to a minimum. We are meant to be helping him, not beating him up. He's our guide, and right now we need him to trust us long enough for us to get to the Ashé Ryders. Truck needs to keep her damn fists by her sides.

"Sorry about that." I offer him water from my bottle. Nena carries extra clothes for him and a sleep sack. Resentments grow within the others but they keep their complaints to themselves. Truck can't hide her anger over how I'm handling the ANT. Again, she is allowing her impatience to blind her from the big picture. We need him.

"We stay on this path till the end of the day. We head toward the waterfalls by a place once called Salem Center," he says. "Right before the falls, that's where we will find Los Bohíos. We got to rest in between there, because I can't walk for too long. My legs hurt. I'm in pain. I need more."

"Not a good idea. We need you to be awake enough so you can direct us. Besides, sueños are the devil. Remember?"

When we pressure him to give us more info, he clams up and begs for sueños. There is a sweet spot when he's in an in-between state, when he's not completely lost to dreams. Reaching the right amount of chemical configuration is hard to guess. Even Shi, who is the queen when it comes to mixing drugs, can't get the right dosage.

Smiley and Shi whisper to each other. Nena walks alongside me. This is Cemi Territory. If I turn back now, I can be back by the D in no time. This thought offers only a tiny bit of comfort.

"I can't walk anymore."

Jesus, this guy is freaking deadweight. It's been only a few minutes and he continues to whine. I give him a sueño to tide him over. He doesn't bother to drink water and greedily swallows the tab whole. The ANT has got it bad. I try to hide my disgust. I've never been addicted to anything. Neither have my girls. I run a clean crew. Drinking is fine. There are nights when I want to cut loose, especially after a throwdown. The drinks at Luna Club can mess you up. The next day you drink a bunch of water and you are good to go. Sueños doesn't do that. It blurs your brain. The effects are slow to take but once they do sueños can ravage a person's self control. Cravings are so intense addicts are willing to do the unspeakable to ride back into a dream.

"If you want to reach Zentrica, you've got to help us," I say. "Our plan will fail before we even make any headway. You understand?"

"I need more."

I'm not giving in to him. I don't care how bad off he is. Smiley nudges him forward so he can continue to lead the way. If anyone guns for us, he'll get it first. We will let him be bait. The ANT quietly hums a tune. I recognize the song from when we were at the Rumberos. It is a sad melody perfectly capturing how I feel leaving Mega.

The sun rises as we continue to walk. Nena distributes food pellets at the times I allocated for us to eat. We don't stop. I want to make sure we get a substantial distance away from the city. It's hard to do so when the ANT must rest every thirty minutes or so. He slows his pace again, never once asking whether or not we want to stop. Instead, he plops right down in the dirt, not noticing or caring about the garbage surrounding him. The ANT closes his eyes and starts to snore.

"Are you kidding me?" Truck yells. "What the hell are we doing? We are never going to get there with this piece of shit."

"Relax," I say. Truck isn't helping the situation.

"If it were up to me, I would force him to show us where to go instead of feeding him sueños. What kind of gang are we if we continue to be soft?"

Smiley grimaces. Shi motions for Nena to move away from me. Truck is out of line. I have to pull rank on her.

"I don't remember declaring an open floor," I say. "I won't let a soldier, even my second-in-command, contradict my decisions."

Truck shakes her head.

"Speak your freaking mind," I say. "Are you having doubts? You had more than enough time to state your case back in Mega."

"We need to move this along. We got only seven days. Less. We got five, since we spent two days trying to find him. The way you baby this man-child is exactly how you baby Nena."

"I guess I got to baby you, too. You're forgetting I'm la mama of this crew. Take your frustrations elsewhere. Get out of my face."

There is a pause. It lasts for only a few seconds, long enough for me to question whether Truck has leader ambitions. No. She doesn't want this responsibility. She's nervous. Up until now her life has revolved around throwdowns and wrestling papis. This is new. I understand her frustration. We are all scared. It doesn't mean I will let her second-guess me. She walks away.

The others lay down their sleeping mats. They try their best to ignore the angry Truck, who stews on her own off to the side. I didn't realize how tired I was until I lay down near the ANT. We will rest for only a couple of hours. Without me having to say a word, Truck keeps watch for the first hour. Smiley will replace her after.

The dream with my sister startles me awake. For a few seconds I'm not sure where I am. I hate how this hazy vision now travels with me to Cemi. A reminder of loss and of grudges.

I nudge the ANT awake. It takes a couple of tries.

"Chief Rocka. Enough with the poking," he says. "It might be hard for you to believe but I'm no animal."

Who does he think he's talking to? I've never allowed any man to speak to me this way. It takes everything in me to not punch his face. From the distance I can hear Truck snickering.

"Let's go," I say firmly.

As much as Truck may want to deny it, we needed the rest. The sun is beating down hard. We slowly shed our layers. The ANT begins to sing. It is a popular song about watching a papi dance at a boydega. Nena loves this song. She mouths the words while continuing to keep her distance from the ANT. He has a beautiful voice. Strong and melodic. This must be the reason why we found him with the Rumberos. Singing is part of their spiritual practice. There is no room for the arts in Mega City. We are too busy rebuilding. Culture is a luxury.

"The sun feels glorious. I've spent too much time in Mega City wasting in the dark," he says. "There is an allure to the night. I used to be captivated by it. Seduced. In the glare of the sun, it's hard to hide who you really are, don't you think?"

He caresses his arms as if the sun's rays are kissing his skin. Again, it is hard to figure him out. The ANT speaks to us as if we are the same. Men in Mega City are only for service. There are no meaningful conversations. Does age give him the boldness to speak so freely? No. The old timers I've encountered only show respect to women.

"Are all men allowed to move around and speak without fear in Los Bohios?" Shi asks. She's been clocking him ever since we started. With Shi, she doesn't let on what she's thinking. She mentally takes notes on his behavior and every word he says.

The ANT pauses. He gathers his long hair into a low ponytail.

"You girls are on the wrong side of the border." He ignores

her question. The ANT has a bit of pep to his walk. "Things pop on this side."

"There's not much out here," Smiley says. "All I see is the garbage Mega City no longer wants."

"In Los Bohios beauty is celebrated, all types, not just what Déesse deems attractive," he says. "If you take the time to truly accept each other, to allow for men, women, and others to be, then there is room for dialogue that goes beyond the superficial. Uncomfortable and truthful conversations about gender. How many ways can you brand yourself to prove who you are? Like those tattoo freckles or the ink on men turning them into properties. Mega City is too busy with the brutality of throwdowns. Where is the beauty? What kind of life is that?"

I need to muzzle him. I'm through with men saying I'm living my life wrong. Always giving me suggestions. Men made this hell we're in. We're trying to rise above it.

"Do the Ashé Ryders throw down, or are they simply too good to even train?"

"There's more to life than fighting," he says. "You'll see. Fists and bruises are temporary pleasures."

"Like sueños," Truck says. She throws a rock, barely missing the ANT. It is a little act of intimidation.

"You don't partake. You are smart," the ANT says to Truck. "It's probably why Déesse loves you guys so much."

His sarcasm is dripping. Truck is not the type of person

who appreciates a smart mouth, especially coming from a guy. Before I can even stop her, Truck barrels toward him.

"Who do you think you're talking to?" she yells before shoving him to the ground. She lands a punch on the side of his stomach before Smiley and I can pull her away.

"Stop it!"

The ANT laughs. Soon the laughs convert into tears. My stomach turns from this sight. What is going on with him?

"Keep hitting me. Maybe it can stop these cravings."

He wants this. He wants us to beat him to a pulp. Is the addiction that bad? I will never understand.

"I don't care about your dreams or how sueños ruined your life," Truck says. "You are just our map."

His body starts to convulse, as if he's having a seizure. Damn it.

"Will you hold him down?" I yell. Shi and Smiley try to help. Truck just stands in judgment. With his convulsing and acting crazy, I can barely hear what Nena says.

"Oh look. It's so cute," she says. "Can I keep it?"

I follow what she points at. It's an innocent-looking doll with golden curls. Old-timers sell them at the mercado. They are super rare. No one makes them anymore. This one looks new. Standing out in the garbage with a sweet tiny blue dress. It doesn't make sense. Why would a doll so new be here in this garbage?

Wait. There is something wrong.

"No! Don't touch it." I tackle Nena. The tip of her baton manages to touch the hem of the doll's dress. The explosion levels us to the ground.

We slowly pick ourselves up. Our bodies are covered with garbage and glass. Before I can even take inventory, I notice them. Waxed masks, torn baby-doll dresses, and creepy red hearts painted on their cheeks. These girls are demented marionettes with weapons aimed right at us.

The Muñecas Locas have got us surrounded.

CHAPTER 12

LIVING DOLLS

The Muñecas Locas wear Kewpie masks and dusty wigs styled with golden ringlets that mimic the porcelain doll bomb. This crew are what nightmares are made of. Their bats and machetes are at the ready. They are not messing around.

"That was very, very scary."

Are you freaking kidding me? There's not much intel on the Locas. What we've read has been pretty laughable. I thought it was only a rumor the way they spoke. It's one thing to dress in a strange tribute to dolls; it's quite another to incorporate a creepy baby voice with it.

"It went *boom*," another Muñeca says in a syrupy, coy tone. Their torn floral dresses are so short you can see their ruffled pants. Breasts are practically hanging out. Maybe a long time ago this would have been considered a man's fantasy. As a fighting crew? There is nothing hard-core about them.

I do a quick check of my girls. Truck is in the back of the formation. She has the least amount of rubble on her. She must have sprinted out of the way right before the bomb hit. Smiley, Shi, and Nena have only minor scratches. The ANT's convulsions have ended. He continues to lie on the ground. His face is in ecstasy, riding the high. Wait. What high? I didn't give him any sueños. Is he playing dead? The punk. This is probably how he gets himself out of predicaments. There's more to him than meets the eye.

"Everyone cool?" I ask.

Smiley shows me her tronic, hidden from view of the Muñecas.

"Let's not waste it. With only one charger, we have juice for only a couple of days. Let's see if we can make a clean break."

"You're sure, Chief Rocka?" Smiley says. "These girls don't appear to be much."

My crew is itching for action. They want to unleash, and why not on these girls? No. We need to hold off on the violence. It will be foolish if we are wiped out and unable to throw down if we run into real trouble.

"No, let's take it easy," I say. "Are you getting anything, Shi?"

"The Codigo's connection to the main server is coming in and out," she says. "I downloaded most of the library, so we are good with information. Other than that, our connection won't last for long."

In the meantime, I got to figure a way to get us out of here. If this is Muñecas territory, we're just plowing through.

A Muñeca who appears to be the leader starts walking toward me. This is a guess. Unlike the others, who have white ribbons on their wigs, her ribbons are red.

"Not one word," I say. "I'm doing the talking."

"Which one of you was a bad girl today?" the Muñeca asks in the creepy baby voice. From where I stand I can tell it's not her real voice. It's a microphone lodged on her clothes. They're about as menacing as a crew of zombie babies. Whatever. I'll play nice. I just want to move on.

"We're sorry. We don't mean to disrespect you or your house," I say. "We're just walking through."

"Walking through? You can't walk through here. You woke us up from our nia nia. Now we're grumpy from not sleeping enough."

Nena laughs at this. Smiley hushes her. I get it. These girls are a bit on the kooky side. How long have they lived here? Are these girls outcasts from Mega, garbage tossed aside? The whole baby-doll voice must be an act, a way to scare people into thinking they're a threat. They would not last in Mega City, not with their cutesy girly act. Without real protection from Déesse's army, the Muñecas must feel the need to invent unusual ways to safeguard themselves from harm. Are the Ashé Ryders the threat? The Gurl Gunnas?

"We are down to trade, if that's what you want." I look around. "I can see your dresses can use an update. We have accessories you might like."

In Smiley's bag, we stored a few trinkets for such an occasion. Shiny baubles picked up from the mercado. Smiley opens her bag and pulls out a gaudy necklace. These girls must be trading. There is no way they can maintain this getup by scrounging through garbage.

A Muñeca walks toward Nena. Nena anxiously glances over. I don't give her a sign. I don't do a thing. Instead I wait to see what Nena's reaction will be. Before the Muñeca reaches her, Nena jogs to the girl and pushes her with all her might.

"Don't even think about it!" Nena yells. She uses a deep voice to try to make herself sound way older than she is. Good girl. Shi pulls Nena back to formation. Nena's force is a minor display to alert the Muñecas we are not above getting rough.

The Muñeca adjusts her mask and fixes her dress. I can't tell if she's ruffled from the push or not. Dealing with masked enemies definitely has its disadvantages. Even with the mask I can see the Muñecas are a healthy bunch. Where are they getting their food? Are trades being made across the border? And if they are, what does this mean to Mega's powerful reputation?

"That's enough," I say, pretending to scold Nena. "We're Las Mal Criadas from Mega City. We're bringing this ANT back to his home. Just taking a walk."

"I know who you are," the Muñeca says. "We know every-thing because our mama tells us everything."

Mama. So this idiot is only second-in-command. Wher-ever Mama is, she's the one directing these clueless amateurs. I need to get to Mama before I can pass go.

"Where's Mama? Can I speak to her, tell her how sorry we are for disturbing you? Maybe she'll want this necklace. It comes straight from Mega City."

"Where's Mama? Where's Mama? Where's Mama?" They start to repeat this over and over in their baby talk, tilting their heads left to right. Smiley shows me her weapon again. I decline her offer to stun them.

"I'm right here."

She appears from within the garbage. I can finally see it. The Locas have made structures, dwellings camouflaged with debris. It is amazing. They have found a way to create a home with the abandoned trash of my city.

Mama has a mask of an old woman on. It's a total contrast to the scary baby faces. The bata she wears is so thin you can see right through it.

"It's nap time. If you're going to pay us a visit, you should have at least come with treats," Mama says. "Maybe lollipops or gum. We love chocolates, don't we?"

They chime in agreement. This is what I'm negotiating with? We have no sweets to give, and even if we did, I sure as hell wouldn't be wasting it on these freaks. I'm losing my patience.

"As I mentioned to your, umm, Muñecas, we're walking through. I'm Chief Rocka, and these are Las Mal Criadas," I say. "We've heard of Las Muñecas Locas. You girls rule this area. We're honored to step through."

Mama shrugs. She adjusts her bata.

The ANT continues to be spaced out on the ground, oblivious to the negotiations going on in front of him. He pretends to be injured to avoid the drama. I see through his tricks.

"We're offering this in exchange for a walk-through," I say. "No drama. Just taking a walk."

"No!" Mama yells. "We are Las Muñecas Locas. We don't need a shiny new toy to make us pretty."

Okay. A necklace won't work with this bunch.

"You woke my babies," she says. "You make it right. Give us treats!"

Her crew starts to cry. Not any ordinary crying. They've thrown themselves on the ground and are having full-on temper tantrums. I've had enough. We need to give these dolls what they are in dire need of—a big pao pao.

"You girls want chocolate? Let me see what goodies we can share. Be right back."

Without me having to say a word, Smiley and Shi get the malasuertes ready. The Muñecas thought the cute doll bomb could cause damage. They haven't seen what our malasuertes can do.

Smiley holds the malasuerte in the palm of her hand. Shi moves the lever down.

"Nena, get ready to head east with the ANT."

Nena grabs hold of his arm. He finally seems awake.

I flick my head east to the direction I want Truck to go. She gives me the nod. The Muñecas Locas are done with their temper tantrum and are now swinging their machetes again. The machetes are rusty, and the bats look just as pathetic. These fools are harmless and should be placed right back in the waste they crawled from.

"Chocolate. Chocolate. Chocolate," they chant.

Is this what happens when you no longer live in Mega City? The baby-doll getup is a strange way of bringing back the childish things we aren't allowed to indulge in. It is truly sad. The malasuerte is ready to detonate. I nod, and Shi tosses the box behind us into the middle of the Muñecas. We've got to jet. I run, following close behind Nena and the ANT. The bomb is going to rock these girls' world.

The explosion propels our movement even more. I don't need to look back to see the Muñecas have scattered. They wanted chocolate. Toma chocolate.

I run past Nena and push the ANT farther. I scan around to make sure there are no other surprises, no other Muñecas waiting to talk their baby talk. When I feel my chest is about to burst open, I run even more. A few yards ahead I see the crumbled facade of a building. I duck in. I try to catch my breath and wait for the others.

The first to come through is Nena with the ANT. Nena coughs. She is completely winded. The ANT? He laughs as if he's on a fun ride.

"What the hell are you going on about?" I yell as I grab his shirt. "You think this is funny?"

He doesn't stop. I let him go and he drops to the floor.

"What's funny is you think you are so different from the Muñecas. Those girls are only following what Déesse has created in Mega City. Don't think for a minute they are not stealing every one of those ideas straight from the source. It's tragic. So are the LMCs."

Nena is worried I'm about to thrash this ANT. He hates what Déesse has created. There was a time when he lived in Mega City. He believed in Déesse once. When did that change?

"Wait outside for the others," I tell Nena.

She hesitates, then leaves.

I scrutinize him. "You lived in Mega City before. It wasn't a place of hate for you. There was a time when you had confidence in Déesse's vision."

"Can I see the necklace you wanted to trade?"

I hand him the piece of jewelry.

"This is what Déesse is selling—an unattainable object

that appears beautiful and luxurious. If you look closely, though, you notice it has no true value.

"If you want to live in Mega City, you are forced to abide by rigid rules on what it means to be a man and a woman," he continues. "There is no room for fluidity. Do you think violence makes you more of a woman? Does forcing papis to work at boydegas make them a better ally? Déesse's vision for Mega doesn't allow for differences. It doesn't allow for true self."

Has he been speaking to Books? The sueños are confusing him as to what is right and what is wrong.

"Did living in Mega cause you that much pain?"

Instead of responding, he puts the necklace on. He raises his chin, defiant.

"You've said Déesse abandoned you," he says. "Is this the real reason why you left Mega?"

"Of course," I say. "I got tired of watching others gain entrance to the Towers."

He nods. He seems to believe me. I need him to. He is going to take us to the Ryders. I try a different approach to reach him.

"We're going to be together for a couple of days," I say. "I should know your name."

"Oh, how nice, Chief Rocka. Wait. That's not your real name, is it? Your name was a gift from Déesse," he says. "Being christened by her also means she owns you.

"I'm owned by no one," I say, angered by what he implies.

"My name is Chief Rocka because I am the leader of this crew."

"What happens if I tell you my name? Do we become friends?" he asks. "I am more than what is displayed, more than the clothes I wear, more than a name or a pronoun. I was never allowed to be both in Mega. Déesse and her people want everyone to emulate only her. There's no room for someone like me."

His words are confusing. I don't understand him. Déesse flipped gender roles around. Women are in power. This is what matters.

I search in my bag and toss him a sueño. "I only want to know what I should call you," I say.

He stares at the tab. Instead of gobbling it down, the ANT stores it in a pocket.

"I'm Miguel for now."

For now?

"What did Déesse do to you?" I ask, nervous my question may betray my real motives. Yet I can't deny this longing to know.

"She fed me a lie," he says. There is a tiredness in his voice. "I believed her when she said I can do anything. Another lie. This is what we do to each other. We feed off of deceptions that are as sweet as these sueños. It's never quite the same as reality. Isn't that what you do to keep going?"

"No."

Miguel chuckles at my response. When did he fall down

this rabbit hole of sueños? Self-preservation. It's what each of us is trying to do. Survive. Align yourself with those whose fists are drawn. Create the family who will ride or die for you. These are the truths I live by. Blood family don't mean a thing unless they are fighting beside you. He is truly misguided if he doesn't believe these simple facts.

From where I stand, I can see his eyes are hazel. His hollow cheeks, shrunken from consuming too many sueños, overshadow what good looks he might have had. Maybe the Ashés are simply a bunch of addicts trying to regulate the sueño business.

"I saw what you did back there. You're not fooling me with this whole philosophical sermon," I say. "Why don't you take the sueño I gave you? I can tell you're thieving for it."

His eyes cast down to the ground for a second. There's shame there. "I wasn't always an addict. When I denied my truth that's when I started using sueños," he says. "How old were you when you were thrown in the training camp? Eight, seven? Not much of a childhood. Not much time for laughing or playing, or even figuring out who you want to be in this life."

"You think Zentrica found a way to maintain innocence?" It's my turn to laugh. There is no childhood because of the foolish decisions made by men long ago. If that is what she is selling, then the Ashé are as good as squashed.

"No room for differences, for love," he says. "No room for empathy. Huh?"

"No," I say. "There's no room."

"Keep swallowing the lies, Chief Rocka," he says.

I hear a rustling sound. The others must be on their way. Shi and Smiley come in, with Nena following behind.

"Truck, where you at?" Smiley yells into her Codigo.

"She was right behind me. When I turned around, I didn't see her," Shi says.

They check their Codigos. This is not right. Truck is always on the wire. The connection must be bad because of the malasuerte. We can't stay here. This building will not protect us. Who knows what else we'll run into.

"Who saw her last? What the hell were you guys doing?"

"We were running. That's what you told us to do," Shi says.

Did the Muñecas get her? I can't see Truck being unable to escape those losers. I tinker around with the Codigo. I'm not getting anything.

"Let's go back and look for her," Smiley says.

"What about the Muñecas?" Nena asks. I take two quick strides and eyeball her.

"Are you hesitating? Because if you are I will dump your ass right here," I say.

There's no denying there's not much love between Nena and Truck. She'd better rethink her reluctance.

"Shi and Smiley, roll back out," I say. "Make sure to check in to let us know what's going on."

Right before they leave, the Codigo makes a noise. I feel a sense of relief. Truck must have found a better place to hide. It must be the reason why she isn't with us.

"What's the word, Truck?" I say. "Where you at?"

The face that appears on the screen isn't Truck.

CHAPTER 13

TRUCK STOP

Hey, we got the ugliest of your girls right here."

Shi and Smiley tune in to the same frequency as my Codigo. Everyone looks into their goggles.

"You better come correct or we're hitting repeat on this."

Four girls have Truck pinned and are holding her arms and legs. Truck tries her best to pull free. It's no use. They've got her real good. The weapons on this crew look shiny and new against their all-black tracksuits. A tall girl walks into the frame of the Codigo and smiles. She then turns and flips a kick into Truck's stomach. Truck has nowhere to go to protect herself from the blow, and she can't fall down to take the hit. Truck's rage rises, which in turn gets her another roundhouse.

"What do you want?" I say.

"Go north for a mile and meet us at the crossroads," says a faceless voice.

"Don't listen to them . . . ," Truck says before the transmission goes black.

The Muñecas were the obvious distraction. This crew waited on the sideline to make their move. Truck pays the price for us not being extra vigilant. The tracksuits look familiar. I need to be absolutely sure.

Shi quickly gets the intel.

"Hurry up and confirm!" I say, almost certain Truck is getting the beatdown of her life.

"Gurl Gunnas," Shi says. "They're not in it for the fight. They are in it for the trade."

Santo warned me I would run into the Gunnas. What I don't understand is why they are holding Truck if they trade. Smiles and a welcoming attitude is what I remember from my interaction with the Gunnas during their pop-ups. It doesn't make sense. We are at a disadvantage here. Mere visitors on these streets without a good enough guidebook.

"Miguel, is there anything you can tell us about the Gurl Gunnas?" I ask. The others turn to the ANT with a confused look. They don't approve of me taking into account his opinion. I don't care what the LMCs feel right now. I need answers.

"Well, I avoid them as much as I can," he says. "They're quite unpolished. They don't take kindly to my kind."

"What does that mean exactly?" I'm so over his cryptic statements. Why can't he just be straight?

"It means they follow Déesse's rule and hate men as much as Mega City does."

I don't hate men. This is also what Déesse has warned us about in her monthly sermons before throwdowns: Men are clever manipulators who use whatever tactics to question women's capability. I could care less how the Gurl Gunnas treat men. My concern is and will always be Truck.

"Where's their leader?" I ask. "Where's Vanessa?"

Shi shakes her head.

"It happened a few months ago," she says. "A change in administration. Vanessa got the ax by one of her own. It was pretty bloody. It's the reason why it's been a minute since we've seen the Gurl Gunnas in the boydegas."

Not good. If I don't know the new leader, then I will be walking in with a deficit. Taking Truck means they will be asking for more than I might possibly be able to give. The bag of sueños Santo gave me seems too small of a trade, not when Truck's life is on the line. Will it be enough?

"Another thing, Chief," Shi says. "The leader of the Gurl Gunnas goes by OG and she's twelve."

"That's real trouble, then," says Smiley. "Undisciplined trouble. No wonder she's flexing her muscle by taking Truck. Truck is by far the strongest LMC. When we walk, Truck is the one who stands out."

Twelve years old probably going on thirty. Dealing with a young gun is scary. I don't know what will set her off. Her taking Truck means they are playing outside the rules. She hasn't lived long enough to know there's a process to everything. Offing her leader was probably her first violent act. To maintain her rule is going to take a whole lot of carnage because the older girls are probably counting the days until they can off her, too.

I can estimate on one hand the number of young leaders who tried to head up crews in Mega City. To prove themselves, these young guns strike in big ways that defy logic or understanding of the game. They want to skip past rungs every soldier must follow to make a name for themselves, including battling other crews until they've reached a certain level. Instead, these young leaders steal and beat unsuspecting toilers. Start fights outside of the scheduled throwdowns. Déesse sends her army to disband these minor gangs before they become too much of a nuisance. Is that how the Gurl Gunnas ended up in Cemi Territory? After Vanessa, did the OG try to expand the Gurl Gunnas to be more than just sellers?

It's a bloody game they're playing, and now they've thrown the LMCs into the mix.

My crew looks at me, eagerly awaiting my word on what our next move will be. I've got to think fast. I've got to make this better.

"Take inventory," I say.

The girls go through their things and start rattling off items for Nena to write down. Four Codigos.

"My Codigo stopped working," says Smiley. "It probably has to be reset. Kind of worthless."

Nena marks it down. There are food pellets. We can't give those up. Our tronics are too valuable. I won't trade them. The sueños will have to do.

I gather the girls away from Miguel. He seems only mildly concerned with what's happening. Or is this yet another performance from him, feigning disinterest as a form of survival? I don't trust him.

"We give them the sueños," I say. "Under no circumstances are we to give them anything else. Not the tronics and not him."

"What would the Gurl Gunnas want with an ANT? We barely want him."

"I don't know. I don't know what to expect from a stupid kid. Do you?"

"Let me hole up with him, then," Smiley says. "So it's not even on the table. They won't see the ANT, so it won't be an issue."

"No. They saw us and they picked Truck. They know exactly what they are doing. OG may be twelve, but she has the smarts to have gotten this far."

I pace. I have to think a few moves ahead. What do the Gurl Gunnas want? As a new leader, OG needs to prove herself. It's why she's acting out with Truck. This is more of a show, a power play to flex her newfound muscles. The Gurl

Gunnas will want to ransack us for sueños. If they are traveling back and forth to Mega City, sueños are the only currency that matters. We will give them what they want. The sueños will be our ticket to getting Truck.

"We can't mess around," I say. "We stick together. It's imperative. They took Truck because we allowed the mess with the Muñecas to trip us. We can't have a repeat performance."

"I'm sorry, Chief Rocka," Nena says. She is shaking.

"What are you sorry about?"

"If I hadn't found the doll bomb, then we wouldn't have been confused. It's my fault."

"You two gather our stuff," I say. "We are leaving in five minutes."

I take Nena aside. She seems so young. I can't have her freaking out on me. This is different from when Miguel caught her. Ever since we left Mega City she has stayed clear away from him. I notice her flinching whenever he addresses her in any way. Truck hasn't picked up on it because if she had, she would have never let Nena hear the end of it. I need her to get hard and not be fooled by dolls or any shiny objects.

"Nena, you have to soldier." I say this firmly. "There is no room for mistakes. Truck's life is on the line. I will cut you loose if you make any more. Do you hear me?"

"I'll be a true soldier. I won't mess this up. I promise."

"You're afraid. So am I," I say. "The Gurl Gunnas cannot

see your fear. No matter what, you go into a new situation strong as a mountain and quick with the rage face."

She shows me her rage face.

I caress her cheek. Baby Nena. I can't lose any more of my girls. Not on this trip, not because of silly errors.

"You are an LMC. Don't let anyone ever tell you different. Do you remember what I said to you on the day I let you stay with us? We are sisters, family, and we look out for each other."

I won't let what happened to me happen to Nena or to Truck, or to the others. I won't abandon them as my sister and father abandoned me. Nena has to channel this dread she has into anger. Let it be a slow burn.

"You stepped to the Muñeca when we needed you to. Summon that feeling again. Follow my lead. Don't forget your training."

"Yes, Chief Rocka."

Her voice is strong. Let it stay strong.

"This goes for everyone. We need Truck. Let's do what we were born to do. Let's go."

A young kid tries to make a name for herself. It's not much different from the crews in Mega City except for one thing—Déesse. The Gurl Gunnas and the demented Muñecas are leaderless. At least Déesse guides us. She provides order. I'm navigating a place with its own set of rules. There's no map here, only my gut telling me to go left or right.

It's been only a couple of days. It feels an eternity since

the battle with Destiny. How am I going to make it to the Ashé if I can't protect my strongest soldier? There's so much doubt surging through me. I can't share my fears with anyone. Truck isn't here to talk this thing through.

"Let's be ready to offer him," Smiley says. There's no usual jokes or last digs coming from Smiley.

"No. We need him," I say. "We won't give up Miguel unless we have to."

"Thank you, Chief Rocka," Miguel chimes in. Here I am protecting a stranger, an addicted ANT. Why do I feel my sense of purpose has been twisted ever since I said yes to Déesse back in the healing center?

We need to get Truck back. I will do what I must to make it happen. Our mission is true. The Gurl Gunnas are just another crew blocking my way.

CHAPTER 14

GURL GUNNAS BE LIKE

A heavy smell of burnt rubber replaces the earlier stench of garbage. Abandoned buildings dot the area. This doesn't surprise me. What does is that I can see Gurl Gunnas situated on the roofs. They keep their tronics by their sides. My soldiers are aware. We keep tight to our formation.

"There's so many," Nena says.

"This is Cemi Territory," Shi explains to her. "They don't abide to the five girls to a gang rule. Who knows how many Gurl Gunnas are part of their outfit."

Two Gurls greet us at the crossroads. The tronics on them look state of the art, equipment we wish we could score from Santo. As far as I know, tronics are made in Mega City. Santo said Déesse has an "understanding" with them. Does it include weapons? I am left with more questions and a feeling of dread.

"Empty them, Chief Rocka," one of them says. She rolls the "R" in "Rocka," really emphasizing it. What a jerk. There's no respect. This should be about business. It's bad news if these scrubs are following what the OG is dishing.

"We don't empty for no one. Stun if you got to," I say. "Your boss isn't going to give you high fives for dropping bodies without making currency first."

This Gurl Gunna will play it right if she knows what's good for her. They are smart enough to understand the value of trade. As for our weapons, they're not laying one finger on them until we get Truck. And not even then.

"We got to pat you down, Rockas," she says. We hold on to our weapons. They won't feel any of our secondary toys, our knives and blades. They're well concealed inside our garments. I get patted down first.

"Sorry to hear about what happened to Vanessa," Smiley says. She baits them to talk, gauging how chaotic the changes are inside the Gurl Gunnas headquarters.

The one with the bald head talks. "Vanessa. Haha. She was a joke. A come mierda who needed to be put down. It was easy."

The other one has a squat build. Her hair is up in elaborate braids. She doesn't say a thing. I noticed the flicker in her eye. She had an allegiance to Vanessa. Smiley sees what I see and directs her question to her.

"If the shift of power was done smoothly, then there's no loss of sleep. Right?" Smiley asks her.

The Gurl Gunna looks away.

"We haven't seen you girls at the boydegas," Smiley says. "The Luna Club is fire right now. You've been there?"

Smiley acts friendly. She's good at conveying that. The baldhead girl isn't interested. The squat one, on the other hand, is curious. Maybe she wants to leave the Gurl Gunnas and sees in us a possible exit. Smiley is planting a seed.

"You think Mega City is the only place with boydegas?" the domed one says. "Life doesn't start with you. We got our own boydegas."

"That's not what I said."

The domed one shakes her head. Was she born here in Cemi Territory? Perhaps this is where her loyalty lies. I guess you have to fool yourself into believing what you have is good enough.

"Next time you find yourself in Mega, the drinks are on me." Smiley directs this to the quieter soldier. The Gurl barely nods in recognition. This may never work to our favor. The Gurl Gunna might be too entrenched. It doesn't hurt to try.

The bald-headed Gurl Gunna checks Nena.

"Aww, look at this new cub." She rubs her bare head. "You might as well put a collar on her because she's about to bail."

Nena has the look of flight for sure. Even after my earlier talk, her baby face still gives her away. Shi comes between the Gurl Gunna and Nena in defense mode.

"Leave her alone," Shi says. "Or the one getting cuffed will be you."

There's a long, tension-filled moment. After a beat, the Gurl Gunna laughs off the threat. They're sizing us up, getting intel to relay back to the boss.

Satisfied, the Gurls walk down a few blocks. Around a corner we see their headquarters. A large tent is made out of colorful sheets. Their emblem, a tiger with two tronics, hangs above the tent.

"OG is in a meeting. She wants you Rockas to chill over at our boydega," the Gurl Gunna says with a snarl. "You can see how we play."

As much as I hate this, I can't refuse.

"Keep close," I tell Nena, and she does.

Inside one of their tents, the music is deafeningly loud. The boydega doesn't compare to the Luna Club. There are skinny, emaciated boys dancing on various elevated stages. They look as bored as ever. Who knows how long they've been at it. The place is packed with Gurl Gunnas placing bets on the papis dancing. I can't tell who is judging.

"Serve these Rockas drinks," she says. "Not him. He only gets drinks if he dances."

Miguel glares at the soldier. This is what he meant by the Gunnas. The papis are forced to be here.

"No thanks," I say. "We're not thirsty."

There are tables of soldiers eating, and my stomach growls. I won't touch the food. I don't know what type of game these people are playing. We don't do a thing until I see Truck.

"How long before OG is available?" I ask.

"Soon." The Gurl Gunna walks away and checks out a boy with flaming-red hair dancing in silver shorts. She guzzles down her drink. "See! You guys aren't the only ones living the high life." She yells to the papi to move faster. He doesn't. Other Gurl Gunnas point and whisper to each other. The whole display is pathetic.

Shi sidles up to the quieter Gurl Gunna. Although Shi is doing the talking, the Gurl Gunna is listening. On another stage, papis gyrate while Gurl Gunnas holla at them.

All I can do is wait. Count the minutes while Truck endures who knows what. Nena fidgets with her LMC tattoo.

A young Gurl Gunna runs to the loudmouth soldier. The loudmouth doesn't stop staring at the dancing papi. She answers only with a nod.

"It's about to happen," Smiley says. Even when I am in the middle of chaos, there is a dance being carried out. This is a performance. I'm being forced to wait while Truck is close by. The OG has the upper hand, and I am part of the show until the very end.

"Do you want a little aid to calm you down?" A papi serves shot glasses with sueños in them.

Miguel grabs a glass and places the pill in his pocket before I can stop him.

"Damn you."

"Just following the leader," he says.

This freaking guy. Miguel will soon ride high and be utterly useless. Why go under when we are walking into the unknown? Or, perhaps, this is the reason why he does it.

"Let's go, Rocka!" the loudmouth soldier shouts. "OG is waiting."

Nena scurries to walk with Smiley and Shi. I follow the Gurl Gunna. She leads us away from the boydega to a large tent. Gurl Gunnas stand guard in the front of it. They give the nod and we walk in.

It's as if we've stumbled upon a boydega fantasy room. The tent is stacked with books everywhere. There are walls of books, more than I've ever seen before in my life. Piles used as tables and chairs. My papi chulo Books would have fit right in. For an instant I am drawn back home and the life I left behind.

A Gurl Gunna keeps a fire pit going by feeding it with books. Tied up in a chair sits a slumped-over Truck. She's been getting the beatdown for who knows how long. She is a bloody mess. They took things too far.

Sitting atop a massive chair made of books spray-painted in gold is the twelve-year-old OG. She's weighed down in chains, around her neck, her arms, her waist, her teeth. Her hair is cropped, with one gold stripe across the top.

"I'm Chief Rocka of Las Mal Criadas. Your situation looks tight, minus, of course, my girl Truck right there," I say. "Let's cut her loose and get down to numbers."

The OG pats an oversized pet iguana that sits beside her.

The iguana is a mechanical animal similar to the piñatas hanging at Luna Club. Built to last forever, or until its batteries die. These toys are not cheap to come by, and it doesn't appear to have been handmade. Are the Gurl Gunnas living that large to be able to afford this opulent plaything? This goes beyond selling multicolored wigs and Codigos. The iguana jets out its tongue and props its head back down on the floor.

"Naw. You're in my house now. I'll tell you what is what." With the self-inflicted scars on her face and body, I can see how an outsider might be fooled into thinking the OG is older. No matter how much gold she throws on herself, she can't hide the baby fat on her cheeks. "Your girl here was out of order. Not checking herself. We talk numbers when I'm good and ready to talk numbers."

I came on too strong. I've got to pull back or there will be no rescue for Truck.

"As I mentioned, your house looks nice. I'm good sitting down with your people, if it's a sit-down you want. I'm coming to you identical to the way you're coming to me. As two warriors, two soldiers with one agenda, getting what we want."

There's a long pause. I can almost hear her brain working overtime, trying to figure which piece to play first. I refuse to step down from this scrub, even if we end up getting jacked. She'll be the first to get a taste of my hidden knife.

Smiley speaks, breaking the uncomfortable silence.

"It's been a while since I've seen you, OG," Smiley says.

"I trained with you right before I left the camp, remember?"

Smiley knows her. This is news. I wish we'd known this before getting here. OG is a Mega City girl. She has roots in our city and she's managed to upgrade her situation by carving space in Cemi Territory. There's no way she could have done this alone. I don't see what makes her special. The chair made of books engulfs her small frame. History between Smiley and her might work in our favor, unless they got beef.

OG gets up and walks over to Smiley. It takes OG a second to place her. When she does, her expression is far from a welcome surprise. Instead, her scowl grows.

"You know me? So what? I remember you being a punk-ass zero who couldn't fight to save her ugly face. You hanging with this sorry crew? That tells me everything. Step back before I truly wreck you." I probably won't be the one to beat this girl. It will be Smiley for sure. If their history goes back to the training camp, then Smiley knows exactly where to hit.

"You forgot it was me who saved you from getting a beatdown from the Rompe Cocos," Smiley says. "I remember too well who played the punk that day."

The OG laughs this off. One of the Gurl Gunnas grabs Smiley and tries to wrestle her down. Smiley is quick to outmaneuver her. She grabs the Gurl Gunna's head and pushes it into her raised knee. Another Gurl Gunna rushes to tackle Smiley. Shi joins in by grabbing the nearest Gunna. More enter the fray. Nena jumps in. The fight is clean. My hand stays settled against my tronic just in case the ugliness escalates.

While the ruckus continues, OG and I play the staring game. Her gold teeth gleam even in the darkened tent. OG waits for me to be the first to blink. I try to re-create her time-line. Did she fail in the training camp and decide to become a freelancer? To be a seller you must be on the pulse of what people desire. She needed to fill a void. What is she selling out here in Cemi Territory? It can't be this extreme force.

Pleased with the show, OG strokes her iguana. There's no protection here, no cover. This is her house, and we're battling our way to find a seat at the table. Truck moans.

Smiley has knocked two Gunnas out cold. There's a slight reprieve for the LMC, enough for Smiley to hold down a Gurl. Then four more Gunnas join the fray. They take Smiley, but not before she lands a blow to the side of a Gunna's head, sending her careening to a table. Books are toppled to the ground. The OG isn't pleased by this.

"We're done," I say. My girls stop fighting. The OG knows what we are capable of. Maybe now we can sit down and plot the rest.

"Good," she says, chuckling a bit. "Get the LMCs drinks."

I am led to her negotiating table, which is made of books painted in gold. The Gunnas bring water to my girls. After catching their breath, Smiley, Shi, and Nena stand erect behind me.

"You're a long way from Mega City. Where are you heading, and why have you dragged your asses over here?"

OG should be more concerned with her own troops than with where I'm going.

"We're marching toward the interior of Cemi Territory. No drama, no blood."

"Cemi Territory isn't for everyone. Only the cold-blooded and ruthless can survive. You guys don't seem either of those things. Too much time in Mega City. Why are you in my hood?"

"That's our business."

"The thing is, your business is now my business. I'm in no rush to cut your soldier down, especially after the way she mouthed off to my people. This girl, Truck, is bad news."

I don't doubt Truck mouthed off. OG's lying soldiers surely provoked her first. Truck probably fought everything and everyone around.

"It's neither here nor there whether my soldier disrespected you. Let's talk about how your Gurls took Truck without negotiating first, while we were dealing with those sorry Muñecas. We can go over the rules broken and see which one of our crews is more on the wrong. It's a waste of time."

The giant iguana circles my feet. Santo had one before. He was gifted a tiger. They are made in the Towers. The latest trend. It can't hurt anyone. Still, I don't appreciate it lingering near me.

"This is true. I still don't know why you are strolling through Cemi Territory."

She won't let up. I have to give her an answer.

"He's my blood." I point to Miguel. "I'm escorting him to a new life in Cemi Territory."

The lie I made up on the spur of the moment. The way they treat their men here, I figured he wouldn't be much of a draw. Miguel nods off. Once again, he pretends to be oblivious to what happens around him.

"A new life. The sueño-gray complexion he has matches perfectly here. If he wants a new start, I can get him a job as a dancer."

"No thanks," I say. "Now you know what we are doing. What is it you want?"

"Your weapons are worthless, so you need to offer me a good and lively trade. You know what I mean? If you want to soldier through our land, you better submit a token of appreciation, a guarantee your trek is temporary."

"Cool," I say. I don't want to appear too eager, so I act as if I'm thinking through our options. I let Shi show her what we've got.

"We'll give you these sueños."

The OG is not impressed.

"I don't need sueños. We have plenty of those. What I need is extra muscle."

I don't follow. The OG wants a person, one of my soldiers. Why? She has enough Gurls. I'm not giving her my strongest. I won't give up Truck. It's just not happening.

Before I can respond, the OG points to Nena.

"This one will do. She's fresh," OG says. "We can use new-ness on our team."

"Not my soldiers. We'll storm through this area on our way back from dropping him off. We'll share the loot we snag along the way."

"What can you possibly get out of Cemi Territory we haven't already taken? We've got sueños and better tronics than the ones on you. This cub will do. We will hold her as a guarantee."

Nena's nails dig into my arm. She's not about to let go without blood.

"No. She's mine," I say. "I'm not trading her."

We eye each other.

"Then no pass."

If I want Truck, my strongest soldier, I need to let Nena go. This is insane. What can she get from holding Nena? What is she trying to prove?

"We will give you the sueños, tronics, and these Codigos," I say. "Take it. You can't have her."

"And here I thought I was negotiating with a real player."

I won't give them Nena. They can't take her. She's family. She's an LMC.

"This is what we call a . . . what's the word?" OG asks the room. An older Gurl Gunna leans in to the OG and whispers in her ear. "An impasse."

Nena's nails dig deeper into my skin. I won't let her go.

There is no reason for her to keep Nena. None at all.

"Her stay here is temporary," she says. "A guarantee for soldiering through."

"No deal."

"Listen, if you do right by us, then who knows what we can do for you later. I'm tight with Déesse. You never know."

She points to one of her gold chains. A choker with the letters "GG." The lettering is the same as the choker given to me by Déesse's people. She is connected to her. A reminder of what Santo told me. This is important. If OG is traveling freely back and forth to Mega City and has an audience with Déesse, I can't afford to alienate her.

"Give me your word you will not harm her," I say. "And that this is temporary."

"No. Wait a minute," says Shi. Smiley slams her hand against the table, ready to lift the whole thing and throw it. I quickly turn to them. They step down. There is no debate. I'm Chief Rocka. My word is bond. We need to move forward. We must leave a type of assurance. I have no choice.

"Give me your word," I say.

"You've got my word. I won't touch a strand of her hair," OG says. "She'll be your guarantee for passage."

I nod in agreement.

Nena cries out. I love Nena. I do. We will get her back. When we return from dealing with the Ashé Ryders, we will come for her.

"Please, Chief Rocka, don't do this. I'm an LMC. Don't send me away. I'll be better, I promise. I won't mess up ever again. Please!" She shrieks, punching wildly to anyone who comes close. I take her in my arms and hold her tight. There's no alternative. I'm securing our future. We will be back. I'm sure of it.

"Nena, we will come for you," I whisper. "I swear to all that is Mega. You won't stay here for long."

She clings to me. It's hard for me to pry her hands off. The knot in my throat chokes. I am outside of myself as I hand Nena over to the Gurl Gunnas. The Chief Rocka part of me is heartless. She will cut Nena loose because she knows it's the right thing to do. The other part of me, Nalah? She thinks I'm desperate.

With the help of the Gurl Gunnas, I give them Nena. The rage from my crew burns. The Gunnas drag Nena from the room. She's so light. I'm doing this to her.

"Let Truck go."

A Gurl Gunna unties Truck and the rag covering her mouth.

"Get out," I say to my crew. "I want to finish our business here. Bounce."

They take Truck. It's time to seal this deal. The OG got what she wanted. She got my Nena. I don't want to dwell on this deed. It hurts too much.

"We need to move this along. We've already dealt with the Muñecas, and my crew is tired and hungry," I say.

"Why are you in such a rush? Your crew can chill here. Lie back."

I pull my knife out. There is real fear on her face. I quickly slice a cut on my hand. Before her soldiers can stop me, I make a cut on the OG. I force our hands to touch. The agreement is official. Now she can't break it.

"When I come back, Nena better be exactly the way I left her. Not a hair misplaced, not a brand on her skin. If not, I'll be coming for you alone."

The iguana tears into my pants. I kick the iguana out of my way. He malfunctions. His tongue stays frozen. I walk out.

Losing Nena hurts more than anything. I did exactly what my sister did to me many years ago. I abandoned her. I never thought I could reach this low.

I encase everything soft within me with a coldhearted layer. It will be my new armor.

CHAPTER 15

HEARTBREAK KID

What are you talking about? Where is Nena?"

It's been a few hours since we left the Gurl Gunnas. Truck needed the time to recover, so we stopped at a clearing. Shi and Smiley will not look me in the eye. Their anger is palpable. They tended to Truck's injuries without saying a word. Ignoring me even. Now Truck is awake and her first words are accusations. We gave in, Truck thinks. She's dead wrong. I made the right decision. I negotiated her freedom.

"How are you going to give them one of your soldiers?" she yells. If Truck weren't in so much pain, she would throttle me.

"I did what I had to do," I say, gritting my teeth. "I saved you."

"After what them Gurls did to me, you rewarded them for their actions? What kind of negotiation is that?"

"You were unconscious. You don't know what went down."

She grabs Smiley's collar. "What happened?"

Smiley sheepishly looks at her. "The OG wanted Nena."

"Naw. Not good enough."

She takes Smiley's Codigo and punches in information. The others gather around her. I know where this is heading. Nowhere. I build up my mental defenses.

"We can sneak in around the back. I think I know where they'll keep Nena," Truck says. "We'll need to empty our tronics. It will be quick. They won't even know what hit them. If we send Smiley in front, create a sort of diversion, then we can sneak around the . . ."

The others are in on the plan. They don't bother to question whether Truck's motives make sense, whether or not it's even a good idea. They've forgotten the mission and are willing to jeopardize how far we've come. I'm not letting that happen. Truck has to come to her senses.

"No," I say. "My deal is sealed. I don't break it for anyone. Nena will be fine. Now let's move. Miguel, where do we go from here?"

"You shut your trap," Truck says to Miguel. He moves away from us. This is madness. We can't act this way. Why aren't they listening? The deed has been done. There is no turning back.

"No one breaks a trade," I say. "I made a pact with the Gurl Gunnas. My word is bond. This thing with Nena is temporary. We will get her back."

Truck stomps toward me, grimacing through the pain inflicted by the Gunnas. We stand toe-to-toe.

"How dare you use Nena? I would have never given up an LMC. As our leader, your job is to protect us, not sell us out."

My hands form into fists. I don't care if before me stands the only person I trust. I will knock Truck out if I have to. I quickly raise my clenched hand. My reaction is immediate. It's what I do with anyone threatening me. Truck doesn't flinch. If I throw this punch, I will cross a line. Our partnership will dissolve right here and now.

Time stops.

She glances over to my fist. What am I doing? Am I about to fight Truck? My hand goes down. Truck shakes her head in disappointment. She turns her back and takes a few steps in the direction of the Gurl Gunnas.

"I'm going back for Nena."

"Stop, Truck. Listen to me," I implore. I didn't make this decision lightly. She has to understand. I run up to her and pull her aside, far away from Miguel. He can't hear us. I talk to her as a friend and not Chief Rocka.

"Truck, OG's connected to Déesse," I whisper. "We need her to be our ally."

"You don't know what their relationship is, if it even exists. It could be a total lie."

"It's not. Santo confirmed it," I say. "We've got to play by their rules."

"What freaking rules? There are no rules in Cemi Territory. If there are none, then I'm going to make my own."

There's no point in trying to persuade her. She's made up her mind.

"Weren't you the one who kept telling me Nena was deadweight? We should have never accepted her in the LMC. Isn't that what you said? Now you've changed your tune."

Truck's face is red with anger. No one wants to hear the truth. "She might be deadweight, but she's still family. What gives you the right to dictate who is of value in this outfit?"

"I'm Chief Rocka, that's what," I say.

She goes back to the others. My crew glares at me. Defiant. Are they ready to jump me? I will never apologize for my actions. Never.

"How much farther, Miguel?"

"We are close," he says. "A five-hour walk."

"I'm heading toward the Ashés. It's where we belong," I say. "If you want to go back and get Nena, you're doing it without me."

Smiley looks at Shi. Maybe this hasn't been the first time they've questioned my authority. This is definitely the first time they are willing to cut connections. They've forgotten I'm the only one who holds the key to the Towers.

"Speak your mind, soldier."

"The LMC will continue with or without you," Smiley says.

"Is that a threat?" I don't care who I plow down. These girls, the Gurl Gunnas, the stupid Muñecas. I will get to the Ashés, finish this job, and end in the Towers as planned. No scrub soldier, not even Truck, will stop me.

"Not a threat, Chief Rocka. The truth," Smiley says. "We are with you until we can't be with you anymore. Set the scenario straight. Are you willing to give us up too?"

"Are you serious!" I yell. "You're all going soft."

I see what's coming down the road. It's as real as Truck's bruises. It's all of us, working the Mega City streets. The LMC will no longer be the chosen ones. Just regular toilers. Why can't they see that? There is a price to pay to align with the powerful, and right now we are paying our last dues.

It's useless. They only see I betrayed Nena. Even Shi, the quiet soldier who manages to disguise her feelings, can't hide her disgust. I'm through explaining myself. I'm done.

"Listen. You, too, Truck. The next soldier to doubt my move can do it with blood," I say. "You feeling me? Shut it or crank the violence. Don't come to me with any more dumb plans. I'm moving forward."

Smiley bares her golden grin, the same smile she gives to her worst enemies. The tense moment feels endless. It's only when Shi places her hand on Smiley's shoulder that Smiley backs down.

I'm gutted. I can't believe this is happening. Leaving Nena was the hardest decision I ever made. Truck questions me placing value on my soldiers. She's doing the same thing to me. They are abandoning me as quickly as I left Nena.

"This is it, then. Huh?"

"We're not deserting you, Chief Rocka," Shi says. "We're going back. We are sisters, family, and we look out for each other. Remember?"

She repeats the exact words I said to Nena right before our meeting with the Gurl Gunnas. It's a punch in the gut. I meant what I said. Every word. Life is not black-and-white. Why can't they see sacrifices must be made to reach the top? I stare at them. They continue with their ridiculous plans. I am left alone. Again.

Miguel makes a noise. An innocent sound. I yank his hand to follow me. He's my guide, and I won't give up. We walk until I can no longer hear Truck tapping on the Codigo. Walk as far away from them as possible. Miguel doesn't say a word. When exhaustion sets in, I pick a building and push him in. There are remnants of furniture and mementos forgotten by a family who once lived there. This will do. We will rest here until I calculate my next move.

"One word and I will bust open your whole face."

I need to think. My sisters have turned against me. How can they do that? We're family. I've never lost sight of that even at the very moment I handed Nena over.

The Gurl Gunnas outnumber them no matter how Truck tries to crunch it. She's not thinking straight. Poisoning the others. She hasn't even healed from the beatdown they inflicted on her. You don't go back on a trade, ever. It's dangerous what she's doing. I couldn't get through to her. To any of them. How did I reach this point?

I pace up and down, not sure what to do.

"They are acting out of anger," Miguel says. "Perhaps what they need is time."

"I don't have time." I angrily brush away the tears.

I never once cried at the training camp, no matter how many times I was punched. Before then? I bawled when my mother passed away. I was a kid. Did I cry when Yamaris left? I can't remember.

"You should be proud. The LMCs are a true family," Miguel says. "They fight and love with every ounce. This passion flows from their leader."

I feel so lost that I'm willing to listen to Miguel. The tears flow even more.

"There was a time when I didn't believe in family. I only believed in myself. I lived that way for a long time," he says. "It's funny how you can convince yourself your actions are benevolent, especially when there are eyes looking adoringly up to you. Power is very seductive. You lose sight of what is important."

"Why are you telling me this? I have no control over my own crew."

"You are a nurturer. Families are not simply molded after us. They grow and contrast. They also test us. You are being tested now. Try to remember the good within your family. You have caring traits. You are not as hard as you think you are or as Déesse wants you to believe."

"Please, shut up," I say. "You don't know what you're talking about."

My head hurts. I don't want to hear about family. I'm not a nurturer. I'm a fighter. If I learned anything from my blood family, it's that people will always fall short.

Miguel gets up and finds a chair to sit in. It doesn't take long for him to doze off. I do the same. My eyes grow heavy, although my mind races.

Yamaris returns to my thoughts. This ghost. I try to wake up. To move my body so to be free of this vision. The dream will not leave me. Instead, it morphs into another vision, one I don't remember ever having before. We are in a field of green. The colors are practically neon. A grand open space, large enough to run. I don't recognize it. My sister lifts me. The sun feels warm. The palms of my hands are sweating.

She plops down on the dirt and directs me to do the same. She uses her fingers to make a heart on the ground. Inside the heart she guides my finger to write our initials. Y & N.

The grass is so tall. I feel as if the green grass was made for us alone. A special place no one knows exists. We've played here before.

Yamaris begins to snap her fingers. I try to snap mine and grow impatient for my failed attempts. "Practice," she says. "Keep trying. You'll get it."

She is much older than me. Things come easy to her. I have so much to learn. When will I catch up?

Yamaris sings a song. I mouth the words.

Help me find the sun. I will follow you, child. I used to know the way. I forgot it all. I used to be you, child. . . .

We are now running. It's raining. We are caught in the rain. We can't stop laughing. She finds coverage under a large tree. Yamaris points to the raindrops on the leaves. This place is magical. I let the drops fall on my forehead. The rain creates a trail down my cheek.

"I will love you forever, Nalah," Yamaris says. "Forever and ever."

The dream shifts again. We are no longer outside. Yamaris stands in front of me, crying. She is scared. I am scared too. I grab hold. I won't let go. I cry, beg her not to leave.

"Nalah, we won't be apart forever. I promise. We will find a way back," she says. "It's important you remember everything I told you. You can do this. We are counting on you."

What is happening? Remember what, Nalah? What did I forget?

She turns away from me. A faceless person calls to her. There is no more time.

"I love you, Nalah. Forever and ever."

Yamaris is gone. I am left alone. I scream as loud as I can, loud enough to rock my room. Loud enough so my voice can leave her a scar. Why did you leave me?

CHAPTER 16

HUNGRY GHOSTS

Wake up," he says. "You're having a bad dream."

Confused by my whereabouts, I instinctively reach for my tronic and aim it at the silhouette. Miguel stands over me. How long has he been there? Is he going to make a move? My hand keeps steady on the weapon.

"You were screaming," he says.

"Move." He stays put. Miguel's not afraid of my tronic or of me.

His expression is hard to decipher. He is the one person on this trip I can never read. The occasions I've spent with sueño addicts have been limited to breaking nights. There have never been meaningful conversations. But mutiny is contagious. Miguel could be plotting to take me down.

"Move away," I repeat while I turn the tronic's laser beam on. This is how we met, with my tronic aimed at his fore-

head. The encounter seems ages ago. Back then I had no idea I would be tied to this man and we would be on this hellish journey. Now I'm alone with him, the last person I want to be with.

Miguel slowly walks back to the farthest corner of the room. He could have easily left me to fend for myself. Hit me at my lowest point. Again, I don't understand him. When he returns to his seat, I put the tronic away and pull my knees to my chest. These thoughts of the past are too much. They are wounds that never heal.

Yamaris. Flashes of green grass and rain. I am left to decipher these haunting thoughts. Did they happen, or is it wishful thinking?

A ray of sunlight descends on the room, illuminating Miguel's thin profile. How long have we been asleep? I think of Truck and the others. Did they reach their destination, or have the Gurl Gunnas already thwarted their foolish plan? Maybe they're devising a way to reunite with me.

Yeah, right.

"Do you hear that?" Miguel asks.

I hear it. It's barely audible. A tapping sound, as if a person knocks on a door.

"Gather your stuff quietly." I grab my bag and make sure he does the same. He's lethargic. My stomach growls. It's been a while since we've eaten, but I don't want to be confined in this space while there are others out there.

I walk to the back of the room, toward a window. Slight murmurs can be heard. It's low. Definitely a voice. Miguel stands next to me. We both take a peek.

A man and a boy are a few steps away from us in a sort of courtyard. The man digs a hole in the ground while the little boy watches him. Every few seconds, the boy taps on a rock as if playing a tune. The man ruffles the boy's hair and smiles. They are both oblivious to anything or anyone else, completely in their own world. The man does not wear the normal toiler overalls, just regular pants and a long-sleeved shirt. He continues to dig while talking to the boy. A few moments later a woman calls to them from the building across the way. She wears a long dress that reaches the ground. The mother, perhaps? There is nothing hard about her. Maybe it's the way the sun slowly rises, creating a sort of haze to the surroundings. It feels as if I'm watching a play, an idyllic scenario that exists only in books.

The boy shouts to her. He lifts his hand and shows her the rock.

"Maybe they have food," Miguel says.

"Yeah, and maybe they're Gurl Gunnas."

Miguel shakes his head. "They aren't Gurl Gunnas. It's a family. Cemi Territory is not populated with girl gangs. That's a city thing. There are many who live here and are simply surviving. Not everyone lives by their fists."

The mother has now joined the man and the boy. How

sweet. Maybe I should go out there and trample their so-called garden. Grab the rock from the kid and hurl it against a window. Destroy this perfect image.

"Let's go."

Miguel stays by the window while I open my backpack and eat a food pellet.

"Los Bohios is close," he says. "Those food pellets aren't very tasty. Let's talk to them. Eat real food."

I grab his shoulders and push him toward the entrance. He hasn't asked for a sueño in a while. In fact, I didn't see him take the sueño offered to him at the boydega. Why is he hoarding them? "Don't eat."

We move into the streets, and the family quickly takes notice. The man stands clutching his shovel. The mother places a hand on the boy's shoulder, keeping him near. She doesn't want any trouble. Neither do I. Miguel waves at the family. The boy waves back. I don't even crack a smile. Instead, I nudge Miguel forward.

"They seemed nice," he says. "Wouldn't have hurt to try to communicate now that it's just the two of us."

"Lead the way and stop trying to think outside of your sueño capacity."

As we walk past small buildings and shacks, families take note of the strangers. Some ignore us and go about their business. Others stare. I imagined Cemi Territory to be a desolate wasteland similar to what Mega City used to be before

Déesse and her family cleaned it up. Instead I find there is actual life, or the semblance of one. It doesn't matter. If the boy is lucky, he'll find work at a boydega in Mega City. If he is smart enough.

We press on.

The path Miguel leads us on ascends slightly. It's not strenuous. However, my ankles feel the strain. The air seems crisper. Cooler. No more piles of garbage. Instead, wildflowers in bright colors line the path. In the distance there are large mountains. There are barely any buildings obstructing the view. Mega City and the LMCs are so far away. I am reaching my destination, and my anxiety increases with each step.

When we reach Los Bohios, I will offer myself up to the Ashé Ryders. Miguel thinks we left Mega City because we were tired of how Déesse was running it. The Ashé Ryders will need to believe this too. The azabache stays tucked deep in my pocket.

There is a stone archway ahead. The grass that surrounds it is overgrown. It looks as if the area is abandoned. I hesitate.

"We are entering Los Bohios," Miguel says. He walks to the archway. I stop. What will it mean once I go through this entrance? I'm not ready.

"No," I say. "We need to regroup."

Miguel tilts his head to the side. Confused. "Isn't this what you want?" he asks. "What we both want? I'm ready to go home."

What is wrong with me? I am so afraid. I want to go over what I'm going to say, the lies I'm about to spill. I'm scared of what I will find once I walk through the archway. I never thought I would be doing this by myself.

I remember seeing a shack tucked in a field filled with wildflowers. It's on its last legs.

"There's a structure back there. I want a break from the sun." Miguel eyes me. He doesn't believe my excuse. He follows me anyway.

Sunrays peak through the cracks. I give him a food pellet and water. He has a bit of color on his face. He is losing the sueño pallor.

As we sit and chew on our pellets, I go over my plan. I will lay the Déesse hate thick. This shouldn't be a problem. What will be hard is finding enough time to gather information. I only have a couple of days. This would have been easier with the LMCs. We would have divvied up what to look for—weapons, strategies—and calculate how many are in their army. Now I will have to do this on my own.

"What are you looking at?" I catch Miguel staring at me. "It's been a while since you had a sueño. Why don't you take one?"

"Have you ever taken a tab before?" he says. "You should try it since you're such a strong sueño advocate."

He closes his eyes as if he's reliving the sensation. "It takes a second for the tab to dissolve in your mouth. The taste is sweet. Smart move on Déesse to make them that way," he continues. "Then slowly the barriers holding you down start to melt. The hateful words that constantly pound your head fade. Edges lose their grip, and you start to feel weightless."

"That's your problem right there," I say. "Those feelings don't exist outside of a sueño."

Miguel opens his eyes and flashes a look of anger. "That is not true. I've had that feeling once before. Singing. I once brought happiness to many. No ties. Just from pure love. And they loved me back. Have you ever felt that way?"

"Sure. Whenever I win."

"I am not talking about throwdowns," he says with a huff.

It's strange to have him ask such an intimate question. My thoughts immediately turn to my sister and my recent dream. The vision is not solid. It's more of an impression A feeling that we were once happy together.

Déesse has said this before—men want to explain away when they should shut up. Santo does the same. Always wanting to steer me as if he has the answers. We will arrive at Los Bohios and Miguel will no longer be a thorn in my side.

"Take this and escape." I toss him a tab. He holds the sueño in his hand. "Why don't you take it? What's holding you back? You love sueños."

"I want to be clean when I return home," he says. "Don't you understand?"

Miguel leans against a wall. He takes a deep breath in and

out. This version of Miguel I can't relate to. Who is he if not an addict wishing to score another dream?

I also find a wall. My thoughts drift to the LMCs and the happier moments when we were victorious. I miss Mega City. Streets I owned for a good two years. The Luna Club and Books waiting with my bath. Most of all, I miss Santo, even though this angers me.

Maybe I'm not strong enough to do what has to be done. At the training camp, instructors taught me how to survive the streets. Only a few were born with the smarts to lead. How smart am I to have lost Nena and the LMCs? I don't agree with Miguel. Ambition is not a bad thing. Ambition compelled Zentrica to leave Mega City and strike out on her own. My dream is what I have.

Forget this nostalgic thinking. If I don't move now, I'll never do it.

"Let's go." I tap him with my boot. "Wake up. Let's do this."

He ignores me. I lose my patience and kick him.

"There's so much anger in you," Miguel says.

I laugh at his stupid statement. He's not making any revelations there.

"I don't care. Move."

"At least I have a love. Zentrica loves me." I should kick him again. Love doesn't exist.

"How's love working for you?" I say. "I'm not the one being led around, fed sueños whenever I feel compassionate enough to treat you. You're not even human, just a poor addict."

"You are also trapped."

"I'm going to tell you what's going to happen when we reach the Ryders," I say. "Zentrica is going to take one good look at you and cut you off for the last time. If she doesn't, I will surely do it for her."

He shrugs off my hateful words. We're the same in that sense. No matter what's thrown our way, we only see the prize. His eyes go wide. He smiles.

"I know who you are," he says. "Who you really are."

I don't change my expression. He's bluffing. Trying to get me angry. Playing with me. What else is there left to do? We're at the end of this journey. He must feel it too.

"Zentrica told me all about you."

My reaction is quick, automatic. I pull out my knife. I press it to his neck, right beside his pulsing vein. "I'm Chief Rocka of the LMC, that's who I am. You? You are part of this nightmare."

He moves his head, unafraid of how the blade cuts the skin. "Your name is Nalah."

"What did you say?" My stomach drops.

"I knew the moment I saw you that night. You both have the same expression when you're upset," he says. "The crinkle on your forehead."

I push the knife into his skin. Blood trickles. "You are lying," I say. "I don't know a Zentrica."

"Everyone hides behind different names. Dig deep. You know who Zentrica is and what she means to you," he says. "She sang this to you, didn't she?"

He hums the song from my dreams. It is the same song from the night we went searching for him at the Rumberos.

Help me find the sun. I will follow you, child.

No. I don't know a Zentrica. This is a lie. Zentrica is my enemy and the enemy of the people of Mega City. It can't be. I hate him for screwing up my head with songs and tales of his life. He won't contaminate me. I won't let him.

"I'm going to kill you for even uttering such a lie," I say. "My sister is dead. She's not an Ashé. She's not Zentrica."

Before I plunge the knife in, I hear footsteps. I push away from him and crawl on my hands and knees to a window.

A string of girls line up in formation. They wear long flowing dresses similar to the one worn by the mother we saw earlier. They are not dressed for a throwdown. How can they fight in such a getup? Their relaxed stance shows a crew that will patiently wait for us to come out. The one in the back pulls out a malasuerte and throws it in the direction of the shack.

I take cover.

CHAPTER 17

JOURNEY'S END

The explosion is deafening. Pieces of the ceiling come crashing down around us. I'm not hurt. Not yet anyway.

"You can't stay in there forever," a voice yells. "The shack is going to collapse. You better come out."

Miguel gets up. I tackle him to the ground. We're not leaving yet. I don't care how many malasuertes these girls throw. They'll have to drag me out.

"Let go," Miguel says.

"No," I say. "We are not going."

Miguel wriggles underneath me. I manage to hold him down while sneaking a peek. A girl in a sky-blue gown and combat boots carries a small microphone with a disc surrounding it. The others begin to place objects in their ears. A sound weapon. Mega hell. I need to protect myself from the noise. I open my pack to find a piece of cloth to use. I'm too slow. Miguel pushes me off as he tries to run toward the entrance.

A high piercing sound instantly fills the air, blasting inside my head. The pain is blinding. Too much. I can't protect myself. I cradle my head and try to stop my insides from spilling. The noise is relentless. I whimper on the floor. Every part of my body clenches.

The noise suddenly stops. I'm unable to tell the difference. Worn leather boots surround me. A person takes my tronic and Codigo. I have no strength to stop them. I try to lift my head. I'm too weak. I can't hear a thing they're saying. Only bits trickle in, syllables. The ringing in my head continues. Tears stream down my neck.

I don't know how long I cower on the floor. The pain is too great for me to even care. I turn to the side and throw up what little food I had in my stomach.

Two girls drag me outside. They drop my body to the ground. My breath is ragged. It takes forever for me to find my bearings, to stop my hands from shaking.

"What the hell do you want?" My voice is raspy.

The girl with the sound weapon answers. I'm scared she will use it again.

"Sorry. We don't know who you are," the girl says. "It's best to take things slow when meeting. Are you able to walk?"

Before I answer her, I ram my body into the girl. The weapon topples from her hand. I raise my fist and punch her in the chin. I'm no punk. I don't care how many there are. Hands pull me away. I don't stop. I pull at their dresses. I throw wildly.

"Damn, girl. Calm down," someone says. They grab hold of my arms. "Relax. We are only going to escort you in. There's no need for this drama."

The girl with the sound weapon stands. She rubs her chin and walks to me. "It will take roughly forty minutes to reach our destination," she says. "We can knock you out and pull your lifeless body over rocks. Or you can walk as a human being. You choose."

I'm no fool. I obey.

Three girls surround Miguel. They tend to him with such care. This fills me with rage. I take a closer look. There are five of them, ranging in ages. These girls don't have a soldier's frame. They're not completely soft, just different.

"Where are you taking me?" I say.

They don't respond.

I turn to Miguel. He looks away. Instead, he takes the hand offered to him. They pat his shoulder. They know him. The simple act confirms my suspicion.

"You're Ashé Ryders."

"Yes. We are Ashé," she says. "Shall we begin the trek?"

When Miguel walks past me, I spit at him. The spit lands right on his cheek. He knew all along who I was. This was a setup. There was never an "accidental" meeting the night Miguel took hold of Nena. He knew what I meant to the Ashé. He knew about my sister.

"Enough," the Ashé says. She pushes me forward. Now I am the one being led.

We walk silently. My head tries to calculate how I can salvage this. The angles point to how much of a suicide mission I was on to begin with. What was I going to accomplish without the LMCs by my side? On my own I am useless.

"Thirsty?"

The Ashé closest to me offers me water. I don't accept it although my lips are parched. The others act as if we are taking a family stroll on our way to a picnic. Their kindness only makes me paranoid. I'm waiting for the knife to be plunged into my back.

We walk through the stone archway. There's a sweet smell in the air coming from the blanket of blue flowers growing on the ground. The path leads us to a hill. I can't tell if the birds chirping in the looming trees are actual living birds or decorative animatronics. There aren't many birds in Mega City.

Once we reach the top of the hill, a new set of Ashé Ryders appears from behind the trees. They greet each other and Miguel. They don't address me. Miguel doesn't join in with their happiness. He is deep in his own world. I hope he rots. As they chat about nonsense, I look down to the camp. I can see where the Ashés live. Hundreds of circular dwellings made of wood are arranged in the center of a type of village. The buildings, if I can even call them that, appear flimsy, not durable. This must be what Miguel meant by bohios. My sister is down there. Where is she? What will she do to me?

"Almost there," the Ashé in the blue dress says. We begin our descent.

A woman alerts the others of our arrival with a whistle. Tons of kids come screaming. Back in Mega, there is no time for kids to play outside. If they're not in the training camps, they're working. These children don't have the harsh street look. They appear healthy, not ready to fight or steal.

Men walk out of the bohios wearing light colors. Some are bare-chested, with no visible symbols of their crew. Where are their allegiances stating they are property of the Ashé? Where are the medallions? They must be branded in a place where I can't see.

An older woman sees Miguel and runs to him. He allows himself to be held. Is that Zentrica?

"We missed you," the woman says. I search for a sign telling me this is my sister. I don't see any resemblance. "She's been so worried."

Miguel shakes his head. "I can't see her. Not yet." He presses down on his hair.

It's been ten years since I last saw my sister. How old would Zentrica be now? I've tried many times to calculate the exact timeline of when she left. That must make her twenty-five or twenty-six. This woman is much older. No. This is not Zentrica.

Everyone seems too in the open. There are probably a

multitude of weapons hidden in this community. An ominous vibe creeps from underneath their smiling expressions. They are too confident to not be completely armed.

Miguel walks away with the older woman while I'm left to follow my escort. She leads me past a communal eating area. The families here don't seem to be preparing for an uprising. Everyone is way too chill. Perhaps their war rooms are located elsewhere. Another thing I notice, there's no difference between the bohios. One thatch house is identical to the other. Where is the sense of hierarchy? I case the area and search for escape routes.

Eventually the Ashé with the blue dress stops in front of a bohio. "We will come get you."

"Where's your leader?" I ask. "I want to see her now."

The girl displays an uneasy grin. "You'll meet her soon enough." She motions for me to enter. I hesitate by the door. Is this girl Zentrica's second-in-command? I can't work out the order of this crew. I insist on seeing Zentrica. She responds by opening the door. She waits for me to enter. I finally do.

"Chief Rocka."

Smiley is the first person I see. Next to her sits Shi. She quickly stands. As for Truck, I can hear her snores. A nudge from Shi wakes Truck. I smile foolishly. I'm happy to see a familiar face, especially now when I'm at my lowest. One look from Truck and I'm reminded of their betrayal. No. They are no longer my sisters.

"Word up, Chief Rocka." Truck looms large before me. The anger hasn't dissipated. In fact, the rage has increased.

There are several makeshift beds in various corners. Wooden boxes made into chairs and a table. I grab one and mark it as my own by dumping the contents onto the floor. I will sit where a leader should sit. I start to take off my jacket.

"I guess you didn't get Nena, huh?" I say this knowing full well my words will hurt.

Before I can protect myself, Truck jumps me. I'm barely able to hold back the punches, the concentration of them landing on my stomach. I manage to punch her on the side of the face. The blow stops the onslaught for only a second. It's enough for me to roll away. She rushes at me again.

Shi and Smiley pull us apart. My lip is split and the pounding in my ear is now replaced with a pain in my gut. Anger keeps me in the fight. Truck will not win, because this battle is bigger than both of us.

"This is your fault," she screams. "The Ashé Ryders were on us before we could even hit the Gurl Gunnas."

"I'm not that powerful," I say. "I couldn't foresee this."

"Oh yeah?" Truck says. "Then why is Zentrica acting as if she knows you?"

I shake my head. "I don't know what you're talking about. I just got here."

"You are lying. They've been waiting for you to come

home. Those were the words she used. 'Come home.' You know what's going on. You knew all along and you're still holding back. We're going to get iced in here, and you're giving us nothing to pull us out of this hole. You're providing them with the knife."

"I don't know Zentrica or anyone from the Ashé Ryders," I say. What does Truck want from me? I'm in the dark as much as they are.

"We took an oath," Truck says, her voice cracking. "LMC meant for life. Secrets among sisters equals death. Who is Zentrica to you?"

She wants me to confess. How can I when I don't believe it? There is no way this can possibly be true.

"Miguel says Zentrica is my sister," I say. "He's an addict. He obviously fabricated this whole story to get a rise from me. You traveled with him. He's not the type of person to be trusted."

I can't face the truth, not when I am still grappling to understand it myself. It doesn't matter. I can explain away every single thing that has happened since we last saw each other. It won't make a difference. Smiley holds her head. The hate on Shi and Truck's faces can ignite a room.

"You don't get it, do you? Ever since we left on this journey, you've been swearing up and down we were in this together," Truck says. "If we were, you wouldn't have brought us here to die."

"Listen. The mission holds. We gather information and report to Déesse. Zentrica is not my sister. It's a lie," I say. "We stick to the plan. We need only a day. Together we can scour the area, really scope Los Bohios."

Truck laughs. "What are you talking about? She's your sister and the leader of the Ashé Ryders. You honestly think we're going to leave here in one piece? You deserve whatever fate is bestowed on you. I only hope it's a painful one."

"I haven't changed," I say. "I'm the same person from two days ago. The same sister who asked you to help me create the LMC. The one who recruited you to join me."

Our mission can work. Whoever Zentrica is, she is not my blood.

"You also chose Nena," says Smiley. "Look what that got her."

We should be exchanging notes on what we've seen and heard. Devising our next moves. I want to know how they ended up here. To tell them how Miguel tricked me, how it was a ruse to get me here. Instead, Truck and the others glare at me. I'm the enemy now.

"This isn't my fault," I say. "The sooner you guys get that through your heads, the quicker we can strategize."

"We are no longer listening to you," Truck says.

They turn their backs on me. The second time is no less painful. When they realize the mistake they've made by shutting me out, it will be too late. I will continue to do this on my own. The Towers are real. I must hold on to the dream. What else do I have?

"Excuse me." A young girl no more than nine years old waits by the entrance. "Zentrica will see you now."

This is it.

No one says a word while I gather my things. I pull on my jacket and adjust my cuffs. I leave scared out of my mind.

CHAPTER 18

ARMY OF ME

My legs feel heavy. Every fiber of my being tells me to run. I bury the fear. Exchange it for hate. My sister died a long time ago. Zentrica is not family. She is a stranger. Just an obstacle I must overcome to get back to Mega.

Instead of taking me to a bohio befitting a leader of a notorious crew, the Ashé walks me in the direction of a structure that is smaller than the rest. My mind overanalyzes the significance of this. Is this a way of faking me out into thinking the leader is humble? I'm aware of the tricks.

The girl pauses before the entrance. "One second," she says.

I hear murmurings. Laughter. I recognize Miguel's voice. He's in there probably joking about how easy it was to dupe me. How I pose no threat to the Ashés. Deals are being made. I need to be in there before I'm counted out of the game.

"I missed you more than you'll ever know." A woman's voice. "More than anything."

Is that the voice of my so-called sister Zentrica? I can no longer wait. I push open the wooden door and step in.

I hold my breath.

Miguel stands before this woman. They are both so engrossed with each other. The woman utters such personal things, I feel embarrassed at having to witness such a display. I stare at her. This is not the girl in my dreams. Not completely. The curly hair is a lot lighter, longer. Her face is much thinner. It is not until I notice the eyes and the shape of her lips that I can see the resemblance. Those features are identical to mine. The only signs that connect me to her.

There are others in the room. The older lady who earlier embraced Miguel. The girl in the blue dress and a couple of the others who found me. They will be witnesses to this farce of a reunion.

Zentrica cups Miguel's trembling hands.

"I didn't realize how hard it would be," Miguel says. "How much of a hold the sueños had. It was as if I had never stopped taking them. I'm sorry."

I can't help myself. I snort at this confession.

They both turn.

"Nalah," Zentrica says. She says my name as if she's trying it on for size. "I can't believe it's you."

Words will betray me, so I keep quiet.

"Do you remember me?" Zentrica says in a gentle tone that makes me want to punch her face.

"She was a tiny one. So small." Zentrica now gestures to her soldiers. "She would follow me everywhere, pulling on my shirt. I couldn't even go to the bathroom. I used to call her my sombra. Now look at her. I can't believe it."

They laugh at her stupid lie of a story. It never happened. Whoever that girl was back then, the one who followed her around is dead. Zentrica won't get the satisfaction of having me acknowledge an anecdote she so casually shares with her crew. This woman before me means nothing.

"My sister was never a Zentrica," I say. "Nor was she ever the leader of the Ashé Ryders."

Her smile melts away. "We'll catch up soon enough. You're tired. Go rest," she tells Miguel. "You made this happen. I can never repay you enough."

As Miguel walks past me, I notice the tears. He told me he wanted to be clean. This was the reason he kept storing the sueños I handed to him. The sueños took him down as soon as he entered Mega City. Why would Zentrica send Miguel if there was a risk? It doesn't make sense. Then again, what does?

The others leave. I'm alone with her, with this stranger. I don't know where to put my hands, so I keep them in my pockets. The azabache is still in my pocket. The first of many lies Miguel set in motion.

"Sit. You must be hungry." Zentrica points to a wooden table with two plates of food. "Sorry there's no meat. Everything you see on the plate will give you energy."

I resist the invite, although my stomach growls.

"There's no need to be afraid." She sits down to eat. There is a rosy tinge to her full lips. I can't get over this. She acts so casual. This moment is unreal.

Zentrica moves the chair in front of her with her foot, urging me again to sit down.

"We are trying to figure each other out," she says. "You're more than welcome to stick with your fears and starve."

I can't deny my hunger. I grab the chair and sit across from her. I don't realize how famished I am until I start plowing into the food as if there's no tomorrow. There might not be.

"We grow everything here," Zentrica says. "Nothing is processed."

She talks as if she is doing a presentation. Selling me on this place. This is the big, bad, scary leader of the Ashé Ryders? She sings the praises of her organic garden as if I would give two sueños about it. I've seen toilers try to grow stuff back home. The soil is crap and doesn't take. It doesn't work in our concrete home.

"Who cares?" I say as I eat the last of the vegetables.

"Many care. If you can grow your own food, you don't need to depend on anyone."

What in Mega hell does she mean? She's talking gardening? I push my plate away.

"Do you remember me?" Zentrica asks. "You must remember Yamaris. Yamaris was my given name. Mami and Papi said the name meant 'wished-for child.' I heard your friends call you Chief Rocka. Now, that's a great name. Nalah also has an important meaning. It means 'beloved.'"

She wants me to be sick. This is no family reunion. She's better off trading hugs with her addicted ANT. Get him to kiss her hands, not me. I'm not going to break down in tears and wish to rekindle a long-lost family relationship.

"What do you want? A pretty picture of our childhood together?" I ask. "The only thing I remember is hitting bodies until they stopped hitting me."

She continues to eat and doesn't flinch from my tone. She acts as if we're two friends having a misunderstanding. This whole wearing long dresses and planting seeds is a ruse. We are both vicious fighters.

"Yamaris seems a lifetime ago. I had to change my name. I didn't have a choice. I didn't want her to find me," she says. "Those freckles aren't real. Are they?"

"Yeah, well, you look like a rat. What are you planning to do to us?"

There is a long pause. The silence in the bohio is punctuated by people talking outside.

"Nalah."

"Don't call me that. You have no right to my name. You don't know me. You and me, we're strangers."

She sighs. "Chief Rocka, then." She places her fork down. "Don't underestimate me. I will defend my family. Bloodline or no bloodline."

A family I don't belong to.

"Let's do this. I'm ready right now."

She shakes her head. A slight smile. Anger rises.

"There's no battle. No one is going to fight here. We made this place because everyone needs to get along. If one of us fails to carry their load it affects everyone else. We are on equal standing. No one is the leader here, not even me."

That is a lie. There's no doubt she calls the shots.

"If you're not the leader, then what are you selling? A better life? A new beginning? If there are no battles, then how do you recruit for your army? There are guards here, albeit weak-ass nobodies. You're protecting your crew."

"We are protecting ourselves from your so-called leader. Déesse. She's holding on to the Towers for dear life. She can't afford to share her wealth. My way of living, the Ashé way of living, will end Déesse. There are too many mouths to feed. You think the Towers will protect you. You're wrong. The toilers grow more desperate every day, and they're going to need more than food pellets and sueños to survive.

"Those battles are eating away at the masses," she continues. "You don't see it because you're convinced two fists can bring you hope. The rest of the people, they are the ones waging a true war. A war to end inequality and bring about a just world, where young girls are no longer forced to risk their lives to survive."

There is no such thing as an equal society. She wants Déesse to topple. That would mean the end of my way of living. It would mean the end of everything I've fought for.

"The Towers should be for only the people who deserve it," I say. "Don't be jealous because I'm on the list."

She shakes her head. "How unfortunate."

How dare she judge me?

"I remember you," I say, "You were there one second and gone the next. You haven't asked me about Mami since I stepped into this room. Typical. A person who professes unity has no time for their own blood. So what if you created a type of utopia here? One forceful crew will tear it down."

I grab my plate and chuck it against the wall. This is what I think about her way of living. Where was she when I was in the training camp learning how to take a punch? Creating this dumb-ass world where everyone shares their meals. Is she kidding me? Has it been so long that she doesn't realize how tough life is? There are no options. Work or battle and claim a space you can call home. It is the only way.

"I was there. You might not remember this. I saw what they did to Mami," she says. "At first they told us it would help with her back pain. We gave her sueños, and it did alleviate her suffering for a while. It didn't take long for Mami to develop a tolerance. She needed more. She soon became addicted."

"She wasn't an addict. Why are you lying? You weren't there. It was an accident."

I remember Mami's blue lips. Her painful death. Then Déesse taking me to the training camp. Zentrica was never there.

"Your leader did this to our family," she says. "Food pellets. Sueños. Tiny morsels doled out to the toilers to keep them in check."

"If that's true, then why didn't you stop Déesse?"

"I was old enough to see what was happening. Brave enough to speak out. Déesse doesn't welcome talkers."

"I don't believe you. This is a story to add to your mythology," I say. I'm yelling now. "At the end of this tale you end up a winner, don't you? These greens were cooked by a person. I see your fine hands. Those aren't hands made to work in the dirt. There are no bruises or scratches on you. No, others are doing the deed for you while you preach."

She looks down on her plate. "I can't change what happened. Whatever version I tell you, you're not ready to accept. Maybe you will later, maybe years from now," she says. "I'm not asking for forgiveness. What I am asking is for you to open your eyes and really see what's going on. Fighting won't get you anywhere. It's not working. No one—and I mean no one—wins."

She kneels down to pick up the mess I made. Unlike me, Zentrica is out of shape. Flabby arms. No muscle. Too much salad. She's been living a content, lazy life.

"You can stay here for as long as you want," she says. "See what we are doing before you jump to conclusions."

Anger courses through my veins as I watch her. Here she is trying to school me. She is blind to the real world. The Towers may not be her reality, but it's mine. I stand over her.

"Why did you send Miguel to Mega City to look for me?" I ask. "Why now? Clearly you were fine with me throwing down all those years. Why the hell now?"

She looks up. "It's a long story and you are not ready. We can continue this conversation tomorrow."

"Not ready? Get up."

She continues to clean. "I won't fight you, if that's what you're expecting. You might not see the connection, but one does exist between us—as much as you want to sever it. No one—not Déesse or your crew—can break our bond. I won't fight you, and I won't give up on you."

"Stand so I can show you what you've missed while you were away. Let me give you my own welcome-home party, the only way I know how."

She finally looks up. Her hands cup the salad remains.

Those are my eyes. Tired and red. If I stare long enough into those deep brown eyes, I will be taken back to my dreams. I resist. I won't let these nostalgic tricks stop me from using this knife I now yield.

"I'm sorry, Nalah. I had no choice," she says. "I left because I had to."

Pathetic lies. This place. These people. Her view and my trembling hands betraying me.

"Think I'm going to fall? I'm no sucker. Look to your boy Miguel for that."

"If you do this, it won't stop the pain," Zentrica says. "And you won't leave here alive."

Zentrica suddenly throws the pieces of plate to my face. Within seconds, she twists the hand with the knife and presses hard enough for me to drop it. She yanks my thumb back. I am down on my knees, trying to break free. She let's go and kicks the knife away.

Her people come running into the bohio. The only thing I feel is rage.

Before her crew pulls me away, I see it. The azabache is around her neck. How had I not noticed it before? I yank the azabache off. This medallion will not protect her.

"Aren't you happy to have finally met me?" I scream while her crew drags me away.

I want to thrash. To destroy with my fists. Years of wishing for my sister to return. I was a stupid kid with only resentments propelling me forward. I don't know what I expected. It definitely wasn't this.

The Ashé Ryders make sure when they toss me back into the bohio I land smack on the ground. The door is closed, and I am left sprawled on the floor. My crew doesn't move to help me. Not a one.

I brush the dirt off my face. My so-called sisters don't say a word. What is there to say? Accusations have been made. Sides taken. I stake claim to a cot.

CHAPTER 19

LOST ONE

It is the crack of dawn. An Ashé Ryder stands before me, patiently waiting. I barely slept last night. How could I when my thoughts raced back to Zentrica? I must have finally slept only to be assaulted by my recurring dream. The vision was a nice dose of cruelty to complement meeting her. A vision full of happiness. In the dream Zentrica and I ran in the vast field of wildflowers. She led the way. My hands brushed against the flowers. The sun warmed my cheeks. Zentrica sang the song again, and this time I sang along. The Ashé woke me before I could see more.

"It's bath time," the Ashé Ryder says. "The whole bohio must go together."

There is an Ashé Ryder for each LMC. Our very own personal escort.

"What if I don't want to?" I ask.

The Ashé grins. "Everyone takes showers. We are on

a schedule. Each bohio has a turn. Afterward, there will be breakfast."

Will this schedule always be supervised? To see what the Ashé Ryders are up to will prove difficult with people monitoring my moves. I'll have to do my best. I'm continuing with Déesse's order. I'll leave in a day, enough time to get back to Mega City before Déesse completely writes me off. I keep playing in my head what Zentrica said last night. "The toilers grow more desperate every day, and they're going to need more to survive." She's aiming to liberate them. How and when is what I need to find out.

I let the other LMCs walk ahead of me. We didn't say a word to each other last night. I don't imagine that will change. When Truck and the others want to talk, they huddle away from me. To share a room in complete silence with people I rolled with for years is painful. The first person I wanted to talk to about my encounter with Zentrica was Truck. Now we just ignore each other.

There is a lot of movement happening this morning. We walk behind an older Ashé who leads a group of young kids. The children are chatty. They go left and enter one of the bohios. Is this their version of a training camp? No. They were carrying books. In Mega City, training camps teach kids what they will need to know to survive. The anatomy of a body. The best places to throw a punch. What can the Ashé Ryders be teaching these kids? To be gardeners? Weak.

I notice another group of Ashé Ryders gathering in an open space. There are roughly about twenty, a mixture of men and women. The girls are the same ones who captured me. A man stands in front of them. He leads the group into kicking exercises. So this is their Ashé army? More and more people join them. Soon it's not just young men and women. The elderly and little kids too. A whole community practicing their kicks. Déesse will want to know this.

We stop in front of a tent. An Ashé shouts for the space to be emptied. A couple of men dry themselves. They exchange jokes with each other. The men seem as if they are on equal standing with the woman. Another mistake the Ashé Ryders are committing.

"The water needs to be heated again." A man who looks to be in charge appears. "You know that."

The Ashé Ryder nods. I would never let a man talk to me that way. She doesn't seem to care.

There are stalls lined with buckets of water. The man sets off the heating devices situated underneath the buckets. After a few minutes, we are made to enter the stalls one by one.

"Go on," the old man yells. "It won't stay hot for long."

We are ordered to strip and step into the bucket. This is far from a boydega bath, but still, the hot water feels good. It's been days.

I dunk my head and wet my hair before being told to get out. We are handed a cloth to dry ourselves.

"Your clothes are being washed. You can wear this."

My escort holds out a dress. I shake my head. I will not wear their uniform. Never. I would rather walk around naked.

"No," I say.

Truck, Smiley, and Shi follow my lead. They can't force us to wear their stupid gowns. The escort sighs impatiently.

"You know better than that. You should have asked them what they preferred first," the old man yells. "Go to the stockroom and tell Mari to give them options."

The man is not yelling at us. He is yelling at our escorts. Shi and Smiley exchange confused looks. I don't get it. Is this how they treat their prisoners?

Moments later a girl comes in with stacks of pants and shirts. She hands them to us. A simple rope is used to keep the pants from falling off my slim hips.

"Mari said not to get used to them. She's collecting them right back when your clothes are dry."

"Everyone out. Baths are closed," the old man yells. Truck is this close to getting in his face. Truck's escort glares at her, almost daring her to try it. I wonder how many times Truck has tried to bash her way out of here. She will not follow along. It's not in her nature. Truck eventually backs down.

They walk us over to the communal dining area. Large groups are taking to their seats with plates filled with a type of mushy warm food. Women and men serve meals from large pots. I notice how not all of the women are wearing dresses.

Some wear pants. They go about their business, not paying much attention to the new visitors. Is this common? Are they always so welcoming to new people? A young boy serves me a plate of food.

"What is this?" I ask.

He laughs at the question. "Oatmeal," he says. "Those are berries."

I wait for the others to eat first.

Zentrica is not around. I notice a few other bohios with Ashé Ryders in front of them. What is behind those doors? Is this where they are storing their weapons? The Ashé Ryders do not walk around with their tronics visible. Their dresses are too long. There are men and women who carry machetes tucked in their belts. Are they weapons or simply tools? They could be both. A machete can't do as much harm as a tronic or a sound weapon. Sound weapons are kind of archaic. Nothing beats a good throwdown.

A bell is rung to get everyone's attention. The Ashé Ryders stop what they are doing. An older person stands and makes an announcement. I don't catch what she says. Instead, I get ready to run. This could be it. For all I know the Ashé Ryders may be delivering me to my doom after a nice bowl of oatmeal.

Then I hear a familiar voice singing.

Miguel is on an elevated platform. He's different. He wears a beautiful long dress. His face is made up. His long hair is now parted in three elaborate buns. Red glistening lipstick on his lips. His beauty is breathtaking. I am transfixed by what I'm seeing, unable to look away. I don't understand.

"We missed you, Graciela!" someone yells. The Ashé Ryders are beside themselves. They stand and clap as if they have been waiting their entire lives for this very moment.

He sings and his voice goes beyond what I heard while we were together. This is something else. There is passion and sadness, a depth that touches me so deeply that I too feel mournful. How can it be?

All the things Miguel told me while we were on this journey come back to me. "You have to abide by rigid rules on what it means to be a man and a woman. There's no room for fluidity."

Miguel is Graciela.

For once I listen closely to the lyrics of Graciela's most famous song:

If I come to you free from absolutes will you shun me.
If I bare all will you deny what is true?
El fuego me llama I'm unable to answer.
El fuego me llama It calls to you.

The longer she sings the more I feel as if her words are coursing through me. How is it possible for one person to elicit this emotion? Because although she sings to everyone, I'm struck by how much I'm moved. What does it mean to be Graciela and Miguel in Mega City? He said people are trapped in Mega City. This is what he meant. You are a girl, you are a papi, or you are a toiler. Those are the options. Déesse believes in female empowerment. There is no room for ambiguity. And yet, here is Graciela singing a song about her truth.

She finishes, and the Ashé Ryders clap thunderously. They even wipe away tears. There is a lump in my throat. I don't know how to process this.

An older woman places her hand on my shoulder. "Thank you for bringing Graciela back."

"I didn't bring her back. I didn't know . . ." I stumble over my words, unable to respond. "It was . . . I was with Miguel."

"Miguel and Graciela," she says.

"That's the problem with Mega City," a voice at a table across from us says, chiming in. "They deny what makes people unique and strong. Music is revolutionary. Art is revolutionary. Men, women, and other will lead. Does your leader ever talk about that?"

The person who says this is a man. Those around him nod their heads in agreement.

"Labels. Names. Déesse lives to control. Her soldiers are made to emulate her. Graciela was loved for so long because she dared to be free. Have you seen others like Graciela? No. Déesse is desperate to crush them out of the city."

"Does she still insist it was her and her family who helped build Mega after the Big Shake?" An elderly Ashé Ryder speaks. "She conveniently forgets the scores of other families.

There was once peace in Mega City. It was never about throw-downs. The Codigo Archives no longer feature this history. She erased that period, didn't she?"

I shake my head. What they say about Déesse can't be true. I don't want to believe. I can't afford to. I turn to my crew and make eye contact with Truck. I need reassurance but Truck looks right past me. The others continue to eat their oatmeal.

This guts me.

I get up. I need to get away from this place. I enter the bohio meant for us. I hate everything. My sister and the Ashé. Miguel and Graciela. The LMCs. Everything and everyone. I was born into this world to fight, to elicit pain. I will not allow these confusing thoughts to trip me. I can't consider a world where Déesse fails. I don't have the luxury of being able to reshape who I want to be. "No room for love. No room for empathy," Miguel said. There are no options. There is only one path for me.

The chair is easy enough to break. The table as well. Once I start, I can't stop myself from destroying the inside of the bohio. Even when my fingers bleed from the splinters embedded into my hands, I continue. Where was Zentrica when I needed her? Sheltering Graciela and Miguel? Creating this home while I fought? Where was Zentrica when Mami died?

A couple of Ashés come to the entrance of the bohio. I throw a chair toward them. They duck before it hits one of them. Soon they are barreling toward me. I wild out, hitting whoever comes near me. I'll take them all down.

The Ashé Ryders pile into the room, and it's hard for me to continue. I'm surrounded, and the Ryders are no longer being timid. They hit, and the punches hurt. I don't stop. I lash out and make contact with whoever steps to me. There are too many. I can't keep this up.

"Get away from her."

It's Truck. Behind her are Shi and Smiley.

"Leave her." Truck tries to enter the room. She wrestles with a couple of the Ashé Ryders. Shi and Smiley do the same. Finally, my true sisters share my pain. They try to get in the fray. The Ashé Ryders hold them back.

I feel less of a human. More an animal. I don't care. I won't stop.

"Hold her down," an Ashé says. "Don't harm her. Zentrica's orders."

"Screw Zentrica! Screw the Ashé Ryders." My voice is hoarse. There is no hope for me. No rehabilitation. I will never be quiet or soft. I will never be Zentrica or Graciela, or Miguel.

The room is a wave of people. I can't win against so many. The Ashés tie me down to a cot.

Soon Zentrica enters. "Everyone leave," she says. "Leave her alone so she can calm down."

My heart hurts. She reminds me of Mami. Stern. How cruel life is to play me this way.

I try to control my breathing. Zentrica stands before me. Her face looks crestfallen.

"This won't work," Zentrica says. "I can't have you and the LMCs bringing violence here."

"You can't?" I laugh. "This hate is especially made for you. How do you plan to get to Déesse? You can't entice toilers out of the city. Our love for our home is too strong."

"I feel sorry for you and the LMC because you can't see past your fists," she says.

"Let my crew go or I will destroy every bohio in this place," I say.

"You are free to go."

"Good. If I see you or the Ashé stepping into Mega City, I will end them."

"You can't stop us, sister," she says. "It's already begun. Look closely at your city. Toilers are finding their way out of the camps. They are searching for a new start. Déesse no longer holds the keys to salvation. People are finally seeing how the sueños are meant to keep them complacent."

"Untie me, then," I say. "Do your last sisterly duty."

She hovers over me. Her forehead is creased with concern. "I never wanted to leave Mami or you," she says after a long pause. "I had no choice."

"Don't cry to me with regrets about your choices. I'm good," I say. "If you are not going to untie me, then get out. I'm sick of listening to your lies."

She ignores my request and walks slowly toward the entrance. She doesn't exit. Instead, she stands there. Her breathing is labored, as if she carries a large weight.

"Listen to me," she says. "Mega City has room only for Déesse, her family, and a select few. You will forever be a pet, no better than a dog. The sueños are meant to keep the masses down. You are either addicted to them or you are working to create them. It's a vicious cycle serving only to keep her in power. Others tried to stop her family. She pushed us out."

"Shut up. Déesse took care of me when Mami died," I say. "Not you. She's been true to me. More than you ever have."

"You are important to her only if you keep moving sueños," she says. "Think about it. Everyone else's visions of happiness can only serve her. I left because I refused to comply. So did these people here. The sueños she forced on Mami killed her."

"That's not true," I say.

"Deep down you know I speak only the truth," she says. "I'm sorry I left Mami. I don't go a day without thinking of her. Do you do the same for Papi? That's an indication of how badly Déesse has brainwashed you and so many others. He's here, you know. Papi wants to meet you."

I shake my head. I don't want her to continue. I can't take this anymore. "Shut the hell up."

"You don't remember our last days together. I took you to Cortland Park. It's no longer open. Déesse had it sealed up.

Too many toilers. Back then we could play there for hours," she continues.

I want to scream, *Please stop. I don't want to relive this hurt.*

"Mami got really bad. We tried to get her clean. It came to a point where Mami would do anything to get sueños, including betray the people she loved. Mami made a deal to send you to the camp in exchange for more tabs. She was convinced we were the enemy. She told Déesse as much. Papi and I had to leave Mega. Déesse was going to end us. The plan was always to come back for you. We tried. I swear to you we tried. It got harder and harder. When my people inside told me you were this close to entering the Towers, I knew I would lose you forever if I let that happen. We agreed to try one more time. This is the truth."

I scream for her to shut up.

"I'm sorry, Nalah. I am."

I can't stop screaming.

She soon walks out.

CHAPTER 20

BETTER MOVE

The hours go by and I remain tied to the cot. Zentrica's words play on repeat in my head. I try to banish them. Burn them. It's no use. How can she say such things about her own mother? Mami never betrayed us. She was sick. The sueños helped her. It was because of Yamaris she overmedicated. It was an accident. I won't let her reimagine history.

My father wants to see me. No. I will never give him the satisfaction. I will never forgive them. He also failed my mother. Their selfishness killed her.

I hear footsteps. I expect it to be another one of the Ashé Ryders, checking in. When they do, they ask me if I'm ready to be untied. I usually respond with curses.

"Leave me alone," I yell. My voice hurts. I'm thirsty. No water and food for who knows how long.

Truck steps in front of the cot. She takes a seat at the

edge. "Hey," she says. Her expression is serious.

I try to loosen the binds that keep me fixed to the bed. They are secured tight. Truck doesn't lift a finger to help. Punishment, for screwing everything. Or maybe she's made a deal with Zentrica. My body for a permanent stay in the Ashé Ryders' garden party? Naw. I can see Smiley doing that or maybe Shi. Not Truck. She is not a joiner. I stop trying to break free.

"What?" I ask. She shrugs. This won't be easy. I must play nice until Truck decides to say what she has come here to say. Payback for my wrongdoings.

"So, I take it you're the leader of the LMCs now?" I say.

Instead of loosening my bonds, Truck tightens them. My fingertips start to go numb. I won't be able to keep this up for much longer.

"I never pictured you for a rat. The salad they're serving must have potent herbs in it for you to buy into this neat story." My hands are falling asleep. A slow burning sensation covers my arm.

"I can't take these straps for much longer!" My neck is the only body part I can move.

"You're an idiot," Truck says after a delay. "Nice work, though. What were you planning to do next? Was that a preview earlier, an opening act to the main event, or was it all part of this fun trip? Because believe me, it's been epic so far."

She loosens the binds. I feel an overwhelming urge to cry.

I concentrate on my wrists, rubbing the rope burns. If I do so, I can push back on this hurt.

Truck pulls my hand toward her and rubs the red marks on my wrists, hard. I don't complain. We sit in silence. I don't know how to make amends for what I've done to her and the LMCs.

"What were we meant to do here?" she asks.

"What I said back in Mega City still holds true. We gather information and relay it to Déesse."

"But . . . ," she says. "Don't you think Déesse will consider you an enemy if your own blood is the leader of the Ryders?"

"I'm sticking to the mission. My loyalty stays forever with Mega. They raised me. Not my sister. Not the Ashé Ryders."

Truck shakes her head. "Then let me finish her," she says. "She's hurt you. Imagine how grateful Déesse will be. Off the leader of the Ashé Ryders. From what I've seen, it should be easy."

I don't know what to say. What Truck offers seems an easy enough solution. I hesitate, which is evidence Zentrica has more of a hold than I can admit. By saying yes to Truck I will cross a line. How different would that make us from the Deadly Venoms? They killed Manos Dura and got away with it. They did it simply to prove a point. Can I do the same with my own blood? Am I that heartless?

"The LMCs aren't punks," she says. "Nena suffers because you're too afraid. Talk to me. Dammit. Your silence has jeopardized the LMCs for too long."

I can't keep the tears from streaming down no matter how hard I try. Seeing how disappointed Truck is with me is too much. I'm too wrapped up in feelings I can't explain. A new revelation hits me hard. Truck is wrong. I am a punk.

"Zentrica is my sister. I can't let you hurt her," I say. "I can't."

Truck chews on my admission. Lets it sink in. She doesn't let go of my hand. I'm brought back to the first time I met Truck. Our friendship wasn't instant. We were forced together, a predicament similar to the one we are in now.

I walked inside the training camp scared out of my mind. Mami was dead. My sister and father gone. I can remember the Rompe Cocos holding court in a spacious room. They were the crew leading the training camps at the time. I was placed next to a skinny girl who sniffled back tears. I paid her no mind and sidled closer to a bigger girl to my right. That was my first mistake.

"Move!" the big girl boomed. Then she shoved me with such force I landed right on top of the skinny girl. Kids laughed their heads off. I couldn't let what she did stick.

Hit first and hit hard. It's what I did to the big girl. I ran on top of her and threw blow upon blow until she was bleeding through her nose. The skinny girl cried next to her, and I lunged for her, too.

We were led to the stage. Blood spilled from the big girl's nose. My shirt was ripped.

"What's your names, young guns?" asked the Rompe Coco.

"Nalah," I said. I tried to steady my breathing.

"Cyn," the skinny girl said.

"Soledad," the big girl said.

"From now on, you are going to be called Baby Rocka and you'll be Truck," she says. "As for you, skinny shit, you're going to be Flaca Nada, because you played bystander while Baby Rocka fought. Now sit down and shut up."

I went to sit farthest away from the newly anointed Truck.

"No, you shit. You three are going to be partners. Sit your ass right next to her."

The Rompe Cocos went over the rules of the camp. When we were meant to wake up (at dawn), the exercise (every day for eight hours), and our meals (two meals a day). Fridays would be fight nights, where the kids would prove their worth. I listened as best I could. It was hard to concentrate with Truck muttering threats throughout the whole speech.

When they told us we would be sleeping right next to each other on the floor, the intimidation continued. However, it was Flaca Nada who proved to be our biggest problem. My eyes were heavy and I wanted to sleep. Flaca lay there whimpering, crying for her mother.

"I want to go home," she said.

Truck hushed her with a fist in the mouth. Any noise and we would get in trouble.

"Shut it or we're going to get kicked out," I pleaded with her. Flaca couldn't stop sobbing.

"I want to go home," she continued. Her voice was so desperate. I felt it too. I wanted to give in to the feeling of hopelessness.

"Stupid. Shut your mouth," Truck said. "This is your home now. Close your eyes before I poke them."

Then Truck started to gently caress Flaca's forehead, back and forth. No one else could see her doing it. But I could. Truck continued until Flaca's eyes weighed down, until she gave in to the exhaustion. With Truck's tenderness, Flaca slept nestled between us.

"What are you looking at?" Truck hissed. I rolled my eyes. We didn't sleep much. I guess we were both nervous Flaca would wake again.

We did what we could to keep Flaca from falling apart. There wasn't enough time. Her days were numbered and we knew it. It came on Friday, the day of the practice throwdown.

"You two, fight each other."

I would beat Truck in a heartbeat. Kick her ass good. No, Flaca had to battle Truck.

"Don't hold back," I yelled. Flaca didn't know what to do. She tried to punch Truck. Landed a pathetic right on Truck's bulge. The hits were brutal, and everyone cheered. I watched. Every blow tore me up, made me harder, too.

One solid jab sent Flaca flying across the stage. No one went to help her, to see if she was okay. Tears streamed down

Truck's round cheeks. I didn't cry. I held the knot in.

"How do you feel about your sister? She doesn't have enough respect to defend herself. Finish her."

Truck shook her head.

"You better finish that girl, or I'll finish you."

The trainer strolled over to Truck, her hands balled into fists. Before she reached Truck, I jumped in front.

"No," I yelled.

I couldn't see Truck or Flaca getting beat anymore. I couldn't let that happen.

"No?" The trainer laughed. "Baby Rocka thinks she's got a say. I'll show you what's up."

The trainer pulled back her fist and slammed it across my face. It was lights out. I found out later Truck got beat too. As for Flaca, they dumped her outside. I don't know what became of her. I never saw her again.

Things changed between me and Truck. We survived the training camp and found others to make Las Mal Criadas. I shed the name Baby Rocka and became Chief Rocka. We clawed our way through Mega City.

"Ever since we met at the training camp, you've shown me underneath the fists and the anger, there is also heart," I say. "I haven't leaned on you as much as I should have. I thought a real leader must do it alone. I was wrong. You're my ride or die. From now on, I will follow your lead as much as you follow mine."

"What about Zentrica? What about your sister?"

"She will never have my back," I say. "She hasn't been through what we've been through."

She squeezes my hand. The tears continue to flow.

"Ugly," she says. "What do we do now?"

"Zentrica is letting us go. It's what she said, and I believe her. We go back to Mega and give Déesse the lowdown," I say. "First, there are a couple of bohios the Ashé Ryders seem to guard. Have you noticed?"

Truck raises her eyebrow. "Definitely," she says. "I overheard one of them say they'll need to expand their storage. Weapons, perhaps?"

I take the glass of water she offers, grateful she doesn't mention anything about my emotions.

I nod. "Yeah. I'm not buying this peaceful hype they keep dishing. It has to be a front."

"Did you see how the men talk? I almost clocked that old man."

I smile. "I'm surprised it didn't go down. They are following the old ways. Déesse always says men will be our downfall. The Ashé Ryders are stupid."

My father is in this camp. I can't wrap my head around it. Zentrica said they had to leave Mega City. I would bet everything it was my father's idea to bail on the family. Only a man would be so cruel. I hope I never run into him.

"Apparently my father is alive. Can you believe it?"

"For real? The hell. This was a bullshit family reunion. Have you seen him yet? Was it the old man at the bath?"

"No. I don't think so. Who cares? You think I want to listen to a man who calls himself my father? It's a meaningless title. He can never redeem himself for what he did to Mami."

"And to you," Truck says.

Truck is the only girl born in a family of three boys. Her father and brothers work at the sueño factories. Her mother tends their station. Truck sees them once a month, bearing gifts. Food. Items she's found along the way. This is why Truck loves the papis so much. She misses her brothers and the way things used to be before she had to enter the camp.

I try to imagine how different my circumstances would have been if my father had stuck to the plan and worked at the sueño factories. For starters, I would not be in this bohío dealing with a hateful sister. Why ruin a good thing? Mega is not an easy city. There are ways to make it great. Work hard. Keep to your script. You move up. I can attest to that. When I return to my city, I'll be rewarded for the many years of grinding.

"Let's gather the others and find what the Ashé Ryders are hiding."

The urgency to leave burns. If the Ashés try to enter Mega City, the whole city will rain on them. I may not be the one leading the charge, but I'll definitely be the one igniting the spark.

"So. Are you happy you found her?" Truck asks.

"No. She should have left me alone in Mega City," I say. "This mistake she will regret forever."

My life will be back to normal. Distance is what I need— and the LMCs beside me.

CHAPTER 21

SET IT OFF

A s promised, our clothes are returned washed. As I slip on my pants and jacket I feel energized. The home-grown threads the Ashé Ryders wear are too thin. They lack protection. I dig through my pockets and find the chain I ripped off of Zentrica right next to the other azabache. Funny how the Ashé Ryders allowed me to keep these souvenirs. Their honor system is deceiving. Zentrica wants me to remember this place. How can I ever forget?

"You know the section you are patrolling, right?" I ask. Shi and Smiley nod. "Good. Walk the camp as if you are break-ing night. Eyes alert. If what you see seems off or question-able, commit it to memory. Stick to your gut."

I notice how much Shi and Smiley have grown close on this trip. They were always good friends. Now they sleep beside each other. Their relationship has shifted to a more intimate one. Will this change once we are in Mega City? I worry about that. Smiley is a notorious player. Maybe Shi keeps her grounded. My concern is how it might affect the LMC dynamic. A close relationship can become an obstacle. I hope it doesn't. Perhaps their connection is only temporary.

"I will go south and follow the trail leading toward the waterfalls," Truck says. "I'm not sure how far I will get. Let's meet back here before the sun goes down."

"Be careful."

We don't have tronics or knives. They also took our Codigos. We must rely on our wits. There are only a few hours left to see what the Ashé Ryders are doing. It's not enough time. Two days to get back to Mega City includes bailing Nena out of the Gurl Gunnas. If we delay any longer, Déesse will surely think we've crossed over. Tonight we leave, no matter what.

There are no Ashé Ryders by our bohio. The time is right to explore. We bounce in opposite directions.

A meal is being prepared by the communal eating space. The men and women are jovial. More greens being tossed into a big pot. The smell is enticing. I won't find much by this area. I set my eye on the bohios with Ashé Ryders in front of them.

"Hey, you," one of the cooks calls to me. "Hey, LMC. Chief Rocka."

When she says my name, she laughs. As if Zentrica is a better name. Jokes. I stop because I don't want to bring any more attention to myself.

"Do you want to give it a try?" the woman asks. "He says

the sancocho is too bland. I think his tongue is broken."

The man has short gray hair and wears the typical Ashé Ryder outfit. The woman playfully rolls her eyes at him.

"Sure." I haven't eaten since my early-morning outburst. This time I will not pass on a meal. The stew is nice and hot. There are large vegetables and potatoes. Our food pellets can't compare.

"Do you want to try this?" I pull out a food pellet. The pellets are made of basic ingredients meant to sustain a person. The woman eyes the pellet with suspicion. I can see a couple of Ashé Ryders walking together toward one of the guarded bohios. The man shakes his head. He won't try it. Spineless.

"What does it taste like?" the woman asks.

"It doesn't have any flavor. There's enough energy in there to keep me going for a few hours."

The woman takes a nibble on the pellet, chews a couple of times, and then spits it out. Unbelievable. The man continues to stir the sancocho.

"There's no way you can eat that without making yourself sick," she says. "Want more soup? This will give you energy, not some manufactured gunk."

"No thanks." The soup has more flavor than the pellet. However, not everyone would be able to afford such a luxurious meal. Toilers need to work. Food pellets get the job done. I leave the two alone and head in the direction of the soldiers.

The Ashé Ryders greet the two already stationed at the

entrance and then enter the bohio. I sneak around the back to get a closer look. Inside there are rows of kids siting at long tables. The soldiers distribute glasses of water with brushes in them.

The children are different ages. Boys and girls. An Ashé in the front of the bohio talks about colors. How to blend two colors to make a different one. Why would the Ashé Ryders guard this room? They are only teaching them how to paint. What makes what they are doing such a dangerous act?

"Protecting their privacy is important."

I turn around to find Graciela. She wears a dress. Her long hair is loosely framing her thin face. No makeup. I walk away. She follows.

"On Tuesdays we teach them dance. Saturday is music. Mostly percussion instruments," she says. "I will start leading the vocal classes soon."

I don't care about the kids' schedule.

"Were you sent to make sure I stay on the right path?"

"No. No one sent me. I saw you and thought you might want a proper tour," she says. "Don't you want to see what we're doing here?"

"Fine," I say. I am positive this is Zentrica's doing.

I stop. "So, Miguel was a way to enter Mega City without being detected. Correct?"

I have so many questions. With her standing before me I find myself timid, unsure on how to proceed.

"I knew if I came as Graciela, everyone would recognize me. As Miguel, I was invisible as so many toilers are in that city," she says. "Who am I? I am Graciela and Miguel. Mega City would never allow for such duality. Today I'm Graciela. You can call me that."

"Fine," I say. "Graciela it is."

She leads me toward another bohio. There is only one Ashé Ryder guarding it. Graciela walks in and asks me to join her. Inside, there are older women who are in class. They are being taught how to read.

"Ay, Graciela. Sing us the alphabet," one of them teases her. "It will help us."

Graciela chides them for not paying attention. We soon exit.

"The Ashé Ryders are teaching kids and old people how to read and sing. Mega City should be trembling from fear." I'm not impressed. This is fluff. I want her to show me where they are making their moves. I'll ditch her soon enough.

"Have you ever wondered why books are only available in the mercados and why they are so rare? It wasn't always the case," she says. "The Codigos you own were generously provided to you by Déesse. The archives in them are limited to what Déesse wants you to know. Mostly propaganda."

"This innocent walk of ours is yet another opportunity for you to lay on me your own propaganda on how the Ashé Ryders are better. I'm not buying it. Definitely not buying these children learning watercolors. It won't help them when you decide to roll into Mega City. Our children will eat them up."

She laughs at this. "You are definitely Zentrica's sister."

Before I use my fist, I walk away. Why is everyone so keen on finding similarities between us when all I see is a vast gulf of differences? So what if we sound the same, if our hair curls in a similar manner? She is my enemy and I am hers.

"Four A-E," Graciela calls out.

"Is that supposed to mean something to me?"

"Four A-E was my apartment number in the Towers," she says. "I was by far one of Déesse's biggest fans. I soaked in the decadence while the toilers below adored me. The dreams the sueños create are sweet until they become nightmares."

"You're an addict. You can't blame your weakness to sueños on Déesse."

"I won't go over the validity of what you are saying. Addiction is a disease. Déesse exploits it for control. I'm not the only person who was born this way. There are many others who are desperate to be true to themselves, to live on their own terms. So many hiding their truth in order to survive," she continues. "When I struggled with my identity, sueños came into play. As I grew more popular and braver as Graciela, Déesse decided I was a threat. All of a sudden she started proclaiming female empowerment at the cost of every single male or other. There's a long history of people like me, and she's erased it."

I give up. Both she and Zentrica are meant for each other. They will continue to fabricate these narratives to pit me against Déesse. I won't stand for it. We leave tonight. Déesse will crush the Ryders with the information I will freely give.

"Is this about revenge?" I say. "You're unhappy because you got kicked out of the Towers.

Graciela tucks a string of hair behind her ear. She presses her lips. The gray skin from the sueños is no longer visible.

"The people who you see here. The young children. The families. They came looking for us. It wasn't easy. Déesse didn't give them permission to leave the city, as she so generously did to you for your quest to find the Ryders. They left behind their daughters. Others left family members sick from sueños. We believe there can be a world that values culture and individuality. A just world for everyone. Can't you envision this possibility?"

They've really drunk whatever Zentrica has given them.

"This is not an easy life, even here. I've spent years exploring who I am, battling addiction and uncertainty. At least I've finally created a home where I can be whole and live among people willing to accept me. I'm not the only one. There are many of us here who strive to make this life better for everyone, not just a few."

I try to walk away. She blocks my way.

"Listen to me. I implore you. This hurt you feel will never go away but there are ways for it not to overtake your spirit.

It is possible to surround yourself with love. Yes, love. I found a compassionate friend in your sister Yamaris and a protective warrior in Zentrica. You can choose a path different from the one dictated by Déesse."

"Bye, Graciela." I say.

Perhaps this place works for Graciela and Miguel. I'm not capable of allowing the Yamaris she knows to ever come to be. To allow Yamaris and Zentrica to co-exist would mean to make room for forgiveness and I can never do that. I do not belong here.

Graciela stands there with a somber look.

A bell rings. Dinner is about to be served. The classes are dismissed. Everyone heads toward the communal space. I see her. Zentrica leads a group of soldiers. Each soldier carries a box. I follow them while making sure to keep my distance. They enter a bohio. They don't stay long. Everyone exits, including Zentrica. I wait until I'm sure no one is around.

There are no locks. Figured as much. Their just world includes trusting everyone. Dumb. I enter and find the room is filled with stacks of boxes. There is barely any space to move. I open one box. It contains tronics. New ones. I open another box. Tronics. Old ones. Hundreds of boxes. Here it is. Their stockpile. They are waiting to use these babies on Mega City. I knew it. This script about culture and a "just" world is a line. They are no different from the crews in Mega City. I got my proof. I grab a couple of tronics and store them in my pockets. I don't have enough room to steal one for everyone. It will have to do.

It's time to get our Codigos. The sun is setting. The others will soon be meeting at our bohio. I might as well pay my respects.

Zentrica sits with an older man. It is the cook from earlier. He notices me and his whole demeanor changes. Of course. I should have seen it before. Papi. I'm transported back to my dream. He was in the room with Zentrica right before they left, his voice urging her to flee.

I ignore him. He can stay in Cemi Territory without ever receiving the satisfaction of his youngest daughter thinking he exists.

"We want our stuff back," I say. "Our Codigos. Tronics. All of it."

Zentrica doesn't stop what she's doing. She continues to speak to Papi.

I grab her arm. "Did you hear me?"

Soldiers stand up, ready to take me down. She alerts them to keep to their position.

"You will get your Codigos delivered to your bohio. You won't get the tronics back."

"Too busy storing them for your revolution?"

She shakes her head.

"You can't deny it. I saw the bohio. The boxes. What's up?"

My father speaks. "Let her go, Zentrica."

I laugh and laugh. This old man. This betrayer.

"We are taking the tronics off the streets," she says.

"You expect me to believe that!" I say. "Don't even think about stepping to Mega City. Your whole life and everything you stand for will be burned to the ground."

I say this loud enough so they can enjoy my words. I stare at Zentrica and my father. This will be my last vision of them. The two conspirators.

At our bohio, Smiley checks on the tronics I stole. They don't have any charge. At least they will appear dangerous even if we can't use them.

"It's time."

Shi pulls out her cap and marks the wall of the dwelling with our initials. We leave Zentrica a gift to remember us by.

While Shi tags up, Smiley piles the furniture into the center of the room. The fire isn't necessary. It's another way for us to leave an impression. It takes a bit for the fire to catch on. Eventually I hear the crackling of the embers. We sneak out and soon hear a scream. The LMCs are leaving, badasses as ever.

The Ashés scramble to put the fire out. While they do, we huddle together behind a bohio and wait for the remaining ones to leave their post. It won't take long. Only a few more minutes and I will walk across the entrance to never return.

"Let's go, Chief Rocka." Truck pulls on my arm.

I take one good last look at the bohios and run.

Zentrica wouldn't send her people after us. Although we are on separate sides of the coin, she won't stop me from leaving. Not now anyway.

My crew keeps a strict watch. The stone archway is mere steps away. We keep bunched behind a tree, listening. I can usually find comfort in the darkness. Not here. What if the Ashés are waiting? Exposed as we are, they can end us.

"We can't stay here," I say. "Let's barrel through."

"Let's do it, then," Truck says.

I walk in a steady pace. I don't run. My determined stride will take me away from this place. The archway is in front of me. I need only to keep moving forward. The others follow close behind.

This archway symbolizes a new way of living for these deluded people. Freedom. The stones appear almost as if they can easily collapse on our heads. I breathe a sigh a relief when the archway is behind us. Let them keep their stones. The Towers are my gateway.

We walk until the sky seems to lighten. Breaking night comes to an end. It feels good to be with my crew. We walk as one.

CHAPTER 22

IN THIS CORNER

Smiley spots them first. Two young men strolling hand in hand a few yards ahead of us. My first reaction is to take them down. Anyone poses a threat. It was Smiley who came up with the idea to approach them on a calm tip. We need a place to rest for a couple of hours. Girl Gunnas are coming up.

"Let me check them out first," Smiley says. "See if they've got a room for us."

Smiley takes off her menacing gold grill and tucks it into her pocket.

Our journey away from the Ashé Ryders seems quicker now that I'm able to recall the landmarks from before. The sun is in full force. I'm hungry and tired.

"I don't know how she does it," Truck says. Truck and I are alike. We prefer forcing people to do our bidding. It's the impatience that drives us. Smiley, on the other hand, uses conversation to manipulate people to change their mind. It's a gift. I guess both Truck and I should take lessons.

After a while, Smiley shakes hands with one of the men. She's struck a deal. I let out a sigh of relief. She jogs back with the lowdown.

"Their Codigo broke. It's an old version. They want to borrow ours for a bit," she says. "In exchange, we get to use their shed for a few hours. Deal?"

"Deal," I say.

We follow the couple as they lead us to their tiny home. Smiley does the talking while Truck, Shi, and I stick to the rear. We keep vigilant, just in case.

"The Ashé Ryders leave the people in the surrounding areas alone," says the one with long black hair. He gave Smiley a funny look when she asked him if his allegiance was with the Ryders. He seems way too eager to talk. His partner stays silent. He watches over us with the same apprehension I watch over him.

"The shed is right this way," he says. "Let me just remove a few things from there."

The shed is small. Nothing extravagant. I wonder how they managed to score their own place. Two men with no ties to a gang. How did that happen?

I sit next to Truck while Shi deciphers the next route to take. Truck hands me a food pellet. She gobbles them down while I take a good look at mine. Whenever we crave real food we venture to the boydega clubs. It comes at a high sueño tab cost. This is the first time I might gag on the pellet. Is Zentrica's judgment contaminating my taste buds?

"Were you guys with the Ashés for long?" Long Hair asks. I am in no mood to socialize with this person or anyone else who is not from Mega. I glare at him until he gets the hint. Smiley tells him she will be out soon to show him the Codigo. She won't leave them alone with it.

The shed is perfect for what we need.

"I don't know. Maybe don't mess with the hosts while we got it good," Smiley says.

My whole body jerks from the unexpected attitude. It's not lost on me how it's Truck telling the others what to do. They listen to her, although as far as I remember I'm still Chief Rocka. I am forced to step back in ways I've never had to before.

"Watch that mouth soldier," Truck yells at her.

"Sorry, Chief Rocka," Smiley eventually says. I won't use my fists on Smiley even though my gut tells me to.

"I'll be back," she says. Smiley glances over to Shi before leaving. It will take time for them to come around. We just need to get home. Once we see the Towers and are among our people, Smiley's and Shi's misgivings will disappear. I'm sure of it.

"If we follow the same road, we can hit the Gurl Gunnas in a couple of hours," Shi says.

"Good," I say. "Go rest. We won't stay long."

After a while Smiley returns. She's anxious to talk about

the couple. How they are living on their own. How they've never worked at a papi chulo club.

"They grow stuff and trade with the Ashé," she says. There's a hint of surprise in her voice. She can't believe it. "It's their home. They own it."

"Until it's taken from them," I say.

Although my final word seems to drop the topic, I overhear Shi and Smiley continue to discuss this while they rest next to each other. Are they seduced by this place? Mega is mine. You need a whole army to protect a home. With Déesse, we have the best chance in creating a good life. Smiley and Shi are attracted to the newness of this place. Nothing new ever lasts. Eventually it is destroyed.

Sensing my uneasiness, Truck lies close to me. When Shi and Smiley sleep, Truck talks.

"Can't believe Miguel is Graciela," she says. "I thought she was dead."

Definitely not dead. Silenced. Déesse wanted her out, and as the boss she made it happen. Being a leader doesn't mean making friends. I can't stop overthinking things. Mega City is a capricious city. Has our short absence already changed the dynamics? Déesse wouldn't renege on her offer to welcome us into the Towers. We accomplished what she asked of us. There is more than enough intel on the Ashé Ryders. I run the scenario again. Déesse won't play me. Will she?

I close my eyes. Truck settles down.

"We'll be home soon," she says.

Within minutes, Truck is snoring and I am left with questions.

The sound of pots clanking wakes us. The sun has set, and it is dark outside. We slept longer than what I had anticipated. I nudge Truck awake. The others follow suit.

"We need to get to the Gurl Gunnas," I say. "Let's go."

We gather our bags. The two men walk out as soon as we exit the shed.

"You are leaving," the one with long hair says. "We prepared a little gift. Dried fruits mostly."

"Why?" Truck asks. She is on the same wavelength as I am. We can never trust men. I don't care how generous they are. I will follow Déesse's rule to always keep men in check.

"Because we have more than enough, and if you find yourself in this area, we will be happy to trade again. I'll be right back."

"I'll wait, if you guys want to walk ahead," Smiley says. Earlier she had explained how the couple wanted to find out about certain boydegas. Names of papis Smiley had never heard of before. Things of that nature.

"No. I'll do it." I don't want Smiley or Shi to continue to be enchanted by these two with their cute little home and their dried fruit. "I'll catch up with you."

I follow him. The house is smaller than it looks from the

outside. The first room has been converted into a bedroom and living space. There are flowers hung to dry on the wall. Old images are spread across a wooden table. The table looks too perfect. It was definitely produced elsewhere.

"Be right back," he says. He has the same vibe most of the Ashé Ryders had, this giving attitude. I will never get used to it. We all have ulterior motives. I can't figure out yet what their motives are. Dried fruits. I don't buy it. I nod, and he walks ahead to what I assume is the kitchen.

I take a closer look at the images on the table. Drawings of trees and the waterfall Truck never reached. Artistic odes to their environment. If this is the art Zentrica teaches young kids, they will surely fail in life. When the LMCs tag up on the walls of Mega City, we are conveying a message. There is a beauty to our signature. No other crew uses the font we use. There is strength in the lettering. Boldness.

Books are stacked against a window. Graciela said Déesse limits the number of books available in Mega City. Which books are considered a problem? Is there a list she keeps? I always assumed the Codigo contained vast amounts of litera-ture and historical text. Whenever we needed to learn about something, we could find a way to download the information and read it for ourselves. Not that the LMCs ever read much. We were too busy fighting.

The Gurl Gunnas don't seem to have a problem finding literature. They burned books without hesitation. Books to

them are valueless. In the boydega clubs, the written texts
are mere props. It never stopped me from wanting to listen
to Books read. I wanted to be transported to other worlds.
Adventures that seemed possible even when the protagonist
was male. I think Books enjoyed reading them. I'm an idiot.
He was doing his job, living up to the papi chulo trading card
I used to collect. Maybe I'll be seeing him soon. So much has
changed, for me anyway.

I pick a book up and flip through the pages. The title of
the book is *Locomotion*. It's true I was schooled in the training
camp. Taught to read and write there. The Ashé Ryders aren't
the only ones dominating education. I read the first few lines.
It doesn't take long for me to follow the rhythm of the piece.

Sometimes I can hear my daddy
calling my name.
Lonnie *sometimes.*
And sometimes Locomotion.
Come on over here a minute.
I want to show you something.
And then I see his big hands
holding something out to me.

My eyes well up. I remember. My father used to read to
me. I can see myself propped up on his lap and him turning the
pages to a picture book. I haven't allowed myself a moment

to grieve the end of my family. The old man who stood there, watching me eat sancocho. What was their life before sides had to be chosen? Did Mami and Papi take walks holding each other's hands? Was there love in this family?

"It's one of my favorite books of poetry." The quieter of the two startles me. I drop the book. He bends down and places it back on the shelf. "Sorry. I didn't mean to scare you. I'm guilty of scaring Beto all the time. He hates it."

"Why did you leave Mega?"

My tone is full of anger. Why do these two get to share a home while I kill myself to get in the Towers?

He is scared. He should be.

"I didn't want to be a papi," he says. "I also didn't want to hide how I felt for him."

"Déesse doesn't care who you love. Only that you put in the work."

He pauses. He is nervous I will hurt them. I can. His partner enters the room with a bag of fruit.

"This might be true for you, for women," he says. "Not for us."

Only a few benefit. That was what Zentrica said to me about Déesse. Graciela said something similar. I take the bag of fruit he is offering. They don't see me to the door.

CHAPTER 23

GONE, GIRL

A deep heavy bass shakes the ground. We heard the music from miles away. Knew we were drawing near. The Gurl Gunnas are partying at their pathetic papi chulo club. My having to return to this place to get Nena is a cruel joke. There is no way around it. The protocol, once again, forces us to wait.

"Right this way, Las Mal Criadas."

Truck mutters to herself. She's on edge. She eyeballs every Gurl Gunna, searching for the ones who beat her. We spoke about this. Revenge is not part of the plan. Truck agreed to keep cool. The tension rises. She is bound to blow. I don't want to spend too much time here. We're so close to Mega. So close. We just need Nena.

"How much longer?" I yell.

The music is deafening. It's funny how much I used to enjoy the loudness found in boydegas. I would crave it. The noise of the clave and congas right before a throwdown. Watching crowded bodies dancing afterward at the Luna Club. I associate this type of music with extreme emotions— lust and violence. At the moment the music is mindless noise meant to drown out every thought.

The Gurl Gunna shakes her head and returns to her drink. The papi chulos seem even more lethargic than last time. A papi stares at me. He has glazed-over eyes. Sueños. I think of Miguel. I also think of Santo. How does he feel about papi chulos? He was jealous when I went to see Books. Was that the reason? Or perhaps the boydegas affirmed how one-sided Mega City is to men? Santo is lucky. He comes from the most powerful family in Mega. I'm lucky too because we are friends.

A papi chulo gyrating in front of me takes a hold of a shot glass with a sueño tab. He lifts the shot glass as a toast. Then he swallows. I look around. Are they all high on sueños? How long can these papi chulos keep taking them? Are the Gurl Gunnas finding addicts, or are they creating them? The papi dances to the other side of the room.

It's not my problem. Since I left Los Bohios, situations that never crossed my mind are being shown to me in a different light. It is unbearable. I prefer ignorance.

Shi has found the Gurl Gunna she spoke to before. They huddle together with Smiley as if making deals. The Gurl Gunna appears to be crying. She is unhappy here. Smiley soon checks in with me.

"Nena is okay. They had her do menial work. Cleaning the bathrooms. Stocking the sueño shots," she says. "She did bear a lot of insults. Not bad considering."

"What's wrong with her?" I ask, pointing to the Gurl Gunna.

"You know. She wants out. Doesn't know how to break free," Smiley says. "I told her we don't have the space for another member. Waterworks soon followed. She's got to live with them poor choices."

"Yeah. I guess we all do," I say. Shi continues to console the Gurl Gunna. "Let's get this moving!"

Our escort slowly sips her drink. We are forced to wait another thirty minutes. The longer I wait, the angrier I become. The intention is to irritate. It works.

"I can't take this." Truck gets up, walks over to a Gurl Gunna, and grabs her by the collar. There is a scuffle. Another Gurl Gunna runs outside. We are finally led to the OG. Let this transaction move quickly. Get Nena and stroll into Mega City as queens.

"Welcome back!" OG screams. The young leader sits in an elevated chair similar to the one Déesse employs. She floats just a couple of inches above her gold table. I've never seen anyone else with a floating chair before, only Déesse.

"Sit down. Have a drink or two or three."

My crew remains standing.

"I see you're admiring my toy. It was a gift from Déesse."

OG taps her fingers on the armchair. "It had to be gold to match. What do you think?"

A gift from our leader. Why is this insect getting so much play? The reason is as obvious as the floating gold chair.

"You are providing weapons to Déesse."

OG smiles a big golden grin. Of course. I foolishly thought tronics were being made in the Towers. Not at this magnitude. There's no doubt dealing innocent Codigos and beauty items can make a freelancer popular in Mega City. Weapons can take a freelancer to a whole other level. A level, apparently, that includes lavish gifts from our leader.

"Cemi Territory is filled with many willing participants eager to conduct business," she says. "We are simply the facilitators."

The Gurl Gunnas must also be trading with the Ashé Ryders. Those tronics didn't just appear out of nowhere. Are the Gurl Gunnas playing both sides?

"How much are the Ashé Ryders giving you?"

OG makes the chair bounce to the beat of a song.

"The Ashé Ryders? Hilarious. Did you hear what Chief Rocka said?" Her soldiers laugh right on cue. "Weren't you just hanging with them girls? I'm surprised you didn't come back rocking a flowery dress."

OG guzzles down a drink. Without even so much as a nod, a Gurl Gunna replenishes the glass by stretching her hand toward the elevated OG. She will not divulge her true motives. Not to me anyway. This performance is to be relayed back to Déesse. How much she loves the gift. How good of a freelancer she is. I don't doubt OG is also dealing with the Ashé Ryders. She just won't tell me. I'm tired of these machinations.

"Ashé Ryders are a fun bunch," OG says. "Zentrica. She's got a few funny ideas. Am I right?"

Behind me Truck breathes heavily. I nudge her to cool it. This will soon be over and I will no longer deal with OG. Then it dawns on me. OG and I may be forever linked. If OG is as close to Déesse as she says, then I too will need to be her friend.

"How long have you known Zentrica?" I ask.

The chair continues to bounce. Her expression never deviates. Regardless of her age, she's quickly picked up on how to work a meeting.

"I don't. You do. I mean, weren't you chilling with the Ryders? I wonder how Déesse will feel about that."

OG thinks she can trade information on me. She has a lot to learn.

"Where's Nena?" I say. "My word is bond. Is yours?"

She chuckles. She doesn't want to lose face in front of her crew. There is a rep she has to maintain. Trade is their thing, and although OG's fishing to know my dealings with the Ryders, I'm not about to give her anything. If she wants to speculate, let her do it on her own time and not mine.

"Go get the cub," OG yells. A soldier runs toward the exit.

"She better be perfect," I say.

"Yeah, yeah, yeah," she says.

Nena trails behind a soldier. There she is. No scratches or bruises. There is a deep sadness, though. She won't even look me in the eyes.

"You okay, Nena?" Truck rushes toward her and grabs her shoulders.

"Yes," she says. Nena only offers a blank expression. Truck lets her go. I catch a hint of disappointment from Truck. She is not one to show affection to just anybody. Nena won't let us in, not for a while anyway. There is too much anger. I will deal with her later.

"We're good, then," I say. My crew turns to go.

The Gurl Gunnas stand in our way.

"You guys owe us," OG says.

My fists ball up. We are outnumbered with no working weapons. OG is desperate to act grown. Every action she takes is a reminder how she is the top dog here. Making us wait. Dropping Mega City names. Here comes another violent dance I am forced to participate in with OG taking the lead.

"Remember the last time you were here. My pet. You broke it. You need to pay for the damage."

The mechanical lizard. What can I trade? The Ashé Ryders took everything from me, right down to my blood family.

"What do you want?" I say.

OG rocks along to the chair. "You'll see."

Before my crew can go on the defensive, Gurl Gunnas rain down on us. They pin each of the LMCs to the ground. It takes a group of five Gurl Gunnas to hold me. Instead of the floor, I am left facing the OG. Nena is the only LMC who doesn't struggle. She goes limp, resigned to the violent spectacle.

"Hold them down," yells OG.

"It's why you got kicked out of the camp," Smiley yells. "If you were a true warrior, you would fight as a woman."

"Muzzle her," she says. "Make sure the LMCs are able to see this."

OG brings her gold chair down. It continues to bounce behind her. She slowly takes off the multiple rings on her fingers. Places them on the gold table. A soldier hands her a gold four-finger knuckle duster.

No matter how much I try to brace myself, I am left out of breath and seeing stars from her first punch. It doesn't matter how small or young OG is, the blow is more than enough.

"Let me go so we can finish this transaction." I can barely speak. She's about to throw another one. Damn her.

"What for? We'll be done soon."

She throws another punch to my gut. Another. The LMCs try to break free. It's not possible. I'm getting jacked by this Gurl Gunna. I pay my exit fee for leaving Cemi Territory with pain. My legs go weak. I am dropped to the ground.

"Escort the LMCs," OG says. "Oh, and, Chief Rocka, make sure you send my regards to Déesse."

Hands lift me. I'm being dragged. I can barely see. There's only a hurt of pain. I close my eyes and black out.

A dream. Mami brushes my hair. Yamaris sits in front of me. She is making funny faces. I hear the voice of a man. Papi. He's cooking. The room permeates with the deep smell of sautéed spices. Yamaris continues with the faces. I am laughing. There is a knot in my hair. Mami tells me to stop moving. Yamaris and I try to be serious. It doesn't work. Papi pokes his head into the room. The food is ready. "Let's go," Yamaris says.

I don't want these visions. This isn't real. I slowly open my eyes.

"You were having a bad dream," Truck says. "You kept calling for Yamaris."

The pain is unbearable. It is more than just the physical. I thought I was done with blood family. I buried them in Los Bohios. New dreams to forever torment me.

"This should help," Shi says.

I take a sip of water mixed with a little pain relief. When I can muster the strength, I look around. We are in an abandoned building a couple hours away from our final destination. I try to stand. I can't. Not yet. Damn the Gurl Gunnas.

"Give it at least fifteen minutes," Shi says.

Smiley stands by the entrance on lookout. Nena sits in

a corner by herself. She has the same dead expression from before.

"Did they hurt you, Nena?" I ask when the pain subsides. Nena looks at me with those big round eyes and simply shakes her head.

"We were always coming back for you," I say. "You're an LMC for life."

She waits for me to finish, then faces the window.

Later, Smiley urges her to share her stories of hanging with the Gurl Gunnas. Nena refuses. There is only frost coming from her. I'm going to give her space. Nena will snap out of this funk and be the same soldier from before.

THE BIG COMEBACK

As we draw close to the Mega City border, my heart races out of control. Truck and the others pick up the pace to an almost jog. They are excited. Happy. I, on the other hand, can't quell this anxiousness.

"Yo, the first thing I'm doing is going straight to the Luna Club and taking the longest bath. There will be no water left," Truck jokes. "Who is with me?"

Shi and Smiley respond with the LMC call. With our quickened pace, the conversation has also increased momentum. They can't get their thoughts across fast enough with all the things they will do once we get to Mega City. Nena keeps silent.

"What? You didn't appreciate showering with the old man screaming at you?" Smiley says.

Truck laughs. "I almost clocked the guy. They had good food though. Doña Chela doesn't come close."

"Their dresses were ugly," Shi says. "Except for the pockets. Long pockets perfect for stealing."

"When I get home I'm going to check on my chillas," Smiley says with her mischievous grin. "For research purposes."

Shi hits her on the back of the head. Truck hoots at this. It's hard not to laugh. Smiley wraps her arm around Shi's waist. They are not hiding their relationship. Perhaps what they have is stronger than what I gave them credit for.

"We need our Codigos fixed," Shi says. "Think Santo will hook us up?"

Santo may not have been on my mind, but throughout this whole trip he appeared in the unlikeliest of places. When I trashed the bohio, there was a moment when my anger was directed at him. This whole scenario began when he asked me to lose the fight. He has to do right by me. I did what the others have never done before. The LMCs ventured into Cemi Territory and met the notorious bruja Zentrica only to find she's a woman preaching clean living and a war against Mega City. This dirt is valuable.

"What's the first thing you are going to do, Nena?" Smiley nudges the young cub. Shi and Smiley have tried everything to get her out of her shell. Truck pulled away as soon as she sensed the cold front. Truck also hasn't barked at her. Maybe the connection is severed for good. Her time with the Gurl Gunnas squashed the last of her childhood and replaced it with extreme anger. That too can be of value. Hate can push you forward in unexpected ways.

Nena purses her lips. "I'm getting ready."

"Ready for what?" I ask.

She keeps her eyes fixed on Mega City, never addressing anyone directly.

"For what's coming," Nena says.

"Yeah! Las Mal Criadas are coming!" Smiley screams while grabbing hold of Nena. She twirls her around. Nena doesn't protest. She lets herself be flung.

"Mal!" Truck says. We yell "Criadas" until our throats are sore.

I let myself enjoy this even when part of me is nervous. The strategy. Déesse wanted results. I'm bringing back information. Will it be enough? Will Santo back me? Stupid. The LMCs will continue to trudge this path together. This simple reminder calms me. It's when I try to do things on my own that I fail. I have to rely on them more.

When the Towers loom large ahead of us there is an adrenaline rush that's hard to contain. Mega City is before us, and we need only to find the fence and climb over. It takes Shi a few minutes to locate it. We've managed to time our arrival at the right moment. The wondrous period before breaking night.

I call for lineup.

"LMC's, we are returning to Mega City. It's been only seven days. Still, a whole lot can change in seven days. You know the drill," I say. "The Deadly Venoms are on top. Keep that in the forefront.

"We march to the D. There is no dialogue with toilers. No telling stories where we've been or what we've seen. You feel me?" I continue. "Information is our currency, and we will trade only with Déesse."

I climb over the fence feeling fortified that my crew walks behind me.

The city is abuzz with action. A throwdown is scheduled to happen soon, and Mega City is preparing for the festivities. When we walk past, people whisper and point to us. The vibe I'm getting is of cautiousness. These are the people who cheered for us to win. Now they look at us as if we are poison.

What did I expect? Not a welcoming party or a parade. Maybe a smile? No. I'm lying to myself. I want the whole city to sing my praises. They did, not too long ago.

Walls are covered with Deadly Venom tags. Destiny is the queen. That dog. It is strange how these walls hold so much power compared to the bohios.

For only a few. Zentrica's voice creeps into my thoughts.

"The LMCs are back." Gata sticks her head out from a mercado. "Cubs are practicing in the courtyard for future placement. Come over, Smiley, before it starts."

"Later, Gata," Smiley says. "I promise."

"It's been dull without you!"

Gata plants her future seeds. It's reassuring to see how

things don't seem to change no matter how much time has passed. I search to see if Shi is affected by this interaction between Gata and Smiley. Those two go way back. Smiley catches up to Shi. Smart move.

The streets are dirty and there is the strong smell billowing from the factories. Sueños are being manufactured. Food pellets too. The cycle continues.

A new papi chulo club has sprung up. The papi chulo posters are surrounded by flashing lights, illuminating the club from afar. The decorations are gaudy and over the top. Promises of way more papis who can dance and all you can eat. The hottest bath. Everything new. To lure customers in, there are giant piñatas of dinosaurs stomping in front of the club. A seven-foot T. rex opens its paper mouth and spews confetti out to the street. The crowd loves it. The boydega is called the Temptation. I chuckle at the name. I wonder how Doña Chela feels about the new competition.

Boydegas come and go. It doesn't surprise me a new establishment is trying to replace the Luna Club. Luna Club has been on fire for six months. A veritable lifetime. The papis will slowly get jobs over at the Temptation. New boys will audition. Crews will eagerly trade sueños for access.

Truck helps bolster Nena. There are remnants left behind of toilers who tried to lay claim to our spot. A makeshift bed at the entrance. Nena appears to be making her best time yet in opening our secret tunnel. No one congratulates her. She is still in a mood.

Today we will stay by the D. Not for long.

Our altar is intact. I have a new offering. The azabache will be my gift, a connection to my history and my future. I lay one down. The other I keep stored in my pocket. The girls place the objects that reflect their journey.

"Smiley, go check the word on the street," I say. "I'm going to set a meeting with Déesse." By now the leader has surely heard of our return. There is no point in waiting.

"I'll go with her." Nena no longer does that thing, adding a question to the end of her sentences. She is not asking. This is a statement.

"No," Truck says. "You are staying put."

Nena walks over to me as I shrug off my backpack. "Let me go with Smiley."

I'm done feeling sorry for her. This is Mega City, and Nena has to let go of whatever ill feelings she has for what we did.

"No. You are staying."

She huffs, angry at my answer.

"Stop being a victim," Truck says.

There is a long pause. We mentally place bets on whether Nena will break down. Whether she will cry. If she curses us out, I can respect that. I wish for anything except this emptiness.

"Yes, Truck." She says this without any emotion. No anger or sadness. Flat.

I motion for Smiley to go. She'll return with intel. As for the rest, they will clean the station. Walk around and make sure things are in order. I need to talk with Nena alone. Once and for all, set things straight, because if not, this new Nena will not work.

"Pop a squat." She does so reluctantly. "I'm giving you a chance on the floor. A private session to expel this anger. It can't go on. What went down with the Gurl Gunnas was for the greater good."

Nena snorts. I let it pass.

"Truck is your second-in-command. She's important to the LMC," Nena says. "I'm not."

How long will she hold this belief? It will crush her because no one cares.

"Did the Gurl Gunnas mess with you?" I ask.

"They kept me caged. They spent hours letting me know how worthless I am."

"Words have no value, Nena. You are stupid to even let it bother you. It was business. I promised to rescue you and I did."

The short buzz we gave her so we could brand the side of her head is already growing out. The Gurl Gunnas used her as a deposit. It was an unavoidable transaction.

"I've got to pee," Nena says. "Can I please go?"

I'm done trying to find an in with her. She can't snap out of this funk. "Sure," I say.

Once Nena is in the Towers, she will forget how the Gurl Gunnas treated her. She will remember how we picked her to be an LMC. She was chosen.

"Shi, how's the Codigo?"

Only one of them works. I tap in and send a message to Déesse's assistant.

"This is Chief Rocka from the LMCs. I urgently need to speak to Déesse. Please let me know when."

The message is sent. Now to wait.

I start to pace. I'm nervous. I go over the dialogue in my head. How should we present what we know in the best fashion? Déesse won't back down on this deal.

Smiley brings food pellets and gossip. The Deadly Venoms have been spouting lies, saying we abandoned Mega City.

"Stupid cows," I say. "What else?"

"The Ashé Ryders. There are people who are slowly voicing their love for this ghost crew, unafraid of the consequences. A group of toilers were caught sporting the azabaches. Déesse's soldiers took care of them."

"What do you mean?"

"They were rounded up and never seen again."

My heart sinks. Never seen again. It's that serious. Déesse is not taking any chances. Violence is imminent for any toiler who finds themself on the wrong side.

"Where's Nena?" asks Shi.

It's been more than a while since she asked to go the bathroom. Where did the girl go? Shi checks around the station. Nena is nowhere to be found.

"I saw her use the bathroom," Truck says. "I knew I should have hollered at her to get back inside."

Nena bailed. I didn't think she had it in her. To leave a crew voluntarily is never seen as a good strategy. She will be considered used, a throwaway unless she proves worthy. She can try to win passage into another crew by selling secrets. She doesn't know about our Ashé Ryder findings. I'm not worried. I'm more upset she was unable to see we were family.

I protected Nena for so long. I was the one who accepted her in even though Truck protested. I overlooked her flaws as a soldier and took her under my wing. How can she quickly dismiss history because of resentments? I tried to get through to her. She was so closed off. It was only a matter of time. She would have seen I was right. Sometimes older sisters are forced to make the hardest of decisions.

A message appears in the Codigo I hold in my hand. *Come to the Towers tomorrow before sundown.*

It's set, then. Nena is probably on her way to offer herself to the Deadly Venoms. She is an idiot for doing so. She thinks we did her wrong. I could have easily left her with the Gurl Gunnas. The Deadly Venoms surely would have. Now she's hedging her bets on a crew about to get ousted. We are hitting the Towers tomorrow, and Nena's losing out on everything.

CHAPTER 25

BALLER BOSSES

State your business." A line of guards form a human barrier. Their tronics shine brightly by their sides. Déesse's army. They exude a hardness that comes only from experience.

"Déesse called for us," I say. Truck, Shi, and Smiley stand behind me. We wear our colors with pride. There wasn't enough time to take a bath. The news of Nena's disappearance sidelined us. Truck and Smiley both hit the streets to see if they could find her. No luck. Nena vanished. We spent too much time trying to retrace her steps. What a waste. It doesn't matter.

"Who are you?" the guard says.

"We are the LMCs," I say.

"You must be a ghost," she says, never once looking at us. "The LMCs are dead."

We can't get past the guards because of rumors started

by the Deadly Venoms. I won't miss our appointment.

"You don't mind if I send a message to her assistant to let her know about the delay, do you?"

The guard slightly flinches, although she manages to maintain her buffalo stance. The few minutes that pass are excruciating. We stand our ground. Eventually she steps aside. We go through the first gateway. This is where we will be patted down by other soldiers. Absolutely no tronics are allowed in. We were not foolish enough to hide knives in our garments. The detectors would have easily discovered them. The soldiers are meticulous. They check our backpacks, our hair, behind our ears. It takes a while.

Aromatic censers blanket the air whenever a new person enters the Towers. No one wants to smell toiler stench. The fragrance consists of orange blossoms, florals, and a little hint of coffee. It smells rich.

I've been to the Towers only once. Santo brought me here after one of the LMC's earlier throwdown victories. We were at the onset of our relationship. He was trying to impress me. It worked. Although I could only wait in the lobby, I couldn't get over the lavishness. Everything was so brilliant and new. Towering marble columns matched the marble floors. Ornate chandeliers loomed overhead. A large indoor vertical garden covered one of the lobby walls. It was the largest garden I've ever seen. There were little nooks with sofas perfect for lounging. Santo found a secluded place for us to sit. A guard brought us food. Even dressed in my LMC clothes, with Santo I felt as if I belonged there sharing a meal with him. I remember it so well. After that day, I began plotting. I had to find a way to sustain the feeling.

Truck will only sit at the edge of the sofa. She's afraid she'll dirty the velour covering. Shi and Smiley sprawl themselves. They can't stop caressing the fabric. They sneak grins at each other. They're practically giddy. This is their first time. I can understand the excitement.

I can't join in on their enthusiasm. I do what I do in stressful moments. I pace. That's when I notice it. Tiny cracks on the marble floors. The paint seems a bit dull, as if it's past due for an upkeep. The lobby has lost much of its luster, or maybe I'm finally taking a good look. I think about the furniture. The knickknacks on the table. These are not Mega made. They were created elsewhere. Strange when Déesse preaches the importance of objects made by hand. The chandelier was surely found and restored even if from where I stand I can see missing crystals. Not everything can retain its effect. I'm fine with this. The Towers are way better than where I live now. The bohios can't compare.

The elevator door opens and Déesse's assistant arrives. She has a hurried air to her. Although she handles Déesse's business, I am positive she is also a fighter. How did she make the leap from soldier to Déesse's keeper of secrets? If she was able to transition to this job and leave fighting behind, there's hope for us.

"You are the only person allowed to go upstairs," she says. "No one else."

"This is my crew. We go together."

I give the signal, and the LMCs walk toward the exit. I'm not stupid enough to go anywhere by myself. We will bail. The assistant doesn't say a word. The meeting can't end this way. Maybe I'm wrong in bluffing. I keep going.

"Wait," she says just as we enter the gateway. She taps on her Codigo. "Fine," she says after a pause. "They can go."

I adjust my cuffs.

The assistant doesn't address us or even glance our way as the elevator takes us up. She presses the button marked "12." We are not heading straight to the last floor, and I wonder if this means anything. Truck decides to eyeball the assistant. Intimidation for no reason. As for me, I watch the numbers light up. We pass the fourth floor. I think of Graciela. This was the floor she lived on. So many people living here. So many lives with a key to their own place. On which floor will I be getting off? I won't make the mistakes Graciela made.

This morning I had the girls pledge their allegiance to the LMC. With Nena's desertion, I needed reassurance from the others. Any doubts I wanted voiced aloud. There is no room for trepidation. We enter the Towers together or not at all. They vowed to keep to the task at hand.

Still, my heart thumps out of control.

The elevator door opens. We're greeted by a long hallway

illuminated by harsh fluorescent lights. There are doors alongside the corridor. Each door has a plaque attached to it. Who lives in apartment 12AE? Apartment 12AD? What goes on behind the closed doors?

A couple of girls unexpectedly leave one of the apartments. They greet the assistant and exchange pleasantries. The girls are dressed in the flashiest of clothes. Colors so dizzying they make sense only in the Towers. The attire is meant for display only. They don't have real pockets to store important items or multiple layers to ward off the cold. These girls dress without concerns. Have they ever been in a throwdown? Probably not. The chosen ones.

"No, it will be only dinner for five." The assistant speaks in her Codigo. She walks in a quick pace. She lists the food to be served at the dinner we are not invited to. The menu sounds delicious. My mouth waters.

"Pay attention." I say this to Shi and Smiley. They take note of the exits. Truck walks behind them and does the same.

We reach the end of the passageway. The assistant pulls out a card and uses it to open the door. She gestures for us to enter, and we do.

The apartment is completely furnished with silver furniture. So much metallic, it is almost blinding. There are various portraits of Déesse hanging on the wall in elaborate silver frames. Every piece of furniture must have been meticulously chosen because of what it symbolizes. Opulence. Yet up close it seems a bit over the top. If I were the leader, would I have portraits of myself? Are other people decorating their apartments the same way? We tag the streets of Mega City to proclaim our clout. A painting of yourself must hold the same meaning. The others love the apartment. I bet they are visualizing themselves eating off the ornate dining room table and admiring themselves in the many mirrors. There are no mirrors at our station. Why do we need the reflections when Déesse always professed interior beauty was all that mattered? Yet, mirrors line up the walls in this place.

"Is this where Déesse lives?" Smiley asks the assistant.

"Wait here." The assistant walks up a set of stairs and disappears. This can't be Déesse's place. Although it has two levels, I sense she would need more room. I try to envision where she lives. Would there be even more portraits, more silver, more mirrors? If I lived here, would I follow an unspoken rule to show my loyalty by professing it loudly with images of her?

"Don't touch a thing," Truck says to Smiley. Smiley places back a wooden sculpture of a female body.

My crew freezes as soon as we hear footsteps.

Santo comes down the stairs first.

It hasn't been that long since I last saw him. Only a week. Why does it feel like years? Santo looks good in his white suit. His beard is thick. My grin is wide. I'm really happy to see him. When he doesn't return the gesture, I quickly drop it.

Déesse soon follows. However, she stops midway on the stairs. She wears a vibrant red dress. Her cuffs sparkle with jewels. It's impossible to count the freckles covering her face and neck. When I decided to tattoo my face to match hers, I tried to tally them. How many freckles would I need so I could emulate her?

"The prodigal crew returns," Déesse says. Santo stands in front of us, almost as if he is blocking access to her. There is no warmth in her words. This cold reception hurts. I try to brush it off. I have value. I am meant to be here.

"How long were you planning to keep your little secret?" Déesse asks. This is not how I pictured the start of our meeting. What is happening? "Do you think I'm that gullible?"

"I . . . I don't understand. We did what you asked," I say. I try to take control of this narrative. "We found the Ashé Ryders. We know what they plan to do."

"Of course you do. When you met her, did you call her 'Zentrica' or 'Yamaris'?"

My heart drops. My crew stops breathing.

"Get ready to bail," Truck whispers. I shake my head. Truck is reading the room wrong. This can be fixed.

"As a crew, the Ashé Ryders aren't much. They are into this whole weak movement in gardening and teaching kids about music and culture. There's a room, a bohío is what they call their structures. It's filled with weapons."

"You didn't answer my question. How did you greet your sister?"

I feel sick.

"She's not my sister," I say. My words seem so weak.

"You sat in that healing room and lied to me about your sister being dead. Your father being dead. When they are living and breathing in Cemi Territory. You lied. Your family is coming to destroy us. You've found a way to lead them here." Déesse holds on to the banister and screams this at the top of her lungs.

"No. It's not true. I didn't know she was alive or the leader of the Ryders. I came back with information. I did this for you."

"You did this for me? Do you think you can come here with your ridiculous tattoo freckles and pretend to be our ally?"

"The Ashé Ryders are located right before the waterfalls. It's a pretty straight path from here." I keep talking. I can't stop. "They don't have many soldiers. They have sound weapons and tronics. I'm almost sure they are dealing with the Gurl Gunnas. You have connections with the Gunnas. You can't trust OG."

I am drowning. I don't know what else to say. The words spill out of me without making sense. Déesse thinks I'm aligned with Zentrica and the Ashé Ryders. It's not true. I came back. I lost Nena and blood on this journey. I lost almost everything. Can't she see that?

"Those in Mega City will not stand by while you contaminate our home with your dissention," Déesse says. "Get rid of them."

With a flick of her wrist, she is done with us. She turns and walks upstairs.

"I already know the plans you've been brewing," Santo says. "It's never going to happen. You and the Ashé will never take Mega."

"Who spoke? Was it OG? The Gurl Gunnas?"

"We got to go," Truck pleads.

If I can get closer to him, he can pull me in and tell me this act is a lie. This hostility can't be for me. This must be a show.

"Santo, you know me. I'm down for Mega City and for your family," I say. "I did what Déesse asked me to do. I went into Cemi Territory, battled, and found the Ashé Ryders. I did what she asked. I never betrayed you."

The space between us seems so vast. If Déesse is upstairs listening, I want her to know I'm no traitor. I didn't pull the trigger on offing my sister. It's my one fault. I fulfilled my duty as Mega City's spy. "Let me speak to your mother. Move out of my way, Santo." I try to push past him. He bars my way.

"You will never speak to her," he says. "And you will never get to the Towers."

Santo's not the decision maker here.

"Déesse! I'm here. I've got intel for you!" I scream.

Truck grabs me. "We need to bounce," Truck says. "Get it together." The rest of the LMC move closer to the exit.

I pull away from her. "No. Santo is not our leader," I say to her. "Get your mother out here. We had a deal."

Santo moves towards me. "You don't come to my house and give orders." With each word, he jabs at my shoulders. "You will never see her. Déesse asked you to find out about the Ashé Ryders. Instead, you're collaborating with them to bring the Towers down. I thought I could trust you."

Hate pours from him. My hands are now fists.

"That's not true. I've been loyal."

"I don't think you ever noticed this. Your choker," he says. "I've been schooled to how Zentrica is your sister. "

Instantly I touch the LMC necklace given to me by Déesse. A recording device? They heard everything. Every conversation I had with Zentrica and Graciela relayed back to Déesse. I yank the choker off.

"Déesse always had her suspicions about Yamaris still being alive. You confirmed it. When Truck asked you to finish her off, you hesitated. Remember," he says. "Just like your sister and your father. You are nothing but the enemy."

Before I could clock Santo with a right hook to get his hateful mug from my face, Truck bashes his head with a fancy silver vase.

CHAPTER 26

CHILD'S PLAY

Santo lies on the floor. It was all an act, a performance. I was just a prop used to further the lie his mother created. I was blind.

"We've got to go now!" Truck says. She pulls on my arm. I still want to state my case. I just need to explain this to Déesse. Everything will be back to normal. Truck grabs hold of me and shoves me toward the door.

"We need to speak to Déesse," I say.

"Are you crazy? The only thing we need to do is run before we are truly iced," she says. Shi and Smiley rush to the elevator. "Didn't you see where Santo was heading? This wasn't an invitation to move in. There was never an invitation."

Truck digs her nails into my shoulders. My legs fail me. *Santo, wake up so I can convince you.*

"Please, Nalah, I'm begging you. Déesse is gunning for us

and we are here in her lair," Truck says. "We have to go. Don't let this be our end."

Footsteps approach from above. I finally snap out of it and head to the corridor. Smiley holds open the elevator, and we pile in. Truck pushes the button. What was a quick ascent seems to drag so slowly. She taps on the button marking the ground floor as if it will help propel the elevator to move faster.

I never had control. I thought I could come back and stroll right into the Towers. All those years of throwdowns and breaking night. I worked hard. We were the best. Santo was never a brother. He chucked those hours spent together in seconds. I watch the numbers light as we continue to go down. Eight. Seven. Six.

The elevator suddenly stops, and an alarm goes off. Truck freaks out.

"Hell no. This is not happening," she says. "We are not going out like this. Help me."

Truck starts to pry open the elevator doors. Smiley and I take the other end. My hands are sweaty. It's hard to get a grip. Eventually we are able to open it. The elevator is situated between two floors. We don't hesitate. While they keep the door open, I crawl through the small space and hit the floor below us. Smiley and Shi follow me off the elevator. Bigger than us, it takes a minute, but Truck eventually squeezes through.

The halls are long and vast. Everything is so freaking

bright. The alarm is blaring. People appear from their apartments to stare at the freaks that clearly don't belong. We don't wait. There is an exit sign above a door by the elevator. We take to the stairs.

We pass the fifth floor, fourth. Truck suddenly stops. There are heavy footsteps coming from the floors below. We can't continue. The soldiers are heading our way.

"I remember seeing a maintenance room. They probably have them on each floor," Shi says. "I don't know how secure they are."

There's no debate. We exit onto the third floor and enter another bright hallway. Off to the left of us, we find the sanitation room. We run inside and block the door. Truck smashes the camera located in the corner of the room. I try to hear above the ringing alarm. People are shouting. Voices complaining about the noise. Others are taking orders. The building is rigged with video cameras everywhere. It's only a matter of time before they can pinpoint where we are.

Smiley covers her mouth. Soldiers. I can see the shadow of their boots under the door. No one moves. The minutes drag. If they open the door they will catch these hands.

The shadows move on. We can't stay here. There has to be another solution. I look around the crowded room. There are buckets and brooms. A shelf with cleaning utensils. I am losing hope until I locate a vent.

"Let's go," I say. I drag a table against a wall and climb on top of it. There is a vent right above me. I'm able to take off the covering easily. We climb one by one. The lightest of us goes first. On our knees, we crawl through the corridor, careful not to make any noise. I must focus on taking light steps.

"What do you think, Shi?" Smiley asks.

"It will probably lead to the end of the hallway. Maybe an exit?" Shi says. "I can't be sure." Shi has studied the Towers before. She loved to discuss where we could find the best views and which apartments are bigger. Sadly, she's going by memories of illustrations she collected from the mercados.

With Shi signaling us to go left or right, we do the slow crawl through the vent, careful not to puncture the ceiling. I will myself to think thin. To suck in my gut and hope we can get through this without collapsing to the floor.

"Damn." Truck curses. She makes a creaking sound. The vent is not steady enough to hold our combined weights.

"Quiet," I whisper. We are going to do this. We are close to the exit. Close to getting out of the Towers.

"It's just up ahead. We got this," Smiley whispers. I can almost feel the grin emanating from her. We're almost out of this hell. Once we are out, we can hide among the people. The crowd will help shield us. Only a few more feet. Truck presses on. We reach the end of the corridor. Below is another mainte- nance room. I climb down. The rest of them crowd in.

"If each floor follows the same pattern, there will be a hallway," Shi says. "At the end, a window. We climb through the window and jump down. Two flights. Not ideal."

"We don't have a choice," I say.

We wait a few seconds and make sure there's no one else in the hallway. The coast is clear, and my heart surges. We are only a few steps away from the window. Pull the sucker open and jump.

"Chief Rocka."

It's Nena. Nena calls to me.

"Hey Chief." Nena appears at the far end of the hallway, in the direction we are heading. She strolls as if she has no care in the world. "You left something behind."

Damn rookie. What is she doing in the Towers? Did she try to find us to make amends? She's too late. We're out. There are no Towers for the LMCs.

With the alarm, I can barely make out what she says.

"It doesn't matter. I'll buy ten more later," I say. "We are leaving."

She now stands right in front of the window.

"Move before I knock you out of the way," Truck says. "We ain't got time for this."

"You are not going nowhere," Nena says. Before I can stop her, before I can change Nena's mind with promises of a new tomorrow, Nena pulls a knife and plunges it into Truck. Truck drops without a moment to comprehend Nena's deed. Truck collapses, and my whole world crashes with her.

"See, Chief Rocka, I'm not the weak one. She is." Her baby

face is hard, unrecognizable. This is not the Nena who has been following me around from day one. This is another. She's assured, certain what she's done is right. Nena poses, ready to yield the knife again. I'm paralyzed, unable to look away from Truck. What has she done?

"You had me wrong," Nena continues. "From now on I'm the starter and the finisher. I'm going to the Towers, not you. Déesse heard me. She trusts me."

Déesse heard me, she said. Is that where she went when she deserted the LMCs last night? Straight to the Towers? Nena doesn't have intel to give and yet she must have fabricated lies to gain favor. My world spins out of control. Nena gets ready to work the knife again. Her eyes are cold. The knife will end inside me just as it did in Truck. I can't move quickly enough.

Nena has an angelic smile. The big innocent eyes. Get hard or get dumped. I drilled that into her. She does what I taught her to do.

Not Truck. Not my girl Truck.

I brace for what will surely come to pass. This violence will definitely hit, and it should, because what happened to Truck should happen to me, too.

Nena wields the bloody knife right toward me. Such anger. Such hate. I close my eyes. When I open to feel the thrust of the cut, I see instead Nena suddenly tumbling to the floor. Time whirls again, back to reality. Sule holds a tronic in her trembling hand. Sule, Déesse's daughter, has stunned Nena.

"You better get out of here," Sule says. "Leave and don't ever come back."

Smiley grabs Nena's knife and places Sule in a bear hug. The knife grazes Sule's neck.

"Why should we listen to Déesse's daughter?" Smiley says. "Your whole family is the problem."

"They're coming. Go through the window now or stay here to die," Sule says. She's not afraid even though this is by far the cruelest act she's taken against her mother. By aiding us she's spitting at her mother's world. "You've wanted to live in the Towers. Well, if you stay here you'll be able to. They'll convert you into a piece of furniture for us to use."

Truck lets out a moan, and I snap into action. Who cares if Sule wants to play the rebellious daughter today? Truck needs me, and we've got to bail.

"Let her go, Smiley," I say. "Tend to Truck."

Smiley and Shi run to Truck and drag her body through the window. Smiley jumps first. We can't cushion the fall for Truck. Shi jumps with her, and they both tumble to the ground.

Blood is everywhere. Truck's not out for the count. Not yet.

"Why are you helping us?" I ask.

Sule's lips are blue. Her skin, an ashy gray. She can't even hide it behind heavy makeup.

"I can't stop taking them. The sueños," Sule says. She leans against the wall, frail and thin. I've seen this look before. The sueños are taking her down, just as they did Mami. "She keeps feeding them to me. It's cruel what she's doing."

I stand before Nena's crumpled body. Do I punch her? Deform the innocent face with my fists? This is what I've been taught to do. My whole life spent defending what little I have. My actions failed everyone and everything, even Nena.

This violence will never end. Not with this young soldier.

I tear off the LMC necklace I gave Nena the night we let her into the crew and throw it to the ground. I feel it crush underneath my boots.

Sule has closed her eyes. She is in a dream. I climb through the window and jump.

CHAPTER 27

BRING THE PAIN

Truck barely moans. The silence is terrifying. Where is the anger that fuels her every day? Yanked away by Nena.

"You're going to be all right," I say to her as we push against the crowd.

The work shift is over. Toilers are busy tending to their lives. Buying things at the mercado. Hurrying to their underground homes to get ready for the amateur throwdown. No one cares to acknowledge the sight of three soldiers carrying a bleeding girl. They don't want to get involved. To them the LMCs continue to be ghosts.

Shi has her hand pressed against Truck's stomach where Nena plunged the knife. We can't tell if the bleeding has stopped. We need to find a place where we can assess the damage.

Smiley tries to decide where to go. She pushes people out of the way to clear our path. We make a sharp turn to the left, away from the courtyard. We are too far away from the D. Even if we were to reach our station, we wouldn't be able to lift Truck through our tunnel. Besides, the medical provisions we have are limited. We haven't been in the city long enough to replenish our stock.

Déesse's soldiers will not stay in the Towers for long. We need to get off these streets and hide.

"Head to the Luna Club," I say. "It will be empty, and it's close by."

Smiley rattles the door to the club. Doña Chela is nowhere to be found. She has to be in there. Where else would she be? Truck starts to tremble. She looks pale.

"Doña, open the gate!" I yell. The others try to figure out another way in. I'll freaking tear the place down. "Open it!"

Doña saunters to the gate.

"Sí?" she asks. "You can't come in here with that."

"The hell we can't," Smiley says. "Open or you'll be missing more than just your front teeth."

She doesn't budge. Smiley grabs hold of one of Doña's wrists from between the gate and squeezes. Doña protests. It doesn't matter. She's tough. She won't bend except for sueños, and we are out of those.

Truck goes in and out of consciousness. The tears start to flow from Shi. Doña isn't moved by them. Truck is going to die because we came empty-handed. I'm desperate.

"Cut her hand off," I say. Smiley pulls the knife she took from

Nena and gets ready to do what she has to do when Doña relents.

"Abren la puerta," the old lady says. The gate opens. Doña spits at our feet. "Malcriadas. You have a half hour."

We push past her and scramble down the stairs. The animal piñatas float above the dance floor to the beat of the garish music. I don't know where to take Truck.

"The rooms are locked," Shi says as she throws herself against a door. They are hiding. No one wants to be contaminated by the bleeding losers. Where are the papis, the ones who love Truck?

"Help us, please! It's Truck, yo!"

Finally, a young papi comes out. I recognize him. One of Truck's favorites. He whistles, and a couple more join him. They lift Truck and take her inside a nautical-themed room.

"She got knifed," Shi says. "We need meds." The blood trickles. This isn't good. A papi rushes to find gauze to stop the bleeding. Shi does her best to check the damage. Truck needs a healer, not a big bandage.

Someone places their hands on my shoulder, and I turn quickly, ready to fight. Books. It's hard for me to keep my emotions from pouring out. He sees me, without malice. A completely different encounter from the one I just had with Santo.

"It doesn't look so bad. We need meds to ward off any infection. We also need to stitch the wound," Shi says. "We don't have anything to trade right now."

As if just the sound of sueños can attract her, Doña barges in, yelling for us to get out. No one moves.

"You need to leave now!"

One of the papis tries to calm her down with sweet words. They'd better leave us alone or I will yank the green hair off her head.

"Help me," I plead with Books. He doesn't owe me a thing. Truck is my sister. I can't lose her. "Please."

Books nods and walks out of the room with Smiley.

"Nena . . . ," Truck says. "Nena needs me."

I lean in. "Don't worry about Nena. She'll be fine," I say. "We are going to be fine."

I squeeze her hand and wait.

Books returns with the papi chulo named Hector. Hector is dressed in tight black clothes, as if he's about to inflict pain on his next client. Why are they sending for him when we need a healer? I immediately want to protect Truck.

Hector reaches over to her stomach. I stop him. "What are you going to do?" I say.

He looks at Books.

"I think it would be best if you leave and let him do what he does," Books says.

"What exactly is he going to do? I'm not going anywhere."

"I'm a healer. I'm going to take care of her. Your energy is not helping. I need you to leave." Hector's voice is deep and commanding. He's not playing. Neither am I. Books gently pushes me toward the door. I try to fight him. I eventually give in.

I hit the wall with my fists. This is my fault. This went down because of me. What am I doing? Destroying those closest for an unattainable goal. Nena did what I taught her to do. She sold us out for a dream I convinced her to believe in.

Align yourself with the strongest or take them down. Lessons I learned in the training camp echo in my head, a cruel reminder that what happened to Truck was foreseen by those rules.

I can't stop crying.

Santo's harshness poisons my thoughts. The Codigos he so gallantly gave me. The bag of sueños for the Gurl Gunnas. He sent us on our way to either find out about the Ashé Ryders or to be swallowed up, never to be seen again. Either way, they would win. I was used by Santo and his family. They want power and will do everything to secure that status. I was a fool to think otherwise.

Books sits beside me. He doesn't say a word. He just pulls off his fake glasses and cleans the lenses with his shirt.

The knuckles on my fingers start to swell. I can't close my hand.

"Do you want ice?" he asks. I want him to stop treating me as a customer. I don't deserve anything good, definitely not the care of a papi chulo.

How long before Smiley and Shi are knifed? This is where I'm leading the LMCs. I can't protect them. I can't even protect myself. Sisters for life. What good is that if we don't live long enough to enjoy any of it? These swollen knuckles are the only thing I own. If I can no longer use my fists, what am I? Who am I?

"He'll take care of her," Books says. "Hector will know what to do. He used to work at the healing centers in the Towers until Déesse . . ."

There's no need for Books to complete the sentence. I know what happened. This is the recurring theme. Names listed in the Towers' newsletter with their offenses. A person was shown the door for malicious gossiping. Another for harboring an illegal tenant. The most common offense: the overuse of sueños. How funny. I never realized it before. For a healer to work in the Towers, trying to care for addicts must prove a problem. No wonder Déesse kicked Hector out. Steady rotation of new healers ensures no one will truly pay attention to the addicts living in the Towers. How does Déesse justify her own daughter's addiction? Sule says she keeps feeding her tabs. She ignores the problem by masking it with manufactured dreams. The line a person crosses is so moveable, there is never security.

Mega City is held together by misguided ambitions that take root only when another person fails. The realization hits me, not as a ton of bricks, but more a slap. Books hands me a handkerchief. I push it away. I want these tears to cover my whole body.

Doña Chela appears doing busywork. Two papis follow her around as she barks orders for them to tidy the place. She is ridiculous. So are the boydegas. I've spent so many hours here with Truck. We loved stunting on everyone at the Luna Club. When we entered the boydega club, we had swagger for days. We believed the club was ours. Ownership doesn't exist in Mega City, not for anyone except Déesse and her family.

Doña mutters how she will let Déesse know we are here. I stand to rush at her. Books stops me.

"She won't. She can't afford to have Déesse come here. Doña is already letting a lot of the papis go," he says. "People prefer the Temptation. Luna Club won't last long."

I face Books. Really pay attention to him. Books is my age. We are on similar paths. We both hustle for others. Where exactly do we think we are heading?

"What will you do?" I ask.

"What I continue to do," he says. "Survive."

Smiley returns with medical supplies. She walks right into the room. I start to pace. This city is a lie and I have fed off of it, knowing if I benefited, then to hell with everyone else. I didn't care what happened to others. The toilers, the papis, the kids entering the training camps. They didn't exist except when they were in my way.

"I can't keep doing this." I say this more to myself than to him. "There's got to be a better way. This path I'm on goes nowhere."

"Did you find what you were looking for on your trip?"

I shake my head. "No one can save me. Not even the Ashé Ryders."

There is a long pause. "Maybe you are right. No one person holds the key to this life. But there are families who are worse off than you and me, and they are waiting for us to change the game."

"I can't change anything. This leader is getting her people taken or iced," I say. "I have no power."

Books stands. "I don't know anything. I'm just a papi chulo who works at a boydega," he says. "I have watched LMCs take whole crews down. One misguided family doesn't seem much. It just takes determination."

He walks away and heads to his room. I let his words sink in. If I listen to Santo and Déesse, I will stay underground. A nobody. If I resist this story, then maybe there is hope for me. I don't know. I am so lost.

After a while I enter the room where Truck is. She is asleep. Hector washes his hands at the boat-shaped sink. He tells me she'll be fine. There's blood loss, and she will be weak. The stitches should hold.

"Unless you are about to throw down," he says, "she should heal."

"I've no sueños to offer. I have this." I hand him a Codigo. It is the only thing of value. Hector takes it.

There's no way around it. We have to move Truck.

Although the Luna Club is losing customers, the place will inevitably see action. Doña will not stand for us converting her boydega into a healing room for much longer.

"I suggest you head to the Rumberos," Hector says. "Tell them I sent you."

The Rumberos. No one will look for us there.

"You didn't hear this from me. Doña has a cart out in the alley," Hector says. "She uses it to move clients who are too high on sueños."

Smiley doesn't wait for him to finish. She's on it. We prepare to move Truck out of here.

I thank Hector again. Shi searches with the papis for clothes to change into. The closet in the nautical room only has sailor outfits. I find a blue robe and gently drape it over Truck.

CHAPTER 28

REDEMPTION SONGS

Not everyone heads to the courtyard to see the amateur throwdown. For the first time I notice families choosing to stay away, more than I would have ever imagined. We walk past them as Smiley pushes Truck, who lies slumped in the cart. The blue robe keeps her covered.

A couple plays a game of catch with their daughter. She must be about nine or ten years old. When the mother sees us, she tries to block my view of the child. She is nervous we will take her away to a training camp. It is obvious the girl is way past due to join. Recruitments start at seven. This family is willfully going against Déesse's orders. How many try to buck the system? Hide their daughters to avoid the camps?

Any other time and I would have dragged the daughter from the mother's arms. Déesse would have surely given me props for delivering a potential soldier to her.

The father looks down. He defers to me. This also has

been my upbringing, seeing men cower whenever I appear. Old-timers feared us, too, as they should. We were stronger. Youth before everything. I feel a sense of shame.

There are toilers enjoying the cool evening air. There is an unsettling quiet, one I am not accustomed to. Silence is a signal that evil lurks around the corner. For these people, it is a moment to cherish. With most of Mega City attending the throwdown, the streets are alive with another type of energy. This is the part of the city I've ignored. It took me leaving Mega to finally see.

"How do we do this?" Shi asks. Her voice is soft. Her bangs practically reach her nose.

"We beg," I say.

A low rumbling sound from distant congas can be heard. The music is not as intense as the last time we were here. Perhaps the players are attending the throwdown. How did Hector know about the Rumberos? As a healer, he must have been taught his craft. Perhaps he learned it in this tent with these people. Nothing is black-and-white.

I stop the girls. The throwdown will end and soon the streets will be overrun with people. We need a place to crash, and this may be our only hope. I absentmindedly rub the azabache in my pocket. I can feel the carved "AR." There are two Rumberos situated at the entrance. An old-timer and a younger woman. They both wear traditional blue tunics. The old-timer gives me a nod and glances over to the sleeping Truck.

"I'm Chief Rocka and we're the LMCs," I say. "We're looking for sanctuary for our fallen sister."

"Take her to the healing center by the Towers," she says.
"It's where people who can afford it go. Aren't you one of the
beloved crews?"

I shake my head. There is a distant roar. The throwdowns.
I want off these streets.

"Hector sent us here. Hector the healer at the Luna Club."

The Rumbero rubs her hands together. She purses her
lips. "Hector's friends aren't soldiers," she says.

If I'm going to get anywhere, I can't continue to play mind
games or find ways to force my way in. The Rumberos are on
a whole other level, and for once I must respect their house.

"Hector helped Truck." I point to my girls. "My soldiers."

The old-timer rolls her eyes. She doesn't care for crews or
soldiers. I try again.

"My friend got knifed because of my failure to see the
truth. Now we are on Déesse's wrong side. They need a safe
place to hide," I say. "Please take them. I will bounce."

The old-timer ponders this. I hear a rush of people coming from the direction of the courtyard. The throwdown is
done. We need to get inside.

The other Rumbero moves forward. Her expression is
serious. I hold her stare and try not to blink. She eyeballs me
hard enough that I form fists. No one comes for me unless
they want to start a fight.

"There is no room for your anger here," she says. "This is a place to heal and pray. You can't seek the Rumberos whenever one of your friends is hurt. The hate you are living in is what will cause your death and theirs."

I take in what she says. Where is the lie? I unfurl my hands. The old-timer places hers on the woman's shoulder.

"They are young. They can learn. You did," she says. "Let them in."

I breathe a sigh of relief.

We follow the old-timer as she leads us inside the large tent. There is a group of women sitting in a circle. I can't understand what they are chanting. The old-timer walks us to another tent. This one is smaller. There are beds on the floor. She directs Smiley and Shi to place Truck on one of the beds. They do so as gently as possible. Truck doesn't stir. The old-timer lifts Truck's robe to see the stitches.

"Hector did a fine job." she says. "The others will be here soon. Leave her be. You three, out."

"What if they find her?" I say. "Who will protect her?"

"I'll stay with her," Shi offers.

The old-timer relents. She leads us back to the big tent. There are people streaming in with their congas on their backs. This is not a joyous occasion. Perhaps they lost a bet. We watch as they come in. The ladies continue to pray. They are joined by the conga players as they line the edges of the tents in a single row.

"I was there when Destiny hit you with the baton," the old-timer says. "I go to the throwdowns to call the spirit. A soltar los caballos. To let the horses free. I pounded on the skin of the conga to pray you were taken care of. I did the same for Destiny. For all the girls."

Why pray for the person about to destroy me? Is it a trick?

"I don't understand."

She motions for Smiley and me to take two seats placed next to the praying mothers. I don't want to be so close to them. I don't want to be on display unless I'm thrashing in the middle of a courtyard. I follow her wishes even though I want to hide.

"We are connected. Men. Women. Children. Déesse. Destiny. Your friend in the tent," she says. "Mega City is not the Towers or the underground stations. It's the people, and it stretches outside these borders."

The old-timer walks to the conga players. She sits in front of a conga and plays. Smiley doesn't smile her gold grin. Instead she is lost in the prayers the women are reciting. I don't want this feeling. More people enter the tent. They take up space.

I believed the conga players at the throwdowns were just part of the chaos. A way for people to join in on the fun. I see now it was more than music. This goes beyond that. It is powerful. What does praying or playing drums have to do with family? My family was torn apart because of Déesse and her rules. Books tells me to fight. So does Zentrica. I'm too scared.

When Smiley turns to me, she has tears in her eyes. "I'm tired, Chief Rocka," she says. "I mean, why can't we be on our own like the couple we met in Cemi Territory? They didn't bother anybody. Nobody seemed to bother them."

There is no way I can reassure her with promises I can no longer keep. I don't have the answer. It's not possible for me to pretend I do.

Rumberos begin to dance to the beat of the congas. There is a sadness to their movements. Not joyful or freeing. While the rest of the city enjoys the same entertainment found in the boydegas and in the Towers, those in this tent lament. I, too, feel a heavy grief. The immensity of moving forward seems insurmountable when there is little left to aim for.

I watch the women play the congas. I allow myself to fall into the music. The prayers become hypnotic. This city doesn't exist unless we are completely in it together. My sisters are with me. Truck and Shi and Smiley. So are the Rumberos who prayed over me when I entered the throwdown. And so are Books and the papi chulos. I have been blind to what the city truly is. It is the people within it that count, not the Towers. It's on me to make this city my own. Not Déesse or Santo.

I loved to proclaim how much the LMCs owned the streets of Mega City. With every throwdown, another notch was added to my skin, ensuring my rank. The embedded number only demonstrated how much of a cog I was. I thought if

I kept fighting, moving up rank, I would be rewarded. Déesse dangles such dazzling prizes—the Towers, papi chulos. I was even hypnotized by the deadly choker. How easy it is for people who have little hope to think she was doing them a favor. I was just incurring debt for Déesse to later collect on. I can highlight the words she repeated in the speeches she gave before the throwdowns—"unity," "together," "our city." "We did this," she would say. That was probably the only truthful statement she has ever uttered. The residents of a city should not be beholden to one person. The city is ours. These streets are ours. How do we take them back without the need to trample one another in the process?

I look around. There are more dancers, both young and old. I don't have answers. Not yet.

"We will figure it out," I tell Smiley. "We will."

I've called Mega City my home for so long. I thought home needed to be tall and luminous, a glowing building with a luxurious setting. Status. What I failed to understand is home is not where I place my head down at night or the color of my furniture. Home is the people I surround myself with, the ones I break bread with. The keepers of my secrets and my fears. It is to be loved and to give love without inhibitions. I won't let Déesse dictate my actions. The fear Déesse has is real. She should be afraid because the change is on me and on my people. Change is going to come, and I can see this just as surely as I feel this pulsating rhythm.

"We're going to be all right, Smiley," I say. "This is the truth."

The dancers swirl and move. Prayers continue throughout the night. Smiley and I remain seated for hours. The music envelops us. I watch the old-timer slap the conga with a force unimaginable.

Santo is wrong about me and the toilers. We are more than his family's plans. We deserve more.

If I repeat this as a prayer, then surely it will form into reality.

CHAPTER 29

COME TO YOUR RIVER

The Rumberos are on the move. Tents are being dismantled and packed away. They move quickly. They've done this many times before. No garbage is left behind. No trace of life.

It is early morning. Tomasa, the old-timer, has instructed me to take care of one of the smaller tents. Most Rumberos do not live in the tents. They come nightly to pray and sing. They have their underground stations and work to tend to during the day. There is a core group who maintain the tents. For the past couple of days, we have been with this group.

"Make sure you have enough rope," Tomasa says. "We don't want the poles to go missing."

"Yes," I say.

"Also, don't forget to fold the tent the way I taught you," she says. "It's the only way it will fit in the backpack." She goes off to explain to another how they will cart away the medicinal plants.

"Does she ever stop barking orders?" Truck mutters beside me. It's been a couple of days since the Rumberos let us in to hide among them. During that time Truck has gotten better. She's not 100 percent. Although Truck wants to help, she can't afford to have her stitches rip open. Instead, her task is simple. She holds the rope for me while I do the rest.

The other night Déesse's soldiers paid the Rumberos a visit. There is a network of sympathizers across the city. From the boydegas to the factories, a slew of toilers communicate with each other through graffiti. Tags on the wall tiny enough to be ignored by most. I've never noticed them before. These people are no fans of Déesse. We were alerted to the raid an hour before it happened. We hid in a nearby station. The soldiers found only chanting. They left empty-handed. To make their search harder, the Rumberos are relocating. I reiterated to Tomasa that we will soon leave. Our stay is a threat.

"Do you need help?" A disheveled man appears. I shake my head.

I made a mistake in calling him an ANT the other day. He came to the Rumberos to get clean. When I called him an ANT, Tomasa had heated words for me. "ANT" is a derogatory term used to debase a human. To turn them into an insect. "He has a name," she said. "Find out what it is it and use it."

Sueño addicts are welcome to stay with the Rumberos

if they are willing to try to kick the habit. It's not an easy transition. There are addicts who don't have the strength to stop. They leave only to return a couple of days later in anguish. The Rumberos don't have a simple solution to break the dependence. They use other drugs, an herbal and chemical mixture. Tomasa has shown me the plants. I can see why Miguel found sanctuary with the Rumberos.

"I'm almost done," I say. I fold the tent and place it in a backpack. The blue tunics we wear are not exactly my favorite. I'm so used to wearing my armor. Our clothes are back in the D, where they will probably stay forever. Nena surely has given Déesse the directions on how to find our station. One day I'll re-create our altar elsewhere.

They do not say aloud what their destination will be. Only a handful is privy to the information. We walk in a straight line alongside the shore. Since Truck is unable to lift anything heavy, Smiley is forced to carry both loads. There is one woman whose legs are not in good condition. She uses the cart we stole from Doña Chela as her private transportation. Shi pushes the cart.

I am grateful for the hoodie attached to the blue tunic. Smiley and Shi are too. We don't see people along our walk. Tomasa says Mega City residents are too busy trying to survive to have time to worry about spiritual zealots. Still, I am nervous. Déesse wants our heads. The longer we stay with the Rumberos, the more my fear of being discovered increases.

"You holding up okay?" I ask. Truck nods. There are times when she grunts from the pain. Only a couple more days and the stitches will be taken out. Then I'll feel secure in leaving.

When I told Truck it was Sule who helped us escape, she couldn't believe it. Her words exactly: "The fea actually moved a muscle for us." Truck wishes she had seen Nena's face when Sule stunned her. After she said that we both stopped talking. The betrayal runs deep. I hate Nena for what she did. I also understand it. I can't blame her for taking a chance. If it were me, I probably would have done the same thing. Well, the old me would have. Now I am not so sure.

Perhaps Nena learned a thing or two from her time spent with OG. They were both finding ways to align themselves with power. They were both making bloody moves with Déesse. When Truck first woke up, she wanted to immediately head over to the Towers to find Nena. The anger eventually subsided. Staying with the Rumberos has a way of making you see how frivolous it is to waste energy on hate.

A little girl tosses a rock to the ocean. She has been skipping for most of the trek.

"Agua es vida, right, Marisol?" Tomasa says.

"Yes, water is life." She tosses another rock.

The girl is Tomasa's granddaughter Marisol. She is the child I met the night we were searching for Miguel. The vessel is what she is known for, a type of messenger. Tomasa explained there are those who are born with the gift of sight.

She believes Marisol has such a gift. I've seen her transform when she dances. It's becoming harder and harder not to believe in the spiritual bachata.

Next year Marisol will be seven, the age when she is meant to go to the camps. Tomasa will never let that happen. Her options are limited. Keep Marisol hidden for as long as she can. Or leave Mega City altogether. Marisol's visions are never about herself. She can see only what will happen to others. Here she is only a kid enjoying herself.

"That girl will save everyone," Tomasa says. She has such love for her granddaughter. Her own daughter works making sueños. She comes on the weekends to visit.

From the Towers Déesse must be able to see the blue of the ocean. Never once has she been seen near the water. Her life is mainly lived perched in her guarded fortress. Because Déesse never gives this part of the city any attention, the residents never venture here for themselves. If Déesse doesn't love getting her toes wet, then we must follow suit. I think there is more to Déesse's reluctance to block the Rumberos from setting up near the ocean. The only excuse I can come up with is she's afraid.

A Rumbero at the front of the group has stopped. This is where they will stay.

"Why here?" I ask.

Tomasa smiles. "Why not? Tonight we greet the super-moon from Orchard."

I've seen the moon many times. When you break night, you develop an intimate relationship with the large star. I felt reassured breaking night would go well with a full moon guiding our way. Since we've arrived, the Rumberos have been waxing on about the supermoon. The occasion is to be marked. Another reason for the new location. A shift is occurring. They are preparing for a change. I assume the supermoon is connected to this.

"Here you go." Truck hands me a shovel. I start to dig. Truck finds another shovel and joins me. The tents will be up soon.

"This is exhausting. I miss hanging at the Luna Club. I miss hot baths. I miss wrestling," Truck says.

"I know this might be hard for you to believe, but I don't."

"Liar. There are things you miss."

She's right. I miss the swagger. The moment when my embedded rank passes muster and there is a sound of a bell proving I belong. My thoughts also turn to Books.

Tomasa inspects our holes. She approves after a few modifications.

"Tell me. Why are the Rumberos allowed to continue?" I ask. "It's just a matter of time before Déesse decides to crack the whip."

"If she ends us, the city will revolt," Tomasa says. "You can only push people so far before they push back. The Rumberos aren't a threat because she doesn't see the numbers. She thinks all we do here is dance and play the congas. Besides, what she's afraid of is already happening. People are leaving Mega City because of her. You can't be worshipped when there is no one around to adore you."

"I guess you are right."

"You think because she is up in that building that she is larger than life. The truth is, I knew her before she became the great Déesse," says Tomasa. "There were five who helped rebuild Mega. Of the five, one was Déesse's father. Mega hasn't always been a man-haters club. This city was open to different types of love. Her father believed, even celebrated it."

"Graciela," I say.

"Graciela was beloved. And when she became too beloved, she had to go. So did Déesse's father," Tomasa says. She thrusts another pole in the dirt. "Is Graciela singing? She wouldn't here. There was too much pain."

"Yes, she is."

"She truly has a gift."

She does.

"Truck. Can you help the pair over there?" Tomasa says. "They don't know what they are doing."

Truck takes her shovel and slowly walks over. As much as she says she misses her old life, Truck enjoys the stillness of being with the Rumberos. For once she is forced to be calm. Even though she gripes about the relentless music, I've seen her tapping her boots to the rhythm.

There is one thing I keep thinking about. I find the courage to ask.

"Your granddaughter told me I was going to die," I say. "That the LMCs would cease to exist."

"Yes, she did. You didn't want to hear that, did you?" She laughs. "Can't ignore a vessel."

"Well, she was wrong. I'm here."

"Oh? The LMCs are not the same crew that left here ten days ago. You are not the same."

She is right. Too much has happened. What if I go back? If I don't have a dream, then what do I have to strive toward?

"The visions Marisol has are messages. They are seeds. You take the seed and you find a place where there is room for it to be nourished," she says. "Rethink your life."

We continue placing the poles. To open the tent, I need Tomasa's help. We spread the sheet and secure it with rope.

"I'm curious to see what will happen next. Aren't you excited? I am," she says. "A rebirth. Chief Rocka, how long before you are only Nalah? Not long, I think. Not long at all."

We are done. There is another tent to be built.

When do I return to being Nalah? Chief Rocka and Nalah aren't interchangeable. They are both sides of me. The innocence and the violence. To let one go is to let go of a part of me. Perhaps I can reenvision a person who is more than just a label or a nickname christened by another.

I've never once been to the beach. Manos Dura would have

loved it here. So would have Mami. While the others continue to work, I walk toward the large body of water. The closer I get to the shoreline, the finer the sand becomes.

The coldness of the ocean is jolting. Sunlight reflects off the water in a bright and sparkling display. The vastness of the shimmering sea seems to never end. I've avoided my own reflection all my life. There was no point in seeing how I looked. My appearance never helped in a throwdown. I equated beauty with weakness.

I see traces of my mother in the reflection. Before the sueños took hold, she was beautiful. She had pronounced cheekbones. Her smile was crooked just like Yamaris and it radiated warmth. My life with her wasn't always full of despair. I remember.

I keep thinking of my sister and what Graciela said to me. How she is both parts protector and friend. Hard and soft. Most of my life consisted of being rocklike, of never permitting anyone to touch me in any way. Is it possible to be both?

There are no black eyes or scratches on my face. For once I'm clean and healthy. My skin even has a glow from the sun. This is the first time I am allowing myself to see parts of my mother in my profile. The cheekbones. The eyes. I can't deny it. I look just like her. If I let go a little, perhaps I can discover the beauty within me.

The waves continue to oscillate. My reflection in the water ripples and moves.

CHAPTER 30

BUFFALO GALS GO

Déesse steps out on the balcony, looking glorious as ever. She is impressive with her long, flowing hair. She manages to take my breath away even now. For a split second I can recall exactly why I wanted to be with her. How much I wished my plans had gone my way. Now that I stand with the other toilers in the back of the courtyard, I have a very different view.

"My beautiful children! If you hear me, let me know. If you feel me, scream it to the sky. All who hear me, far and wide, know that we are in this world for one thing, to make this life right. When everything around us was being destroyed by those lost in their blind ambition, we didn't cry. We didn't ask, 'why?' No, children, we got up and got to work."

Déesse always begins her speeches the same way. I used to live for this moment. Her words fueled me when I entered the throwdowns.

When the applause dies down, she continues.

"I need everyone to pay close attention. There are those who do not want us to succeed."

The newsletter from the Towers made its rounds yesterday in the tents. The list of infractions was pretty elaborate. Laughable even. She is also creating a new narrative hinted at in the newsletter. Déesse has a gift. I can give her that much.

"We've seen with our own eyes how the degenerates in Cemi Territory live. It's important we secure our borders," she says. "Training our young people to fight is vital. I'm here to tell you the rumors are true. The Ashé Ryders want to destroy Mega. We can't allow it."

Standing beside her are Santo and Sule. Sule stands a bit straighter. There is a slight difference in her stature. It could just be me searching. Sule did manage to fumble the microphone when she addressed the crowd. There is more to Sule than I could have ever imagined.

Truck nudges me. "There she is." I spot her. Nena stands in her buffalo stance. Hard face. No longer a baby soldier. She's a full-fledged fighter. She looks very comfortable.

There are no colors on us. No red and gold, nor the Rumberos blue. We left them behind with our hosts. Four weeks of hiding. It felt even longer. I wanted to make sure Truck's wounds were healed even though the stitches were taken out a couple of weeks ago. Another scar to add to the many on her body.

The time we spent with the Rumberos wasn't altogether a smooth ride. Sometimes Truck and I would get caught up in plans on how to destroy the Towers. Anger can make a person irrational. Other times I wanted to revert right back to begging. If only Santo would listen to me, then surely he would change his mind. I did none of those things. Tomasa's rants in her spiritual bachata language would get on my nerves. I don't understand most of it. At least what she says doesn't frighten me as much.

The sun slowly slides down behind the Towers. Smiley cozies up to Shi. She's on stealth mode. We don't want to attract any attention.

"I'm excited to welcome to the fold Nona," Déesse says. "She's proven to be instrumental in protecting Mega City. You're going to be seeing a lot of her. Our first job is to get our training camps in order. We will need every soldier. We take the fight to the Ashé Ryders."

There it is. The big news Déesse mentioned in the newsletter. She is going to go after the Ashé Ryders. How will they defend themselves? The large stockroom filled with tronics is worthless if they are not going to use them. I can't find myself following the Ashé Ryders' decree of nonviolence. When Déesse's soldiers arrive at Los Bohios, will the Ryders simply give up? They must defend themselves.

Everyone in the courtyard cheers except for a single toiler. He yells to Déesse, complains about sleeping in the cold tunnels. The apartments in the Towers look pretty toasty. Back where I stand, those around me are not adding to the adulations. Instead, there is anger. Snide remarks about Déesse. Crude jokes. Funny the things you miss when you are trying to be a good Mega City soldier.

"We built Mega together," Déesse continues. "Together we can do anything."

Nena has a smug look on her face. A slight envious twinge rises in me. Nena stands in my spot. She made it. Déesse introduces the crews battling in the throwdown. There's no point in staying.

"Let's bounce."

Truck alerts Smiley and Shi.

"How long do you think Nena will last?" Truck asks.

"She's got more lives than most of us," I say. "The person she needs to pay attention to, though, is Sule."

Truck laughs at this. "Yeah, Sule and me. When she least expects it."

I pull up my hoodie and dig my hands into my pockets. We keep our heads down. No eye contact, not as before. No rage face. Blend in with the rest of the toilers. That's how we roll in Mega City now. We know how they handle those who betray them. Déesse and her supporters make them disappear or feed them sueños until they can't differentiate day from night. I loved being in people's mugs. Oh well, things change.

There's one more place to hit before we leave.

The Luna Club is dead except for a couple of twinkling lights left on the open sign in the front. I circle toward the back of the club. There's no need to freak Doña out. She must be already hysterical over many other things. As expected, Books waits for me. He has his uniform on. I wonder how long he will continue to work here before it becomes pointless.

The girls give us privacy.

"Did you enjoy the spectacle?" Books asks.

"It's definitely different when you go as a regular toiler," I say. "Interesting, I guess. So how long you think you will last here?"

"Not long. Things are brewing. I'm staying on top of any sudden moves." He pushes his glasses. "Aren't you doing the same?"

I nod.

"I wanted to thank you for what you did for Truck. I can never repay you," I say. "I have only this."

I dig in my pocket and hand him the azabache. "People say it can protect the wearer from harm."

He looks at the charm and smiles. "Who are these people you are referring to?" he teases.

I turn to leave. Books reaches for me. "I'll be right back. Five minutes," he says.

Truck throws me an impatient stare. Breaking night is soon approaching, and we have a lot of ground to cover.

He returns and hands me a book. It's the one he would

read when I came to visit. *The Wonderful Wizard of Oz.*

"This is yours," Books says.

I shake my head. "I don't know how much reading I'll be doing in the future."

"Don't you want to know how it ends?" His smile is genuine. It doesn't seem syrupy or fake. It is stripped of papi chulo pose. Real.

I thank him for the book and place it in my backpack. I'm not sure if I'll see Books again. Tomasa told me people who are meant to be by your side will appear again and again. There are no coincidences.

"Maybe the next time I see you you'll tell me your real name," I say before following my crew.

"Sure, Chief Rocka. Be safe."

"My name is Nalah," I say, and run to join the others.

A sudden chill from sleeping on the floor wakes me. Not wanting to disturb anyone, I quietly walk outside.

To avoid the Muñeca Locas, we decided to take a longer route. Shi found us a place where we can squat for a day or two. A run-down building with a couple of families on the top floors. We traded a few food pellets so they wouldn't call us out.

There's so much to do. Déesse's soldiers will be heading this way. We need to warn the Ashé Ryders. We also have to convince the Gurl Gunnas to work against Déesse. I haven't figured that part out yet. Will there ever be a moment when sleep is no longer a struggle? When will I feel safe?

While we were with the Rumberos, the LMCs each took time to reimagine our future. We shared our visions with each other. Smiley and Shi decided they didn't want to follow us. They want to join the couple we met a while back and try to carve a different kind of life on their own. No more crews for them. It's not to say they won't join in on the fight if we need them. They just want to explore other possibilities for what a home can be.

Truck and I are headed back to the Ashé Ryders. I don't know what to expect. It's hard for me to let go of this feeling that I'm returning as a punk. A failure. I brush it off. Pride will get me iced. The LMCs aren't dead. The crew is just evolving. Only time will tell what the future holds for us.

"You up?" says Truck. She chopped her hair off while we were with the Rumberos. Now her face is a full dark moon. I couldn't believe when she walked out of the tent. She held her brown twisted locks in her hands as if they were her babies. Then she threw them in a fire pit.

"I'm waiting for the sun."

"Why?" she asks, annoyed.

After a few minutes she drops to the ground and sits next to me.

Zentrica and the Ashé Ryders can try to do their thing. I don't know if the Ryders have the answers. I don't know if anyone does. Change doesn't come overnight. It's a slow build. Mega City is my home, and I intend to take it back. Maybe with the Ryders, or maybe we need to start anew elsewhere. I'm just glad my sister Truck sticks right by my side.

"It's cold," Truck says. "Let's go back inside."

"Wait for a few more minutes," I say. "Why are you so impatient? Just wait."

Truck makes a smacking noise with her lips. She stays. I knew she would.

We watch the sky transform from dark inky blue to a slight rose color. The hues we see are so intense. Before, I would never stop to watch day break. Instead I would hole up in a boydega or in a tunnel, eager to sleep off the night's activities. This incredible sight, the transforming sky, will be my guide.

It's slow, this heavenly movement. We huddle in closer and wait for the day to finally break.

Acknowledgments

Dealing In Dreams owes so much to my brilliant editor Zareen Jaffery. While I drowned in themes that seemed too big in scope, Zareen always nudged me to dig deeper. Thank you, and to everyone at Simon & Schuster, including the art department for once again finding the perfect artist, Aster Hung, in creating such a beautiful cover.

Thanks to my agent, Eddie Schneider, for always answering my questions and quelling my doubts. Gratitude also goes to Kima Jones at Jack Jones Literary Arts for going above and beyond in getting the word out for this novel.

This story was first workshopped in VONA with author Tananarive Due in her speculative literature class. It also got much love at Clarion with author Christopher Barzak. I love my 2015 Clarion family, with a special shoutout to Vanessa for reading an early draft.

Sisters are at the heart of this story and I so dearly love my sister Annabel. I'm also here for my other hermanas: Ritzy P, Lady Imix, Aditi, Jean, Brandy, and Isabel. I also can't do this without my family—David, Bella, and Coco—and my forever Bronx Puerto Rican crew.

This story is for all the young ones who wonder where they stand in this world. I hope they find strength in their buffalo stance.